"Don't move!"

Vance was moving swiftly toward her, shirtless, wearing only a pair of jeans. Tess could hear the mud sucking at his feet, the breath slicing in and out of his lungs. He had almost reached her.... Only fifty feet of smooth, flat ground separated them.

And then something happened. Cursing, crying out in surprise, he went down through the surface.

Tess screamed his name as she saw his legs disappear, screamed again as the thick mud sucked at him like a huge, hungry mouth opening in the ground. "Vance... oh, God, Vance."

His arm came up, waving her frantically away. But he only sank lower. Soon she could hear only his muffled cry, "Quicksand."

Dear Reader,

Writing the 43 LIGHT STREET books has been one of the most exciting experiences an author can have. What could be more gratifying than creating a whole building full of characters, each with her own dramatic and romantic story?

But what if there's a tale you long to tell that just won't fit? Like *Bayou Moon*. Both of the main characters, Vance Gautreau and Tess Beaumont, have deep roots in the dark, mysterious Louisiana backcountry. It would be impossible to move them to Baltimore, the setting of the 43 LIGHT STREET series. The only way to approach their story is to go down to Louisiana and plunge into the dangerous black waters of Savannah Bayou.

Getting down and dirty in the swamp was a real change of locale for me. But not a change of pace. *Bayou Moon* is the same kind of tense, fast, sensuous story I love to tell—and you've come to expect from me.

Sincerely,

Rebecca York

Bayou
Moon
Rebecca York

Harlequin Books

TORONTO • NEW YORK • LONDON
AMSTERDAM • PARIS • SYDNEY • HAMBURG
STOCKHOLM • ATHENS • TOKYO • MILAN
MADRID • WARSAW • BUDAPEST • AUCKLAND

Harlequin Intrigue edition published June 1992

ISBN 0-373-22188-6

BAYOU MOON

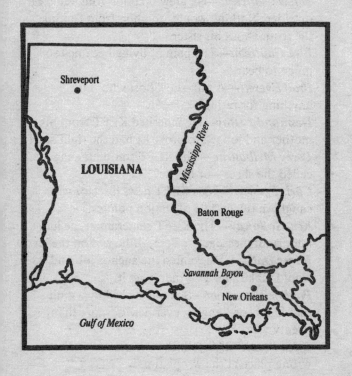

Shreveport

LOUISIANA

Mississippi River

Baton Rouge

Savannah Bayou

New Orleans

Gulf of Mexico

CAST OF CHARACTERS

Tess Beaumont—She was in over her head the moment she returned to the bayou country.

Vance Gautreau—He grew up poor, tough and an outsider. Nothing would stop him from finding the truth about his sister.

Lisa Gautreau—The pain of living became too much to bear.

Brad Everett—A talk-show host who'd do anything for ratings.

Desmond LeRoy—He inherited KEFT from his mother and longed to prove he had the right stuff.

Larry Melbourne—The KEFT station manager called the shots—or did he?

Chris Spencer—This KEFT news director was caught in the middle of station politics.

Ken Holloway—The KEFT cameraman, he had an important message for Tess—if he was on the level.

Roger Dallas—He wanted the anchor job and would make sure Tess didn't get it.

Pauline Beaumont—She was racked by a guilt that had been hanging over her for more than twenty years.

Erica Barry—This talk-show guest was in the wrong place at the wrong time.

Glen Devoe—Was he Lisa's devoted husband?

Ernestine Achord—Vance's aunt may have a piece of the puzzle.

Prologue

A sudden cloudburst peppered the dark surface of the bayou like a blast of bird shot. The young woman standing on the bank shivered as the cold drops pounded against her shoulders. But she didn't step back.

For the first time since she'd stumbled off the set of the *Brad Everett Show,* her tortured thoughts cleared and a blessed sense of peacefulness came over her. The feeling came from having finally made the decision.

The rain plastered dark hair around a face that was white as marble. Then, as if the sun had peeked from behind a cloud, the hint of a smile softened the set line of her lips.

She'd come to the spot she'd been looking for. The ruined icehouse where she and Vance had played. Twenty years ago it had been a heap of moss-covered bricks. Now they'd crumbled even more. Vance had tried to teach her how to skip flat pieces of brick across the water, but she'd never gotten the hang of it. Maybe only boys could get that flip of the wrist.

Reaching out, she picked up a chunk. For a moment her thumbnail grated across the rough surface. Then she quickly slipped the broken rectangle into the outsize pocket of her loose cotton dress. Six, eight, ten others followed.

Wet from the rain, they soaked the thin fabric. The sharp
edges dug into the flesh of her thighs. Yet the ballast felt
reassuring. Solid. As if she were squirreling away emergency supplies.

The bricks were heavy. It was too much effort to stand
up, and she hunkered down on the bank, tucking her skirt
around her ankles.

Vance. For a moment her heart squeezed painfully. He'd
wanted to help, but the grief on his face had stopped her
from telling him any of the details. They would have made
him angry. God knows what damn fool thing he'd have
tried to do.

Struggling to her feet, she took a decisive step toward the
water. She'd made a royal mess of her life.

"Lisa!"

Haunted eyes turned to see a figure hurrying down the
path.

"Lisa, wait—don't—"

She was more afraid of him than of the water. What if
he started in again with the endless questions, the endless
accusations.

"Stop! You can't—"

He couldn't reach her in time, could he? Heart pounding, she launched herself off the bank. The cool water re-
ceived her. The bricks helped carry her down to the
bottom.

Chapter One

Tess Beaumont looked up from the TV monitor and consulted the notebook on her desk. "Give me 6327 again—the sound bite where Jenny is standing beside the empty crib."

Stan Reardon's coffee brown fingers tapped the keyboard on the editing machine, and the young woman on the screen began to speak:

"When you can't have a baby of your own, you'll do just about anything to get one. Even find another woman to bear a child for you."

Tess felt her chest tighten as she listened to the soft, wobbly voice. "That's the most powerful part of the interview. I want to start with it," she whispered.

Stan's Afro bobbed. Usually he joked around when they weren't on deadline. This morning he was quiet.

The tape started again. On the screen the two young women talked in low voices. Tess listened. There was something so powerful about this piece. She'd been drawn to the subject as soon as she'd seen the press release on the surrogate mother program at University Hospital.

Her research had included interviews with wives who'd agreed to have their husband's sperm impregnate a surrogate and with women who were willing to carry a child for nine months and then hand it over to someone else. About the only ones she hadn't questioned were the babies. But she'd held them and cuddled them and played with them—and wondered fiercely what it would be like to find out you were someone else entirely different from the person you'd thought. The notion was disturbing.

More tape rolled. Tess realized with a little shiver that she was scrutinizing her own face on the screen as if she were a stranger. Ash blond hair. Finely molded cheekbones. Lips that were soft, but not too generous. Blue eyes under long lashes remarkably dark for the rest of her coloring. She'd heard it said behind her back that her looks had gotten her the reporting job at KEFT. That had only made her fight harder for the tough stories.

She sensed Stan's gaze on her and sat up straighter. "Let's skip to 9073."

Laurie, one of the surrogates, began to talk about how hard it had been to give away the baby she'd borne.

"Roll back a sentence and cut it off there," Tess directed.

"Don't you like the part about her needing the money?"

"It's a side issue she barely mentioned. And it creates a false impression. We only have four minutes to tell this story. Every second has to count."

The editing took another forty-five minutes. While Stan stretched out his long legs under the desk, Tess slipped into an audio booth to do the voice-overs. When she came out, Stan was snapping his fingers to the jazzy opening theme of the *Brad Everett Show*. It must be ten o'clock.

Tess looked up at the monitors. Rumor was that Studio Seven had been remodeled to order for the talk-show host—to the tune of $100,000. Tess thought it looked like a cross between a boxing arena and the bridge of the starship *Enterprise*.

A tall, agile man came prancing down a runway—a microphone held jauntily in his right hand. His wide brown eyes were his best feature. When he turned them on you, they conveyed sincerity. Probably a trick he'd learned in acting school.

Thunderous applause.

Tess couldn't repress a grimace. While she and Stan had been editing, she'd forgotten about everything except the surrogate mother story. Now she was face-to-face with a larger reality. In the two months he'd been here, Brad Everett had become a symbol for her. A symbol of what was wrong with modern society. And a symbol of what had gone terribly wrong at station KEFT in New Orleans.

From the monitor Brad gave a little bow to the camera. "Thank you, thank you. All week we've been exploring some of the problems and choices of women in the nineties. Child abuse at day care centers. Personal safety on the college campus. Today we're going to take a look at a problem all too many women encounter in the workplace—sexual harassment."

Tess knew how she'd treat the subject if she were running the show. But she wasn't in charge.

On the screen, Brad continued. "With us are two women who say they lost their jobs because they wouldn't—uh—play ball with the boss."

The camera followed the dramatic sweep of Brad's hand to the front of the studio where three women and a man sat in stylish barrel chairs. Sooner or later, they were going to find themselves in the hot seat. It was usually sooner.

"Let's start with Erica Barry, who claims she was fired from her middle-management job at a major New Orleans corporation because she declined to have an affair with her immediate supervisor."

A slightly chunky but attractive woman in her early thirties, Ms. Barry was wearing a buttoned-up silk shirtwaist set off with a brightly colored scarf at the neck. Her blond hair was pulled back in a severe bun. As she told about her late-evening work schedule, frequent out-of-town trips with her boss and unwelcome physical contact, women in the audience began to murmur sympathetically—until Brad interrupted to flash a photograph of Ms. Barry on the screen. In the picture she was wearing a tight blouse that revealed a generous view of ripe cleavage.

"But that was a publicity photo when I was trying out for the Miss Sugar Cane Page—"

Brad cut her off with a rapid series of questions about her after-hours relationships with male employees.

Tess tried to swallow over the tar paper coating her throat. She was suddenly feeling very sorry for Erica Barry.

AT THE OTHER END of the hall in the KEFT executive offices, Desmond LeRoy reached into his desk drawer, found a bottle of antacid tablets and shook out two. You were supposed to let them dissolve in your mouth, but he couldn't stand the taste of minty chalk. So he ground them up with his back teeth and swallowed rapidly before reaching for a cigar. The acrid smoke washed away the mint—but not the fear.

During most of his adult life, Desmond LeRoy had felt a great kinship with Prince Charles. It was damn tough waiting for your mom to bow out so you could take over the reins. Then nine months ago, while Desmond's old lady was on a cruise to Alaska, he'd gotten a frantic call from the ship's doctor saying she'd died of a massive heart attack.

For the first time in his life, Desmond felt alone—and strangely helpless. Sure, he'd resented his mother's power, but she'd always been there. When he was a little boy, she'd kissed scraped knees and made sure the freezer was stocked with chocolate ice cream. When he grew up, she'd bought him a silver blue Jag, a condo with a great view of the Mississippi and a membership in the Pontchartrain Club. Once or twice she'd even fixed things up with the police for him. Her will had left him set for life. It didn't offer a clue how to cope with KEFT on his own.

Without waiting to be announced, Larry Melbourne, his station manager, breezed into the office for their ten-thirty meeting. "So what do you think of the new schedule?" The tone of voice and the cocky angle of the bulldog jaw assumed that approval was going to be a matter of a quick signature.

"Expensive."

"You gotta spend money to make money. See, we needed a big-draw game show for the mid-morning slump," Larry continued as he pulled up a chair. When he leaned over, the top of his bald head looked like a giant light bulb. It was like the light bulb cartoonists sometimes drew over a character. To Desmond, it symbolized the creativity inside.

"One where they give away plenty of cash," the station manager continued. "I would've gotten *Wheel of Fortune,* but *House of Cards* is hotter. And I'm moving *Worldwide Crime Beat* to Tuesday night. It'll play stronger than what we've got up against that new detective show on CBS. And it will help set us up for when Brad leaves."

Larry didn't look too upset about their star attraction going nova. But Desmond felt sweat gather under his collar. Brad Everett wasn't going to be a permanent fixture at KEFT because the talk-show host didn't have a perma-

nent base of operation. Instead, independent stations vied
for the honor of his presence. Three or four months in a
city, and then he moved on before the format got stale.
Which meant KEFT in New Orleans had only six to ten
more weeks before he jumped ship. Of course, they were
still going to run his syndicated show. But it wouldn't be
quite the same once he was no longer broadcasting from a
studio right in the Crescent City.

Were they going to lose the audience they'd built? If they
did, everyone would find out that Desmond LeRoy was a
failure.

IT HAD BEEN A LONG DAY, including a remote taping on the
Stranger Danger program at McDonough Elementary
School Number Four. Tess was clearing the last folder off
her desk when Chris Spencer, the news director, stepped
into her doorway. He was a slender, boyish-looking man,
with a shock of wheat blond hair. Around the station, he
had a reputation for keeping his cool under pressure, except when he was afraid somebody else was going to get the
drop on a news story. The glitter in his green eyes brought
Tess back to instant alertness.

"I've got a drowning in Savannah Bayou," he said,
bouncing lightly on the balls of his feet. "If we hustle, we
can open the six o'clock news with a shot of the police
pulling the body out of the water."

Tess shivered. And not simply because of the graphic
image of a drowning victim that rose to the surface of her
mind. The name Savannah Bayou conjured dark water as
flat as a windowpane. Gum trees and cypress pushing
against each other. Insects choking the air with their
buzzing. Snakes and alligators slithering through the tangle
of underbrush on the shore.

Chris must have caught her expression. "Drowning. Yeah. Not exactly a fun gig for a woman. Maybe I can send Roger." Roger was Roger Dallas, another one of the field reporters. Tess loathed his heavy-handed techniques.

"No. I'll take it." Her voice was stronger then she'd imagined it would be.

"Good. Ken's got the directions. Can you be ready to go in fifteen minutes?"

"Yes."

After closing the door to her office, Tess reached for the zipper down her back—grateful that she didn't have to sit and brood about the assignment. Her dress was wilted from a long day at work, but she'd learned to keep a spare at the ready. After she'd made the quick change, she pulled the makeup case from the bottom left-hand drawer of her desk. Viewers expected a certain look from Tess Beaumont, and she would try to give it to them. When she was finished with her face, she still had a couple of minutes to spare. Before she left her cubicle, she stuffed a pack of Oreo cookies into her tote bag.

"No rest for the weary," Ken Holloway, the cameraman/sound technician observed when she climbed into the front passenger seat of the KEFT van.

As they wove through the first wave of rush-hour traffic, Tess wished she could plan the news report she'd give as she stood at the camera. But with no details, there was nothing to work with yet. After a few minutes of riding in silence, Ken honed in on her tension. "What's the matter, doll?"

"I'm just tired." They were southwest of the city now, in Madison Parish. Bayou country. Tess slid down in her seat and closed her eyes, trying to find the calm, peaceful place where she'd learned to hide when she was a child. It eluded her. Instead, the disturbing images swirling in her brain grew more vivid. Dark water. A trailing creeper curling around her ankle, sending her toppling to the ground. A man's urgent voice. Others joining him in a chorus of anger. Where had that last part come from? she wondered as her eyes snapped open and she forced her mind back to the here and now.

"Chris give you any information?" she asked.

"Just that the woman drowned herself."

They rode in silence for a few moments past fields of green sugarcane. "You—uh—got any Oreo cookies?" Ken finally asked.

"Would I let you down?" Reaching in the bag, Tess fished out a cellophane-wrapped stack and set it on the console between them.

They grinned at each other. Whenever they went out on assignment together, he drove and she supplied the Oreos. Ken polished off six. Tess ate two and had to stop herself from wolfing down another.

She hadn't been to this precise spot before, but she had an excellent idea of what the road to Savannah Bayou would look like. Twenty minutes later, she wasn't surprised when the KEFT van pulled off onto a narrow byway bordered with bay trees and live oaks, their branches thick with gray green streamers of Spanish moss. They looked like witches' fingers reaching toward the van, and Tess unconsciously edged away from the window.

"Chris shouldn't have sent you to something like this."

"I'm okay." She sat up straighter. "I'm always a little spooked by this part of the world. It's so isolated out here. I guess anything could happen."

Ken nodded. "The way people tell it, there's some bad stuff that goes on in the back country, all right."

"What have you heard, exactly?"

"Well, you know, drug pirates. Swamp rats who'd kill you if they thought you'd found their illegal traps. Barns where the main activity is betting on cockfights. Voodoo. What about you?"

Tess pleated the fabric of her shirt. "The same kind of stories. Nothing anyone can prove."

"You think the dead girl stumbled into something she wasn't supposed to know about?"

"I guess we'll find out."

At the end of the lane, the way was blocked by two police cars and an ambulance. A small crowd of onlookers watched as two men in wet suits maneuvered a pale, lifeless form toward the side of the bayou.

Ken swore under his breath, pulled off onto the shoulder and jounced to a halt. Cutting the engine, he twisted around to grab his Minicam.

Tess was left sitting in the van. She didn't want to watch the divers. But there was nothing else to look at besides the wall of vegetation that crowded the windows. The wet green lichens on the bark of an oak tree were so close she could have reached out and scraped them off with her thumbnail.

But she wasn't being paid to sit here scrutinizing lichens. Briskly she jumped down from the van and started toward the water, her high-heeled shoes sinking noisily into the gravel of the road. Maybe one of the police officers or a bystander could give her some background about the dead woman.

Out of the corner of her eye, she saw Ken lift his camera to his shoulder and begin to shoot. The sound of her shoes was drowned out as tires squealed on the lane in back of the van. Tess whirled around just in time to see a tall, rangy man jump out of a red Mustang. His jeans and blue shirt were faded, and his western boots were scuffed. But they were expensive. Alligator, her reporter's eye noted.

As he paused for a moment, his deep-set eyes focused on Tess, and all her carefully collected composure evaporated like drops of water splattering on a hot stove.

She didn't know the man. But she knew the type. Ignorant. Arrogant. Clannish. Dangerous when provoked.

Eternity stretched as he pinned her with his ebony gaze. Then one of the divers climbed up on the bank, and the newcomer's attention snapped toward the scene at the edge of the water. In the next moment, he was striding toward Ken. Under the dark stubble on his cheeks, his skin had gone oyster white. His full lips were set in a slash of a line.

"Hé. Hé la bas!" he snarled at the cameraman. "You there!" Then he was jogging down the path.

Ken's head jerked up as the stranger grabbed his shoulder. "What the—"

"Non télévision. No pictures."

"Listen, buddy—"

The newcomer's large hand transferred itself from shoulder to Minicam. The next second, he'd ripped it from Ken's grasp.

"You can't do that, mister." Ken snatched frantically for the camera. With his free hand, the stranger shoved him to the ground. Then he strode to the bank.

As Tess watched in stunned silence, he swung back his arm. An instant later, the expensive Minicam arced through the air. It hit the surface of the bayou with a loud splash and vanished beneath the dark water.

Chapter Two

The phone in the van wasn't working, and the only place in town open after eight was the Paradise Café, which was more of a bar than a restaurant. As Tess bent toward the scarred wall phone between the restroom doors, a drunken patron jabbed her in the hip.

"*Pardonne,* ma'am."

"Sure."

On the other end of the line, Chris Spencer was speaking. "What? I can't hear you."

"Sorry." Tess didn't bother to explain about the little side conversation. Instead she went back to what she'd been saying before the interruption. This time she tried to pitch her voice above the loud talk from the rough-looking patrons and the recorded Cajun fiddle music. "You should have been here. It took a football team to subdue the guy. They have him in custody now."

"He sure as hell is going to pay for the camera."

"His name is Vance Gautreau. People seem reluctant to answer a lot of questions about him. But I found out he's the victim's brother."

"Anything else?"

"He's a carpenter—restores old houses. Learned the trade from his uncle."

"Think he'd talk to you?"

Tess pushed at a pile of sawdust on the floor with the toe of her beige pump. Too bad she hadn't brought anything more comfortable. "After what happened? I wouldn't count on it. Maybe I could interview some of the local—"

"Forget it. We've already lost our edge on this. Channel Four did it as a special report fifteen minutes ago—with plenty of speculation from the locals. I don't want to come in with anything second-rate."

"Sorry."

"I, uh, was wondering."

"No!"

"You haven't let me ask you the question yet."

Tess sighed. "All right. Ask."

"What if you went over to the jail and bailed Gautreau out? He'd have to be grateful."

It wasn't difficult to come up with three excellent objections. "How can I bail him out when he hasn't been before a judge yet?" Tess asked. "Even if I can, he'll think it's some kind of stunt. And where am I supposed to get the money?"

Chris carefully demolished the arguments. "The sheriff will take your money. I'll bet Gautreau will give you an interview. And use the emergency stash in the van. Ken knows where it is. Tess, if anyone can pull it off, you can."

"Oh, sure."

"Sweetie, it's important. This story's bigger than you think. Trust me."

Tess found she was having trouble drawing a steady breath. She'd given Chris logical objections. She knew they were only excuses. On some gut level, Vance Gautreau represented a threat. And it wasn't just her imagination. She'd seen his violent streak firsthand. But what if she really did confront him? What could happen? He wasn't going to assault a woman in a public place. Was he?

She glanced over at Ken, who was enthusiastically polishing off a heaping bowl of red beans and rice at one of the tables in the back. The thought of eating anything at the moment made her own throat clog, but she wouldn't interfere with the meal. He'd be finished dinner soon. And he'd look out for her if she got into something she couldn't handle.

Chris must have sensed her wavering.

"Tess—please. Doesn't the name Gautreau ring a bell?" the news director asked softly.

"No."

"His sister—the dead woman—was Lisa Gautreau."

"And?" Tess thought back over the recent programming.

"She was the star attraction on the *Brad Everett Show* a couple of weeks ago."

A couple of weeks ago Everett had been going for the sleaze factor. The underbelly of the Crescent City, the ad promos had promised. "She a prostitute or something?"

"No. It was the program he did on rape victims."

Tess sucked in a jagged breath. She'd avoided finding out how Brad would handle that particular topic. "Oh, my God. The poor thing. And now she's killed herself."

"We don't know that for sure. Maybe it was murder. Maybe the husband didn't like her spilling her guts on national TV. Or maybe it was the hotheaded brother. And now he's trying to cover up his tracks."

"I see. But you still want me to spring him from jail?" Tess could tell from the audible change in Chris's breathing that he realized his mistake.

"Look I was just thinking out loud, you know," he explained hastily. "This guy's our best source of informa-

tion. Find out what Lisa was like—as a kid. As an adult.
What kind of a relationship she had with her husband.
And how Gautreau felt about what happened.''

Tess sighed, wishing fervently that she'd turned Chris
down in the first place. Ending the call as quickly as possible, she went to tell the cameraman they wouldn't be
leaving for a while. After he finished eating, he brought
her the money from the van. Then he pulled the vehicle
into a spot where he could watch the action.

A large, rusty Jax Beer sign appeared to be holding up
one exterior wall of the bar. Tess stood beside it, taking in
measured breaths of the warm, muggy air. When she
glanced at the van, Ken gave her the thumbs-up sign. She
nodded and looked across the street at the jail. Convenient. The sheriff didn't have to haul the drunks or the
brawlers too far.

She should get this over with, Tess told herself. Still, she
hesitated. Maybe the odd, green-gold evening light was
making her feel spooky. Or maybe it was the jailhouse—a
small building of moss-encrusted bricks that looked as if
it had been built around the time of the Spanish occupa-
tion. Somehow she couldn't shake the fancy that she'd had
a bad experience there. Or somewhere like it. But in ac-
tual fact, she amended, she was simply anticipating a bad
experience.

She knew she'd been right the moment she pulled open
the sagging wooden door. The office was like a steam room
that hadn't been hosed down in a decade. The wooden
blades of a ceiling fan barely stirred the thick air. The
scarred nameplate resting on the front of the sheriff's desk
said Frank Haney. He was a big man wearing a rumpled
uniform decorated with half-moon patches of sweat at the
armpits. Under a few strands of dark hair, his scalp glistened in the light from the metal desk lamp. Tess knew he

recognized her, because he'd been there when she'd come forward to tend Ken with the first-aid kit from the van. Now he kept her waiting half a minute while he turned several more pages of a battered issue of *Field & Stream*.

"Ain't had many visitors like you of recent."

"I'd like to post bail for Mr. Gautreau."

Haney didn't miss a beat. "Five hundred bucks."

Tess counted the money into his moist hand, pretty sure this wasn't really a legal transaction. Was he going to get her for bribing an officer after he impounded the evidence? She felt a trickle of perspiration inch down her back.

No. Haney didn't seemed concerned with legalities. He counted the bills again, slipped them into his desk drawer and pushed back his chair. "It's your funeral, lady."

While she grappled with her second thoughts and waited for him to reappear through the barred door at the back, Tess studied the little room. The mildew high up in the corners matched the patches of sweat under the sheriff's arms. Starting at about shoulder level, the walls were scarred and gouged. How had they gotten that way? she wondered. Had generations of law officers and their deputies shoved the prisoners around? Or had the drunks hauled over from across the street done the damage?

The barred door clanked and Tess looked up. The man in custody was somewhat the worse for wear. His dark hair was tousled, his blue shirt was torn, and his right eye was going to hurt like hell tomorrow.

Tess realized that she'd unconsciously pressed her shoulders against the damp wall. When the sheriff jerked his thumb in her direction, Gautreau's gaze followed. "This lady's bought and paid for you."

His low-pitched response was in gutter French.

"Paid your bail, anyway."

Chris had suggested the man might be grateful. But Gautreau fixed her with a look as menacing as the first time he'd pinned her with those anthracite eyes. Tess crossed her arms and stood up straighter. Yet it was she who lowered her gaze first. Neither one of them moved.

"Go on, git out of here 'fore I change my mind," the sheriff muttered.

Shrugging, Gautreau opened the door without giving her another glance. Tess followed him outside and stopped short. While she'd been in the jail, the moon had come up. It was large and full, a perfectly round disk hovering over the treetops like a UFO.

As Tess turned toward it, the circle of light seemed to beckon her forward. For a confused moment, coherent thought was swallowed up by the eerie glow. The moon. It had hung above her like this, out here in the bayou country, once before. She felt the orange light fill her head. Drown her thoughts. Then every muscle in her body clenched, and she wrenched her gaze away, back to the present—and to the man she was supposed to interview. His broad shoulders were rapidly receding.

Tess wasn't sure why her heart was pounding. Vance Gautreau was leaving. She was off the hook. As he strode toward his Mustang, she thought seriously about simply letting him disappear into the night. Except that she'd paid KEFT's good money to spring him. And Ken was watching from the van.

"Wait!"

Stopping in the act of opening his car door, Gautreau slowly turned. "What do you want?"

"To talk to you."

His voice was bitter as he spoke in carefully enunciated English—as if using her language were somehow insulting. "You're with that TV station."

"Yes."

"You vultures are all the same. You smell death, and you come circling around to tear off some rotten meat for yourselves."

"That's not exactly fair."

"Oh?"

"The public has the right to know—"

"Why a poor, wounded girl killed herself," he interrupted, finishing the sentence.

"Did she?"

His ebony eyes grew dangerously bright. "What else do you suppose, *cher?*"

"You tell me."

The anguish on his face was suddenly so real that, despite everything else she'd been feeling, a tender place inside her chest ached painfully. She thought he was going to turn away. Instead, he pivoted to face her fully.

"She was ashamed to talk to me about what happened to her, but it built up inside her." As his hurt and anger took over, his words began to slip into Cajun French. "So when that bastard Brad Everett called, she let him parade her in front of ten million people. That's how I found out. Somebody called to tell me Lisa was on TV, her."

She could imagine him standing rigid as a lance in front of the television, listening to his sister's terrible story. "I'm so sorry. I mean about everything." She gestured toward the dark waters of the bayou.

"*Bien sûr.* You're a reporter. You know how to sound sorry." His voice was raw, but he had switched to perfect English again as if making the effort could get his emotions under control. "What you really want to know is how it happened. Why she did it. Well, I'll give you the executive summary. Some masked guy grabbed her in the parking lot of the bank where she'd gone to get some cash from the machine, tied her up, threw her on the ground and shoved her face in the mud so she could hardly breathe. Then he beat her up. And then he raped her.''

Tess had gone completely still, her gaze fixed on the man who stood before her. The harsh words had come to an abrupt end. Despite his best efforts, he looked as if an iron fist had smashed into his chest. The sudden defenselessness knocked the breath from her own lungs. Without thinking, she reached out and clasped his hand.

For heartbeats that stretched into eternity, neither one of them moved. Her flesh closed over his as if there were some way for her to offer him comfort for everything that had happened this evening. His hand was hard and rough and warm. The hand of a man who did an honest day's work. Somehow it helped reshape her concept of Vance Gautreau. That and his helpless reaction to what he'd just told her.

He was a man who felt things keenly, who had just suffered a profound shock. When she'd asked about his sister, he hadn't been able to hold the anguish back.

Earlier his violence had been unnerving. Now his calm was equally disturbing. He didn't stir. Except that his gaze had fixed on her as if he were really seeing her as a person—as a woman—for the first time. In the rapidly vanishing light, she could feel his eyes more than she could see them. Despite the evening heat, the intensity of the moment sent a shiver sweeping across her skin.

In the next second, like a razor knife slicing through silk, he slashed the connection between them. Not just his hand under hers. Everything. And she was sure that any defenselessness she'd ascribed to the man had bubbled up from her own imagination.

Gautreau's lip curled. ''Don't try any more of your reporter's tricks on me, *cher*. If I haven't satisfied your curiosity, you can watch her spill her guts on the cursed tape." He turned and walked away.

Tess didn't try to follow.

FIFTEEN MINUTES LATER, the red Mustang ground to a halt in front of a flight of white-painted stairs. Vance took the steps to the second floor gallery two at a time. At the top of the flight, he unlocked the double front door. Five years ago, the riverboat captain's house had been just another nineteenth-century relic rotting in the cotton fields. But Vance had seen the building's potential immediately.

He'd gotten a crew to truck the hulk overland from the river. Then, on weekends and during slack work periods, he'd lovingly restored the high-ceilinged rooms. Now his Greek Revival home sat serene and proud on the shores of Savannah Bayou. It gave him a lot of pleasure to think that someone who'd been raised in an unpainted shack with a bare light bulb dangling from the ceiling could kick off his boots and sprawl on the couch in a fancy place like this. At least if he knew how to do the carpentry work himself. And if he didn't expect to invite New Orleans high society in for afternoon tea. Of course, social climbing had never been on his agenda, anyway. He just wanted to earn a decent life for himself. He wasn't like Lisa.

Lisa. The whole time he'd sat in that jail cell this evening he'd been trying to keep from thinking about what she'd done. Then that sleek blond TV reporter had started him talking about it. And now there was no place to hide from reality.

As soon as he stepped inside the house, he headed directly for the little study off the front hall. The tight feeling in his chest eased when he saw that the envelope was still in the desk drawer where he'd put it. With a muffled curse, rich in the flavor that only the Cajun can achieve, he crumpled the envelope and the letter inside his large fist. Then he carried them to the kitchen sink. It took only one wooden match from the box in the cabinet to set the crisp paper blazing.

The cleansing smoke made him suddenly aware of the jailhouse stench that clung to his clothes and body. With clumsy fingers, he tore off his clothes right where he stood and stuffed everything except his boots into a plastic trash bag.

He'd vowed he'd never end up in a cell like that again. And for ten years he'd made it stick. But his anger had driven everything from his mind except the need to keep a stranger from filming his sister's lifeless body. Surely she was entitled to that much privacy.

Naked, he stalked to the back door and tossed the bag of clothes in the direction of the trash cans. Then he turned away and pounded up the stairs to the bathroom. The water in the shower was as hot as his skin could stand. He was sluicing a washcloth over his ribs and shoulders when he found the bruises. He'd been too full of anger and adrenaline to pay much attention to the roughing up Sheriff Haney had given him once his hands had been cuffed, but he was going to remember it pretty well for a while.

Throwing his head back, he closed his eyes and let the hot spray beat against his skin. To his surprise, a woman's face immediately flashed into his vision. It was the cursed TV reporter—all blond and innocent and appealing. He still didn't even know her name. But her face wouldn't leave him.

In barrooms and alleys, he'd made dangerous men back off with the look he'd given her. She'd held her ground—just as she'd continued to hold his hand. Or, rather, hold his full attention. She was a polished city lady so delicate she looked as if a strong wind off the river would blow her away. Yet, if he were honest, he'd admit that it wasn't the trimmings that had frozen his boots to the ground in front of her. It was the way she'd reached out to him and let him see her own vulnerability. Not many women had taken that kind of risk with him.

For one crazy moment, he'd flirted with the idea of telling her a little bit about his background—just to see her reaction. That would send her running in the other direction fast enough.

But he'd recognized the impulse for what it was. His own weakness. In self-defense, he'd taken her tender emotions and thrown them back in her face, because he was hurting so much that lowering his guard would be like the first crack in an eggshell. He wasn't about to let anything soft and mushy ooze out. Not in front of someone like her. And not now. He had to hold himself together long enough to take his revenge.

ERICA BARRY HAD SPENT the middle of the day driving aimlessly up and down the streets of the city thinking about all the men she'd known over the years. As a girl, she'd been pretty wild. Thank God she'd calmed down in her old age. Except lately she wasn't sure it really mattered much. Somehow guys always managed to make a fool of her. Talk-show host Brad Everett was only the latest in a long line.

When it started getting dark, and she admitted that she had no place else to go, she turned back toward her little white shotgun house. The down payment had come from the money a former lover had given her when they'd broken up years ago. At least she'd gotten that much out of him.

On the front porch was a basket of fruit and a card thanking her for being on the Brad Everett show. The gift brought a mirthless laugh to her lips.

The phone was ringing as she inserted the key in the lock. Ignoring the summons, she brought the fruit in and set the basket on the dining-room table. As she stared at the polished apples and perfect oranges all done up in red cellophane like a Valentine present, the laughter changed to tears. The phone rang again. She waited until it stopped before lifting the receiver off the hook and closing it in the dishwasher so she wouldn't hear the beeping.

She cried until the reservoir of tears simply dried up. Then she opened a bottle of cream sherry and put a stack of her favorite old jazz records on the turntable. The sweet wine and familiar presence of Duke Ellington were comforting. Neither demanded anything but her indulgence.

The knock on the door came at eleven-thirty.

Erica kept silent for several moments, hoping that whoever wanted to invade her privacy so late in the evening would go away. But the music had betrayed her presence, and the knock came again.

Finally she tiptoed to the door and called out, "Who is it?"

"I'd like to talk to you, Erica."

She was startled by the voice on the other side of the door. Why was *he* here? Why now?

"I'd like to come in," he repeated, his voice soft and persuasive. "Please."

She pulled aside the curtains in the living room window. He looked apologetic and humble standing under the porch light, so she opened the door on the chain. Maybe she wouldn't have let him in if she hadn't killed most of the bottle of sherry. It helped her decide she didn't have anything left to lose—with this man or any other.

They stood looking at each other for several moments.

"I'm sorry about what happened on the program," he murmured.

"My fault for volunteering."

"Did you and Lisa know each other?" he asked in a voice that was barely above a whisper. "Or was it just a coincidence?"

"Lisa who?"

"Just another guest who was at the wrong place at the wrong time."

As he followed her across the living room toward the couch, she wondered why the conversation wasn't making much sense. Probably too much wine.

But even if her mind hadn't been fuzzy from the alcohol, there was no way she could have known about the coil of rope wrapped around his waist or the four-inch switchblade knife in his trouser pocket. She found out about the rope first. The knife came later, after he'd thrown her on the couch and gagged her with the scarf she'd worn on TV that morning.

Chapter Three

The monsters only came when the moon was round and yellow in the midnight sky. They were gray, indistinct shapes creeping through the moonlight. Shadows flickering on the wall. But their voices were loud and rough and solid.

The terror started with their voices in the darkness. No, one terrible voice. Whispering. Urging the others on. Getting them ready to attack.

Then the front door splintered, and the invaders were in the house. Dozens of booted feet drummed on the rough floorboards. Evil. Come to hurt Momma—and her.

"Momma. I'm frightened, Momma."

The only answer was a woman's scream.

No savior stood between the little girl and the attackers. Defenseless, alone, she surrendered to her own blind terror. Get away. Before they got her, too.

The window. Momma had told her if the monsters ever came, she might have to get out the window.

It was a long fall. She tumbled to the ground, gasping to pull the damp night air back into her lungs.

"*Où est l'enfant?*"

"*Arrêtez-la!* Stop her."

Tess shrank into the underbrush until the booted feet had thundered past. Then she pushed herself up.

The moon hung above her, huge and orange in the night sky. It gave enough light so that she could make out the shapes of trees in the inky blackness.

Did that mean the monsters could see her? With a little sob, she started to run through the thick, wet underbrush. On and on, in her white nightgown. Fleeing the monsters with loud voices and tramping feet.

Insects buzzed around her face. Night creatures slithered through the rank weeds. And always, overhead, was the enormous orange disk of the moon.

A green tendril curled around her ankle, trapping her. They had her. Sheer black terror swept through her. They were going to do it to her, too. The terrible thing that started with Momma's scream.

With a shriek of panic, Tess wrenched her foot away and fled on. On and on through the dark underbrush. Until she ran headlong into the dark, still water.

Then she was choking. Gasping. Struggling to keep her head above the surface. But the dark water closed over her—cold and thick—and she was being pulled down, down, down into strangling terror.

Into orange light.

Confusion threatened to swallow her.

The moon.

Tess was standing at the window, breathing in quick, shallow gasps, her gaze fixed on the dull orange disk in the sky.

Reality seeped gradually back into her mind. Somehow she'd been back in the past, fleeing from the half-remembered monsters of her childhood. All at once, her knees would no longer support her weight, and she sank into the antique wicker chair beside the window.

Outside, the huge orange face mocked her, and she
pulled down the shade with a snap. But cutting off the view
couldn't stop the waves of icy cold that rippled over her
skin, nor keep her teeth from clacking together. As if she
were a child again, alone and afraid of the dark, she closed
her eyes, drew up her knees and wrapped her arms tightly
around them.

What in the name of God had just happened to her?

Like a penned animal trying to scratch its way to freedom, her mind dug for an answer.

The bayou. Lisa Gautreau's limp body in the water. The
moon.

The connection didn't make perfect sense.

But it would have to do. Another woman's death in the
dark water had brought back her own very personal
memories of evil.

Her fists clenched. She wouldn't allow it. Not now. Not
after all this time. The monsters in the swamp were not her
reality. Reality was her life in New Orleans. Her job at
KEFT. Aunt Pauline.

What if she and Aunt Pauline talked about it? No, that
was a step neither one of them had ever dared take. They'd
keep the conspiracy of silence, the two of them. All the
long years.

But maybe simply seeing her aunt would help.

AS SOON AS IT WAS LIGHT, she called the nursing home and
told them she was coming.

The huddled figure in the bed was so small and so piti-
fully frail. The voice was barely above a whisper, the
speech slightly slurred. But the aged eyes brightened when
they spotted the early morning visitor.

"Tess!"

"How are you, Aunt Pauline?"

"I'm just fine, honey," the shrunken old woman quavered. She wore a lace bed jacket over her gown. She'd probably still be wearing it when the afternoon temperature had climbed into the nineties. But then Aunt Pauline had worn long sleeves, a straw hat and gloves long after most of the female population had switched to halter tops.

Tess leaned over and they embraced. Her grip was hearty. Her aunt's was weak.

"I watched you on the evening news the other night. It makes me proud as punch every time I see you in front of the camera."

"Which piece was it?"

"Oh, I don't recall, exactly. But it was good. You're the best."

Tess forced a smile. Recent events just seemed to vanish from her aunt's mind like papers scattering in the wind.

The old woman groped for the silver locket around her neck and fingered the delicate tracery on the front. When she saw Tess was watching, her bony hand dropped back to her lap. Tess reached for the sticklike fingers and squeezed, no longer certain whether she was reassuring herself or Aunt Pauline.

"I tried to call him," the old woman murmured.

"Who?"

"I couldn't have any children of my own. Did I ever tell you that?"

"No."

"Who did you try to call?" Tess prompted gently.

The old woman's hand flew to her mouth. Then her eyes grew shuttered. "Call? I—I—must be confused. It's so hard to keep everything straight when you get to be my age."

"Aunt Pauline. Is there something bothering you? Something you want to tell me?" Tess asked gently.

"Remember to water the garden and pull the weeds."

"I do."

"Your mother loved plants, too. At least we had that in common."

Tess tried to use the opening. "What else do you remember about my mother?"

The old woman ignored the question. "You always were such a good girl."

"Aunt Pauline, we never talked about what happened before you took me home with you."

The old woman turned her face away on the pillow. "We will not talk about that," she whispered.

Tess swallowed her frustration. Maybe another time. "I brought you a present," she said softly.

"A present. What fun. Let me see."

Reaching into the bag she'd brought, Tess pulled out a plush pig with a gaily striped ruffle around its neck. Her aunt had a collection of pigs at home. Stuffed, china, brass, wood. Tess had played with them when she was little. She'd helped the old woman add to the collection over the years.

As if the previous conversation had never taken place, aunt and niece smiled at each other, and things were back on the old comfortable track.

"It's so adorable. But you shouldn't have."

"Sure I should. We'll keep it on the dresser for now. But when you come home, we'll put it with the others." She stayed for a few more minutes. Then she reminded herself she'd better get to work before somebody missed her.

THE MANAGEMENT AT KEFT had definitely missed Tess. "Where the hell did you get to? We've been calling your house every fifteen minutes," Larry Melbourne growled as he spotted his only female reporter coming through the door of the newsroom.

Usually the tall, balding program director was genial with Tess. This morning she wished she'd made it to her desk before she'd encountered him. "I was visiting my aunt in the nursing home," she answered.

"Well, you picked the wrong day to be late for work. Chris is breathing fire. Unfortunately, he sent Roger out to cover the city council meeting. And another mobile unit's up in St. Louis Parish covering some alligator festival or something. Now we're up to our ears in murder."

"*Our* ears?"

"Yeah. It was Erica Barry."

Larry thrust his hands into his pockets as he caught the shock of recognition sweep across Tess's face. "That's right. Another one of the guests on Brad's show yesterday. Kind of spooky."

He was watching her face closely, Tess realized.

All she could do was nod.

"The police are on their way over to talk to LeRoy right now. Only he doesn't know that yet. And I'm the lucky stiff who gets to tell him."

Tess hardly heard the muttered complaint at the end of the station manager's speech. She was too busy fighting to drag air into her lungs. She remembered watching Erica Barry and feeling sorry for her when Brad Everett sprang his trap. "But that was yesterday," she managed in a weak voice. "I mean, I just saw her—"

"Right. Murdered the same evening as the show. In her living room. After I talk to LeRoy, I get to interrupt Brad's rehearsal with the news."

Tess tried to pretend she hadn't been plunged into the middle of chaos. "Who've we got covering the murder?"

"George Foster."

He was a recent LSU graduate and green as new sugar-cane. "Tell Chris I'm on my way. Do you have the ad-dress?"

Larry reeled off a number on South Rampart.

"Thanks. Call the van and let them know I'm com-ing." Tess didn't even stop at her office. She simply did a quick about-face and headed back to the parking lot. Af-ter starting the engine, she tuned in to the city's all-news radio station. They were already broadcasting a report on the murder.

Hoping she wasn't going to pick up a police escort, she pressed her foot down on the accelerator. She was going to be on the air herself in half an hour—or die trying.

As she wove through traffic, she considered the story. The police wouldn't have much information yet. What about the Brad Everett connection? It could be an inter-esting angle. But it was probably a coincidence. And no-body down at KEFT was going to thank her if she mentioned it on the air. Let someone else make the con-nection public.

VANCE GAUTREAU RARELY watched television. Especially not KEFT. Especially not after what Brad Everett had done to his sister. So he wasn't sure why he switched on the set in the kitchen while he brewed a pot of chicory-laced coffee. Some mornings he scrambled up eggs and added thick slices of boudin sausage. Today the coffee was all he could stomach.

He could tell that the regular morning's programming had been interrupted by some sort of crime report. The KEFT truck was parked in front of a pretty little shotgun house. But the effect of the nicely done restoration was marred with yellow police crime-scene tape. A crowd of onlookers milled around on the sidewalk, craning to get a good view.

They were better dressed than yesterday's mob on the banks of the bayou. But they had the same wide-eyed, curious look. Spectators jostling for the best vantage point from which to watch somebody else's tragedy.

Vance grimaced. Today *he* was watching somebody else's tragedy. The irony made him reach out to switch off the television set. Then the camera cut away from the residence to the side of the van, and he saw the pretty blond reporter who'd bought his way out of jail yesterday. All at once he knew why he'd turned on the television.

He still didn't know her name, although he realized suddenly that he'd seen her as he'd flipped through the channels before. She looked different on television than she had in person. Not quite so delicate. And definitely in charge.

"This is Tess Beaumont reporting from South Rampart Street."

"Tess Beaumont," he repeated under his breath. The name suited her. The Beaumont was elegant. Tess had a homey, reassuring ring.

"New Orleans resident Erica Barry was found stabbed to death early this morning. A friend, who stopped by on her way to work because she was worried when she couldn't reach Ms. Barry last night, discovered the body."

Sacré bleu! Another woman's life snuffed out. Yet it didn't have the impact it might have had if he hadn't been caught up in his own personal tragedy.

"At this hour, police have no leads in the case," Tess continued, "although they are saying that robbery does not appear to be a motive, and there was a ritualistic quality to the murder."

Ritualistic? What did that mean, exactly? Vance stopped
his mind from speculating. He had problems of his own to
take care of today. But something compelled him to sit at
the kitchen table, watching the rest of the special report.
The murder? Or Tess Beaumont?

"Residents of this quiet, middle-class street are shocked
by the death. Ms. Barry was well liked and has been char-
acterized as a friendly woman who lent a helping hand in
time of need. But she had been despondent for several
months over the loss of her job. We'll have further information on the twelve-noon news."

TESS STAYED with the van until the noon news program.
But when she told Chris they weren't going to get any more
substantive information from the police for several days,
he suggested that she go back to the stories she was working on.

That's what she'd intended, but she heard other words
leaping to her lips. "Since I'm already out, I thought I
might try to get some more information on the Lisa Gautreau case."

She could sense Chris hesitating on the other end of the
line. "You still want to pursue that one?"

He was giving her a chance to change her mind. She
didn't take it. "Yes."

"Okay. You're not on the list of people the police want
to interview right now. Just a second, let me get my notes."
Chris was absent from the line for several seconds.

Not on the list, Tess thought. She hadn't even considered that. They'd want to talk to Brad. And Larry and
Desmond. Who else?

Chris began speaking again. First he gave her some details from the official report. Then he provided some
background. "Lisa was married to a man named Glen

Devoe. Maybe he's more talkative than the brother. Do you want to go over there?''

"Yes."

He gave her an address on Coliseum Street. "Remember, there's a staff meeting at three. You'd better be back for that."

Tess drove slowly down the block, consulting the number she'd written down. As she had suspected from the Garden District address, the house proved to be one of the antebellum mansions built by the English settlers who came to New Orleans in the early 1800s. Like Erica Barry's house it was painted white, but there the resemblance ended. It boasted double verandas supported by ornate columns and enough stained glass in the windows and doors to outfit a small church. The cast-iron fence enclosed a garden lush with magnolias, crepe myrtles and hibiscus.

There was no answer when Tess rang the bell.

Suppose that was a sign, she told herself. Suppose she wasn't meant to stay with this story. Yet she knew deep down that she couldn't simply turn around and drive away.

Tess stood for a moment looking uncertainly at the house, suddenly aware of the eerie quiet. Strange. In an expensively maintained place like this, at least there should be a servant at home. Maybe someone was around the back.

A brick path bordered with clumps of pink-and-white begonias led around the side of the house. It connected with a covered walkway between the garage and the back door.

Normal-looking. Natural. Yet Tess was suddenly aware that this spot was completely isolated from the street. Better leave. She could come looking for Devoe another time. Tess had just made an about-face when a muscular arm reached out from the thick foliage along the white-painted wall and grabbed her.

Before she could scream, a man's callused hand clamped over her mouth. In the next moment she was pulled behind the wild fronds of a banana tree.

Panic rising in her throat, Tess struggled to twist away. She tried to gnash her attacker with her teeth. But he held her fast, his other hand and arm binding her securely against a hard body she could feel but couldn't see.

"Shh! Be still! *Pour l'amour de Dieu.* If you don't want to end up as dead as Lisa."

The warning was no louder than a buzz against her ear, but she knew the familiar, deep cadence. The shock of recognition zinged through her along with the shock of the words. The man who had pulled her into the bushes was Vance Gautreau.

Before she could ponder that, heavy feet pounded along the brick pavement, and Gautreau pulled her further behind a trellis overflowing with lush trumpet vines. As he flattened himself against the side of the house, his breathing stilled.

Two rough-looking characters stopped on the sidewalk. They were both as muscular as bodybuilders. And they were both holding guns. The hairs on the top of Tess's scalp crawled. Involuntarily, she shrank back against the man behind her. His body was tense, as if he were poised to spring.

One of the men on the path turned in their direction. Eyes as hard and malevolent as a water moccasin's probed the screen of foliage, and Tess forgot to breathe. He was looking right at her, and some deep primal instinct told her she was staring death in the face. He was going to pull her from her hiding place and jam the pistol against her head. But the way his eyes appeared to drill into her must have been only a trick of the light. In the next moment he moved on, body crouched, gun arm extended.

"Who was that blond broad? You see her face?"

"*Non.*"

"Where'd she go?"

"Around back."

"*Arrêtez-la!*"

The feet pounded on, and Tess sucked air into her burning lungs. She looked past the broad hand clamped across her lips toward the alligator boots planted on either side of her feet. Neither had moved a fraction of an inch.

Gautreau seemed to realize that his palm still covered her mouth. For just a moment he smoothed a finger across her lips. Then he cautiously lifted his hand. That apparently didn't mean that he was going to turn her loose.

The pursuers had disappeared from her line of sight. Every nerve in her body screamed for her to bolt.

He held her back. "*Non.* When they don't find you, they'll come this way again. And when they do, they'll start beating the bushes."

She couldn't run. She couldn't hide. While Tess's mind scrambled desperately for an alternative, Gautreau pulled her toward the house. There was a low door almost hidden by the foundation planting. In the next moment, Vance pushed her inside. Following quickly, he pulled the door shut just as the footsteps on the path returned.

Outside, hard-edged hands chopped at the shrubbery. Guttural voices cursed—a bastard combination of Cajun French and English. Gautreau must understand more of it than she did, Tess thought fleetingly. Inside the basement, the dank blackness was a heavy, smothering blanket. Mutely Tess turned toward the man behind her and buried her face against the front of his shirt.

They didn't speak. They hardly breathed. But she could feel his heart beating rapidly and knew he wasn't as calm as he'd appeared. Her own heart was threatening to pound its way through her chest.

His weight shifted subtly, and she realized he was leaning against the door. Would that be enough to keep it closed if one of the men found their hiding place? Seconds stretched. She wanted to scream. She clamped her lips together and squeezed her eyes shut.

The doorknob rattled. The pressure of Vance's large body against the barrier held it firm. At the same time, his arms tightened protectively around her.

What would he have done if he'd been alone in this situation. Taken them on instead of hiding? There was no way to know, because he was here, holding her in his arms. She gave herself over to his custody and felt a subtle shift in the way he was holding her, as if he knew she'd granted him trust.

It took several seconds before her muddled brain realized that the footsteps were retreating again. Just when she knew she couldn't stand another minute in the suffocating dark. She tried to draw away.

"*Arrêt.* Wait. They may be out there—hoping to flush you from hiding." The words were so low she had to strain to hear. But she obeyed the command.

Not a muscle in his body twitched. He might have been a statue. Except for the warm breath stirring the hair beside her ear, and the callused hands on her flesh.

If she closed her eyes, she didn't have to probe the musty blackness around them. Now that the danger was receding, every sense except sight was focused on the man who held her in his embrace. His legs were long, his torso hard, his shoulders a broad ledge where her hands could cling.

If she ever had to find him again in the dark, she'd know him.

She felt another change in the way he was holding her. His head bent, and his cheek pressed against hers.

"You were very brave, *cher.*"

"No. I was very frightened."

"But you didn't give us away." He eased his grasp on her and felt in back of him for the doorknob. "I think they're gone. For now."

"Who were they?" Tess whispered.

"We can't talk here. It's not safe."

He opened the door and looked out. Apparently he judged it was all right to leave.

Tess followed him into the sunlight, blinking. He gave her only a moment to adjust before he was tugging her by the hand and leading her swiftly across the yard to a side gate guarded by crepe myrtles. A few moments later they were around the corner on the next street. Vance opened the doors of a nondescript black van and almost shoved her inside. She found herself sitting down hard on the edge of a paint-splattered ladder. Toolboxes were crowded against her feet.

Vance climbed in after her and closed the door. In the dark, they'd been intimate as lovers. Now she was facing a stranger again. But this time she thought she understood him a little better.

She'd been worried about his eye. As she peered at it, his lips compressed.

"What are you staring at?"

"I thought you'd have a shiner."

"*Non.* Haney doesn't like to leave marks that show."

She swallowed. "The sheriff did that?"

"It wasn't your cameraman." He looked at her consideringly. "I didn't think we'd meet again. What are you doing here?"

"I wanted to talk to Mr. Devoe. What are you doing here?"

"I asked first. What do you want with him?"

"I wanted to understand about Lisa, if I could."

"What's Lisa to you?"

The challenge—and the pain—were there in his voice again. This time she didn't make the mistake of trying to comfort him.

"A woman. A human being. Maybe if I can figure out why she felt so alone, why life was intolerable, I can keep the same thing from happening to someone else," she said in a low voice.

"She was alone because she wouldn't let me help her."

"But her husband—"

"Scum!" At least that was a polite translation of his guttural French.

She fought to keep from dropping her gaze.

"Glen Devoe is a dangerous man," Vance continued. "If you want to live to do another live remote, you'll stop looking for him."

"Where is he?"

"He doesn't confide in me. Maybe he's hiding from his rivals in town. As represented by those wise guys who were on your tail the minute you stepped through the front gate. Or perhaps they work for him, and they're doing guard duty while he's out of the house. Either way, if they'd caught up with you, it wouldn't have been good."

"Rivals in what?"

"I told you it's a bad idea to go poking into his business."

"Then I guess it's lucky the door was unlocked."

He hesitated a beat before answering. "It wasn't exactly luck."

Her eyes widened as his meaning sank in. "Are you telling me you were breaking into your sister's house?"

He shrugged. The same noncommittal gesture he'd made when Haney had turned him out of jail. "You say you want to find out what happened. Not quite so much as I do, I think."

"If you suspect foul play in her death, you can go to the police."

His laugh was harsh. "Going to the police doesn't get someone like me very far. Or didn't you figure that out last night?"

"You didn't *go* to them."

"Trust me. It's the same difference."

"Let me help you."

The carefully studied expression on his face didn't drop into place fast enough to hide a flash of surprise. "Not a chance, *cher.* I work better alone."

"I like to pay my debts. Maybe you just saved my life."

He gave her a crooked smile. "Consider it a fair exchange for getting me out of the sheriff's clutches. That was a brave thing to do, too."

The smile transformed the harsh lines of his face. That and the words made her chest tighten. He wasn't a man who gave compliments—or his trust—easily. Not to TV reporters. Not to anyone he didn't know very well. But maybe he was going to change his mind about her. She wasn't sure why that meant so much to her. But it did.

His next words dashed any hope she might have been entertaining. "I'm going to drive you back to your car. And if the coast is clear, that's where we part company, *cher.*"

Chapter Four

"That's my car." Tess pointed to the sporty blue Oldsmobile parked at the end of the block. She'd gotten a good deal on the vehicle because it was a demonstrator with minimum mileage. So far, knock on wood, it had given her no problems.

A spot had opened up in the back of the Olds, and Vance pulled up to the curb, cutting the engine.

Tess watched him roll down the window and inspect the vehicle as if it might yield some secret about her. Next he took a careful measure of the surrounding area, his eyes probing the houses, the shrubbery and the street. His gaze shifted and his head turned slowly. She was reminded of an old trapper she'd once interviewed for a feature story. As she'd watched him walk along the edge of the bayou, she'd had the odd fancy that he was listening to sounds other men might have missed, seeing things in the shadows other men might have passed right by. She felt that way about Vance now. He was more aware than any other man she'd ever met.

Where had he been raised? What kind of life had he led? All at once, a question she'd been wanting to ask him tumbled from her lips. "Where did you learn to stand so still?"

"I beg your pardon?"

Color flooded her cheeks. "Back there in the dark. You didn't move a muscle. Where did you learn to do that?"

"In the swamp."

"You mean so you could look at the birds and animals?"

He laughed harshly. "I wasn't auditioning for a *National Geographic* special. I was stalking game."

"You shoot animals?"

"I did. When we were hungry and there wasn't anything in the house to eat but a half-full sack of rice and the roots Lisa had dug up from the swamp." He stared at her defiantly.

"It sounds like you—you—had it rough. As a child, I mean."

"No rougher than a lot of other dirt-poor kids, I guess. But then you're a pampered city girl. You wouldn't know what it's like to scrape a livin' from the land."

Tess heard the put-down in his voice.

"I think you have the wrong impression about me."

"Oh?"

"I've worked hard for everything I've gotten."

"It's all relative. Where I come from, you don't buy a fancy car like that when you land your first job. You're damn lucky if you can swing a used pickup."

So her car *had* yielded secrets about her. How had he known she'd gone out and splurged on the damn thing to spruce up her fledgling reporter's image? A lucky guess? Or did he have uncanny insights into people's motivations. That was supposed to be her specialty—not his.

She was trained to push the right buttons and get people to reveal their inner selves—without getting involved. So what had she been trying to prove by her protestations a moment ago? That they were on some kind of equal footing?

She wasn't fooling herself. And she certainly wasn't fooling him. She'd had a fair amount of experience in handling people. Yet Vance Gautreau had thrown her off balance from the moment he'd jumped out of his car and raced toward Ken. And he kept doing it.

Since she'd already hit rock bottom, she had nothing left to lose. "Do you enjoy intimidating women? Or just me?"

The tactic didn't work. He laughed. "Maybe I'm just trying to keep you out of trouble."

"Why?"

She had the satisfaction of seeing him look momentarily perplexed.

"I think you're not as hard-boiled as you pretend to be."

"I wouldn't put it to the test." He reached across her and opened the door of the van. But before she could climb out, his fingers closed around her upper arm, holding her prisoner. "I mean what I said. Be careful."

"Why?"

"Two women are dead. Bad luck comes in threes."

Tess felt a chill sweep across her skin. When his eyes narrowed, she knew he must have felt her reaction. But she kept her voice steady. "You don't believe in superstitions, do you?"

"When it's prudent."

He released her, and she climbed quickly down to the ground. Without looking back at him, she unlocked her car. But she could feel his eyes burning into the back of her neck until she'd driven away and around the corner.

A WEEPING WILLOW trailed its delicate leaves over the deck of the forty-foot houseboat, dappling the varnished teak. The stocky man in the lounge chair scraped at the bottom of the bowl of Cajun popcorn. There was nothing left but salt and grease.

Licking the last of the snack off his fingers, he glanced at the television set. The news was over, and the laugh track of a particularly mindless sitcom was cutting through the serenity of the bayou.

"Fermé-la," he muttered. "Shut up."

After wiping his hand carefully on his shirt, he pressed a button on the TV remote control, fading the screen to black.

He felt sorry for anyone who substituted a regular diet of TV for real life. On the other hand, it was important to know what was going out for public consumption. He'd check the news again at five, but so far it didn't look as if he had anything to worry about.

Heaving himself out of the low-slung chair, he shook the kinks from his legs and scratched a hand thoughtfully across his comfortable paunch. He'd come out here so he could be alone to think things through.

Now he had to come to some decisions before he headed back to town. About the Lisa problem. And the Erica Barry problem.

He sighed. It was bad luck the way everything was coming to a head like this. You'd think someone had put a hex on him or something. For a moment the hair on the back of his neck bristled.

Then he shook off the stupid fancy. No one would dare such a thing. He had too much power of his own. No one would risk his wrath.

The thought brought a satisfied smile to his lips. Everything was going to work out. He just had to decide how to handle things. And while he was doing that, he might as well find out what Henri had left for him in the well-stocked galley.

WITH ONLY MINUTES to spare before the staff meeting, Tess shuffled through the pile of folders on her desk. She'd gotten together a list of story ideas she wanted to propose and left it right on top of a stack of pending assignments. Now it was missing.

She distinctly remembered setting it where she could grab it in a hurry. Either she was losing her marbles, or...or what? It wasn't very likely that someone had been fooling around with her stuff. Unless maybe Chris or Larry had needed some material and had come looking for it in her absence.

Glancing at the clock, she muttered a very unladylike expletive. Larry was a stickler about punctuality. The field reporters weren't always included in the senior staff meetings, and she didn't want to be the center of attention when she walked in. Quickly, she thumbed through the pile of material, hoping the wayward folder might have gotten shuffled to a different position in the pile. No luck. And no time to make any notes. She'd just have to wing it.

As she hurried through the doorway of the conference room, she was surprised to see Desmond LeRoy, who rarely came to these sessions, commanding the head of the table. Larry, who had given up his usual chairman's position, was sitting to Desmond's left. Brad Everett was next to him. Chris and Roger Dallas, another field reporter, had their backs to the door.

A man with ambitions bigger than his talent, Roger had been at the station longer than Tess, and he was after the weekend anchor job. In his mind, he'd set up an unofficial rivalry between them. Usually Tess ignored him. That wasn't possible in a meeting like this.

The group was in the middle of a conversation that stopped abruptly as she scraped her chair up to the table. Had the token female on the news staff interrupted a locker-room joke? she wondered. No, from the looks on their faces, it appeared to be more serious.

There were several moments of awkward silence.

"Thanks for stepping in on that Erica Barry thing," Chris said, filling the void.

"But—?" Tess asked.

"Why didn't you make the connection with my show?" Brad Everett got right to the point. Tess had noted weeks ago that in station strategy sessions, he didn't bother with the initial TLC that had such a magical effect on his guests.

"Because of the negative publicity. I assumed you'd want to play it down."

"You assumed wrong. There is no such animal as negative publicity. Anything that calls attention to us—gets people curious, gets people watching—is to our advantage." Brad's steel-edged voice cut into her like a knife. She tried not to flinch. "Maybe there's even some way I can work this into another show."

The station owner shifted uncomfortably in his chair at the head of the table. "I—we haven't set policy on how we're going to handle it, yet."

"Maybe the station hasn't. But I set the policy regarding my program," Brad shot back. "That's in my contract."

Silence again.

Larry raised a hand and rubbed it across his shiny dome. It was like someone rubbing a Buddha's tummy for good luck, Tess thought.

"He's right." Roger Dallas nodded vigorously. "It could boost the ratings. And that's the name of the game in this business."

Tess looked carefully around at the faces in the room. Once it had amused her to assign them roles as if they were the cast of a continuing TV drama about the broadcast industry. The eager but uncertain owner. The ambitious field reporter. The program director who ran the show like a circus ringmaster. The private joke had worn thin months ago. Was everyone else really in favor of this macabre tactic? Was Brad Everett going to do a show now on talk-show guests who died right after their appearances? She shuddered.

"I've been giving this whole thing some thought," Chris said, bringing her mind back to the work session. "What if the blue meanies have it all wrong? What if they're both murders?"

"You're talking about Lisa Gautreau and Erica Barry?" Roger asked.

Brad leaned forward. "Yeah. If they were both given the chop, and we scooped the cops, that would really be somethin'. Beaucoup points for us." He shifted his gaze toward Tess. "You were at the scene on both of them."

She nodded.

"Yeah. So we'll keep her plugging away on the stories," Chris muttered.

"Now wait a minute." The strident objection came from Roger. "Why does she get all the good stuff?"

Chris looked from him to Desmond. "Okay, it might not be cost-effective to shelve the features Tess is already working on. So maybe it makes sense to split the murder assignment."

"Umm. Right."

"Roger, which one do you want?" Chris asked.

"Erica Barry." Without hesitation he picked the newer story, the one he thought had the most possibilities.

Maybe he could just take them both, Tess thought. No, she brought herself up short. She wasn't going to cut off her nose to spite her face. Somehow Lisa had become personal. Partly it was her brother's insistence that a reporter couldn't care. She wanted him to know how wrong he was. Beyond that, she needed to understand why anyone would weight her pockets with bricks and wade into the dark water of the bayou.

Gautreau had warned her away. Now she was putting herself back in the middle of it.

Looking up, Tess saw Desmond LeRoy pull a cigar from his shirt pocket and roll it between his fingers. Usually he didn't smoke during conferences. Now he flicked his lighter. In a moment he was wreathed in a cloud of smoke. *He doesn't want this kind of publicity,* Tess thought. *But he's afraid to go against Brad.*

With the strategic assignments made, some of the tension in the conference room dissipated. But it was hard for Tess to focus her attention on the rest of the meeting. And when she was asked to propose some other story ideas, she knew the suggestions she came up with were lame.

Roger did much better. But she was able to ignore the smirk on his face as the meeting broke up.

STAN REARDON THREW his shoulders back and stretched as the tape rewound. "You really want to run this through again?"

The weary edge in his voice made Tess glance up at the large clock on the wall. Five-thirty. Nobody was going to pay him overtime. He should be on his way home by now. "Oh, Stan, I'm sorry," she apologized. They'd been editing the stranger-danger footage she and Ken had shot. And she'd been listening to sweet little children repeating what their parents had told them they had to do to avoid being kidnapped. In her present state, listening to the interviews had torn her apart. Then she'd pulled herself together and made the theme of the piece the loss of

innocence. She hoped it had the bittersweet quality she'd
been aiming for. But she was too close to it now to tell.

"No problem." Stan ejected the tape and put it back in
the rack with the others that needed final editing.

After he'd left, Tess briefly considered going home. It
had been a long day, but she was still too keyed-up to relax. Wandering down to the canteen, she got a soft drink
and a package of peanut-butter crackers from the vending
machines. If you were going to eat junk food, it might as
well be a treat from your own childhood. Did moms still
pack this stuff in kids' lunch boxes? she wondered. Maybe
she could do a story on that. It might make a cute feature.
Except that tonight she wasn't into cute.

As she munched on the crackers at her desk, she found
her mind turning back to Lisa Gautreau. As long as she
was still here, she might as well have a look at the Brad
Everett segment where he'd interviewed her.

Most of the staff had already gone home as Tess made
her way down the silent hallway to the tape library. Usually the room was very neat—because Larry Melbourne
reamed out anyone he caught putting cassettes back in the
wrong place.

Tonight the shelves that held the tapes from the Brad
Everett show were a disaster. It looked as if someone had
been searching for a selection of the programs and had
shoved things back on the shelves in a hodgepodge wor-
thy of a bargain-basement sale. A number of the tapes had
been stuck in on their sides. Others were turned so that the
labels were in the back.

Tess methodically began to sort through the carnage,
putting the plastic boxes in order and arranging them so
the subjects and dates were visible. Had someone been re-
viewing segments from the show? Had they been in too
much of a hurry to put things back properly?

As it turned out, only one tape was actually missing—the one that had featured Lisa.

If she wanted to dream up an ulterior motive, she could assign it to Roger Dallas—who was probably smart enough to have gone through the same thinking process that she had. Only he might want to throw a stumbling block in her way—by hampering her investigation.

Tess shook her head. She was sounding pretty paranoid. If the tape wasn't here, perhaps the police had taken it. Or it could even have been removed by Brad himself—if he wanted to go back and check on what had actually transpired on the air.

Her face still drawn into a frown, she walked toward the door. Then, some impulse made her turn back for one more look. From this distance, as her gaze swept the material, she could see a hint of a shadow on top of the shelves.

Pulling a chair over, Tess climbed on the seat and reached up to the dusty ledge inches from the ceiling. Her fingers felt a hard plastic corner. She wasn't really surprised when she pulled down the case and read the label. February 20, Rape.

What a coincidence. The missing box. And there was no way it could have gotten up there by accident. But if someone wanted to take it out of circulation, why hadn't they removed it altogether? Still puzzled, Tess tucked the case into her purse and headed through the dimly lit building toward one of the film booths. Only now as she passed each darkened doorway she felt imaginary eyes following her progress.

More paranoia, she told herself. There couldn't be someone watching every few yards. Yet when she got to the viewing room, she pulled the door shut behind her with a sigh of relief.

Running the tape was an eerie experience. First, because Lisa Gautreau was a smaller, feminine version of her brother. They were both compellingly attractive. Although, if you analyzed the faces feature by feature, it was hard to say why. Maybe it was the way the dark eyes dominated. Or the animation. The same defiance she'd seen in Vance sparked Lisa's face as she talked.

Tess found herself leaning forward, studying the young woman's expression, listening to her story with rapt attention. She hadn't wanted to see the show in the first place, because it had struck her as one of those pitiful little displays of human misery Brad Everett loved to dangle before the viewing public. "Look folks. No matter how bad your life is, here's some poor slob who has it worse." Now she found herself wishing she had watched—and talked with Lisa afterward. If she'd still been in a talking mood.

The details were essentially the ones Vance had told her. Lisa had been grabbed from behind just as she finished a transaction at her bank. She'd been dragged through a hedge, folded into a car and taken to a vacant lot where she was raped and left in the mud.

As Tess watched, it was hard to connect Lisa Gautreau with the despairing, humiliated human being who had drowned herself in Savannah Bayou.

This young woman had spunk, grit, determination—despite the terrible ordeal she'd been through. She spoke rapidly, her words following one another in quick succession. She was angry that the police had no leads in the case. She was grateful for the support her husband was giving her. And she had suggestions for the police department on how to protect other women in the city.

About halfway into the tape, Tess began to get a feeling of wrongness about the story. She'd been doing interviews long enough to recognize the little lapses of expression, the subtle shifts of eyes or mouth that indicated a person wasn't telling the truth—or the whole truth.

The show came to an end, and Tess sat for several moments without moving, unable to shake the unsettled mood. Finally, with fingers that were just a little bit shaky, she pressed the rewind button. As the tape began to whir in the machine, she realized that for the past fifteen or twenty minutes as she'd watched Lisa, she'd felt as if someone were standing in back of her silently observing. But that was impossible. She would have heard the door open, wouldn't she?

The logic made sense. Still, she had to fight an impulse to turn and glance over her shoulder and make sure she was alone. Stubborn pride kept her from succumbing. She'd been spooked ever since she'd left the tape library, that was all. However, it *was* late. She was isolated in this part of the building. And she couldn't turn off the tingling sensation at the ends of her nerves.

No one was there, she told herself again. So what did it matter if she swiveled around and satisfied herself that she was really alone?

She turned quickly. Even as she did, her mind refused to process what she was seeing. It was her own distorted fancy. A phantom conjured from her subconscious by a trick of light and shadow. But no. A tall, shadowy figure really was blocking the doorway—blocking the only escape route from the viewing room.

Air solidified in Tess's lungs as she leaped from her seat and back into the corner. Was there anything in the room she could use as a weapon?

She had just wrapped her fingers around one of Desmond LeRoy's heavy glass ashtrays, when a familiar voice cut through her panic. "You shouldn't be in here alone, *cher.* There's no one to protect you if something happens."

Vance Gautreau. It was Vance Gautreau. The man who could move so silently that no one heard him. He had opened the door.

"I don't need protection. And *you* shouldn't be here at all," Tess shot back, anger warring with chagrin. She made an effort to bring her pounding heart under control. It refused to cooperate.

He shrugged with maddening Gallic aplomb.

Tess unclamped the ashtray from her hand and moved back toward her chair. "How did you get in?"

"Perhaps the station ought to beef up its security," was his only answer. Not too many hours ago he'd held her in his arms. Now he didn't come any closer, and she sensed that he was deliberately keeping a certain distance between them. Perhaps he didn't feel as unaffected as he looked. That was something, anyway.

"What are you doing here?"

"You didn't go home."

"Have you been following me around all day?" she demanded.

"Hardly."

"Why are you here?" she repeated.

"It looks like I had the same thing in mind that you did. I wanted to watch the tape," he said carefully.

Still not exactly an answer to the question, Tess observed silently. "Were you planning to steal it?"

"Borrow," he corrected her.

"I assumed that you'd already seen it."

Only the rapid bobbing of his Adam's apple betrayed his emotions. "I needed to know what she really said. When the show was running—I heard some of it. But I couldn't watch the whole thing. This time I made myself pay attention." He stopped abruptly, as if surprised that he'd admitted any weakness to her.

So seeing his sister talk about the attack had been too painful for him to absorb the first time, and he hadn't taken it all in until he'd watched from the doorway just now. She thought she could understand, but she couldn't let sympathy cloud her responses to him. Not when he was standing there admitting he'd broken into the studio. How long had he been there? What else had he been up to?

"Are you the one who shoved the tape on top of the shelves in the library?" she asked quickly, while he was still off balance.

She could tell at once from the flash of surprise on his face that he hadn't.

"You're saying somebody did?"

Tess nodded.

"An interesting development, wouldn't you say?"

"Yes," she admitted tightly.

"Someone who works at the station, do you think?" Vance's eyes narrowed as he looked from her to the machine. "It could become dangerous if they know you found it."

She felt a delicate shiver travel up her spine. "I don't think they could have. It was only an hour ago."

"Then let's put it back before someone comes looking for it." Their gazes met and held. Once more she was the first to glance away. Vance went to the machine, studied the controls for a moment and pushed the eject button. When he turned back to Tess, the cassette was in his hand. She saw his fingers clamp down on the black plastic.

Tess's stomach muscles tightened. He was acting as if he was worried about her. But what did she mean to him? When he looked up and caught her watching him, he crossed to the door again and started down the hall toward the tape library.

Her emotions did a flip-flop as she followed him through the corridors. He moved rapidly, confidently. So her after-hours visitor had already acquainted himself with the building. Maybe he'd lied about hiding the tape, after all, and she hadn't been adroit enough to catch him.

"I thought you wanted to take the cassette," she said as she trailed him.

"I saw all I needed to see. And I'd rather not have to worry about somebody at the station stalking you."

"Why?"

Vance stopped and turned. "Maybe I'm a male chauvinist who needs to protect women."

He'd meant to sound sarcastic. Yet the words brought back the way she'd felt when he'd held her in his arms in Devoe's basement. Safe. Protected. Aroused.

She hadn't admitted that last part earlier. She looked away quickly before he saw the expression on her face.

Vance opened the door to the library and found the shelves without turning on the light. When he'd replaced the tape, he turned back to Tess. "I'd advise you to stop putting in so much overtime. It would be better for your health."

"What do you care about my health?"

Instead of answering, he touched his hand to her cheek. It was the barest contact of male flesh against female. Yet for pounding heartbeats they stood staring at each other as if caught by a force they didn't understand and couldn't control. Her tongue touched her lips. His gaze followed the tiny motion.

They leaned toward each other. Vance was the one who wrenched away. In the next moment, he was striding quickly toward the exit.

Tess made a colossal effort to gather her scattered wits. "Wait. Where are you going?"

He paused with his hand on the knob. "You're going to have to take care of yourself, *cher*. I've got other business tonight."

THE WORST TIME at the nursing home was at night, when the hallways and rooms were swathed in shadows and you could hear the inmates tossing and moaning in their sleep.

Living hulks. Old. Infirm. Useless, Pauline Beaumont thought as she tried to find a comfortable position for her bony body in the narrow hospital bed. She looked at the rails the nurse had swung up. To keep her from falling out. Like a baby in a crib.

She was just like everybody else here—waiting in this twilight way station, praying for the Angel of Death to take her by the hand and lead her out of her misery.

It was strange to end up like this—to think of herself as dried up and useless. But she'd always been a practical woman, and she'd come to terms with her own mortality. And her limitations. There wasn't much left for her in this world. Just Tess.

She was so proud of that girl. As proud as if she were her own daughter. But there was the guilt, too. Always the guilt. Over the years she'd held her demons at bay by keeping busy, but when she lay in bed night after night hardly able to move, there was all the time in the world to think over the past.

She'd done the right thing all those years ago. Hadn't she told herself that over and over?

The old woman squeezed her eyes shut and fought off a wave of remorse that threatened to wash her out of the bed and onto the cold tile floor.

Why had Tess been asking questions? Did she know something? How?

No. That was impossible. There was nothing to worry about. It had all come out right as rain in the end. Tess had a fine head on her shoulders. And she was smart as a tack. She'd had a chance to make something of herself. She'd gotten herself a good job. And she was on her way to a wonderful life. The beginning had been the bad part. But Tess didn't remember a thing about it. And it was over and done. You couldn't change the past. You could only go on marching into the future.

"Pauline."

She remembered that voice.

"Pauline."

Her eyes drifted open. He'd stolen into the room as silent as fog. Perhaps he was just a dream memory.

"You called me."

He was real.

"I did the right thing, didn't I?" she asked in her quavering old woman's voice. The voice that continued to surprise her every time she heard it. "I got what I wanted, and so did you."

"Yes."

She tried to hitch herself up in bed.

He put a restraining hand on her shoulder. "You just rest easy now. You were good for the girl. You gave her a chance."

Pauline sighed, contented. They agreed. It had all been for the best. And if anyone could bring her absolution, this man could.

"You haven't been talking to her, have you? I mean about what happened twenty years ago?"

"Oh, no! Not ever. Didn't we agree?"

"I wasn't sure you remembered."

"I remember everything. Everything."

"It's been a hard burden to carry."

"Yes—" The syllable whooshed out of her.

"And you deserve to lay down your burden."

"Oh, yes. Yes."

The man stepped closer to the bed and raised the pillow that had been dangling from one hand.

"Sleep in peace, Pauline." He brought the pillow down over her face, pressing firmly through the feeble spasms. There wouldn't be a mark on her. It would look as if a sick old woman had simply died in her sleep. Another stroke, perhaps. Or maybe a heart attack.

When he was sure it was over and done, the Angel of Death left the room and let himself out quietly through the side door he'd left unlocked.

Chapter Five

He'd been lying to the pretty little TV reporter, Vance acknowledged as he pulled the truck under the convenient branches of a gum tree and cut the engine. If her car hadn't been in the lot beside the station, he wouldn't have slipped past the front desk where the security guard should have been sitting.

Some need of his own had drawn him back to her. Then, when he'd come face-to-face with her, he'd had sense enough to realize that he'd better keep his distance. The muddled logic wasn't lost on him, yet he knew it was dangerous to examine his feelings too closely. Especially now when he needed every ounce of concentration.

From within the shadows of the branches that hid him, he looked carefully up and down the sidewalk lined with cast-iron fences. The metal barriers made him uncomfortable. He liked the freedom of the back country where willow and oak trees lined the two-lane roads and snowy egrets nestled along the edges of the bayous. But if you had to live in town, Glen Devoe's place was a pretty good choice. The lushly planted grounds were like an insulating barrier from everything but the occasional blare of a car horn.

This time, he could detect no sign of surveillance. Still, he waited patiently for close to an hour before stealing toward the gate where he'd entered the grounds earlier.

He stopped at the basement door behind which he and Tess had hidden. As his hand touched the knob, he remembered the female scent of her skin and the imprint of her willowy body against his.

Cursing softly under his breath, he twisted the knob and tried to put Tess Beaumont out of his mind. The effort was only partially successful. *Sacré bleu!* He was obsessed with a woman he never should have held in his arms.

Now he was absolutely sure he should have stayed away from the TV station tonight.

Once inside, he pulled a flashlight from his back pocket and snapped it on. The high-intensity glow illuminated cobwebs and little piles of dust. The view helped bring him back to reality.

Maybe, he thought with a little snort of self-derision, if the market for custom carpentry dried up, he could make a new specialty of breaking and entering.

This morning he'd been interrupted before he'd had much time for exploring. After playing the light over the floor and the cement-block walls, he located the stairs. Emerging into an alcove off the enormous kitchen, he stood for several moments making sure he was really alone. The only sound of life he could detect in the house was the ticking of the grandfather clock in the hall. It was a tall, handsome timepiece with an engraved moon-and-sun face and a polished brass pendulum. Like everything else in the mansion, from the Oriental rugs to the antique dining room set purchased down on Royal Street, it proclaimed the owner's affluence. And a certain station in life. As if a wild hog from the swamp could buy respectability.

Suddenly Vance felt claustrophobic. He wanted to open the front door and escape. Instead he headed for the broad, curving staircase to the second floor. He'd been here to visit Lisa a couple of times, and he knew where to find her room.

She'd insisted on a boudoir of her own—probably like some rich southern belle heroine she'd seen in a movie—and Devoe had accommodated her. He'd been indulgent about a lot of things at first.

Vance thought he was ready for the stab of pain he felt as he opened the door. But he drew in his breath fast and hard as he stepped into her room. It was different from the rest of the house. Less sophisticated. Childish, even. The furniture was French provincial, and a collection of china dolls in frilly dresses cluttered the top of the dresser. In the semidarkness, he couldn't tell the colors of anything. But he remembered that the wallpaper was a delicate mint green and pale pink.

All at once he could remember Lisa as a ten-year-old in a ragged dress sitting on the sagging back porch of Tante Ernestine's house. An old magazine was spread open across her dirty knees, and she was drinking in the pictures of beautiful people and places.

She'd always yearned for a life of luxury. The trouble was, she'd been too impatient to work toward a distant goal. Fulfillment had to be quick and immediate. While she was still young enough to enjoy it, she'd explained in that logical way of hers that he'd found so maddening because she was so sure she had all the answers. Which was why she'd attached herself to a succession of men with money, and why she'd married scum like Glen Devoe.

But Vance wasn't going to waste his time brooding about that now. Every moment he stayed here increased the risk he was taking.

Swiftly he began to open drawers and search the contents. He wasn't sure exactly what he was looking for, but he was certain he'd know when he found it. However, there was nothing but the obvious accoutrements of his sister's life in the dresser and the bedside tables, nothing under the mattress or in back of the expensive clothes in the enormous closet. There were two exits, one to the bedroom and another to a dressing area outside the bathroom. He realized he'd been smelling the faint odor of decay for several moments. It hit him full in the face when he stepped through into the dressing area. Shining the light around the small enclosure, he realized that the tainted scent was coming from the large basket of fruit sitting on the floor in the corner. It was wreathed with a swarm of fruit flies and must have been sitting here, forgotten, for weeks. How long had it been since Devoe had come to his wife's room? The stench increased as Vance approached, but he wanted to read the white tag thrust into the wicker of the handle.

The words, not the smell, almost made him gag. "Thank you for being on the *Brad Everett Show.*"

Cursing vigorously in coarse French, Vance backed away.

"Yes. Thank you, Lisa. Thank you for giving your life to a talk-show host." Brad Everett might as well have pushed her into the bayou.

He'd been holding himself together for days. Now it took several moments before he could blink away the burning sensation in his eyes. At the bathroom sink, he splashed cold water in his face. It helped. But it didn't do anything to dissipate the odor of the rotting fruit. Wondering how much more he could take, he pulled open one of the drawers in the bathroom and began to sift through the contents.

A bottle half-full of little yellow pills stopped him. He looked carefully at the label. Had Lisa been taking them again? Where had she gotten them? She'd told him once that they helped. Apparently, not enough to keep her from killing herself. He'd better not remove them. Or someone might notice they were missing.

He'd just opened another drawer when his carefully tuned ears picked up a sound that hadn't been there before. A door opening and then a thump somewhere on the floor below.

His breath stilled in his chest. It whooshed out as heavy footsteps began to climb the stairs.

Whoever it was wouldn't come in here, he told himself. Nobody had been in Lisa's room for weeks, or they would have removed the rotting basket. Unless they'd come to the Devoe mansion for the same reason as he. Or unless whoever it was had heard the water running a moment ago.

Hastily he switched off the flashlight. But there was enough light from the moon to guide him to the window. The latch sprang open with a click that echoed like a gunshot in the darkened room. The groan of the sash as he thrust it up was even louder. Expecting to see the door open, expecting to hear a roughly delivered order to *arrêt*—halt—he thrust his shoulder through the opening. Then he was on the porch in the blessed open, breathing the uncontaminated night air.

It was a spectacularly sunny day. But not too warm. Just the kind of morning Aunt Pauline had loved to putter around her garden or disappear into the kitchen to prepare the fancy Creole dishes she loved so much.

She wouldn't be puttering around the kitchen or the garden anymore. Tess tried to feel her aunt's presence as she walked toward the old family crypt in Metairie Cemetery, but all she felt was alone. Completely alone. As if part of her had been hacked away and could never be recovered.

Sorrow was tinged with uncertainty. And also dismay—for the loss of something intangible she couldn't name because she didn't know what it was.

Strange, the way it had always been between the two of them. She'd known her aunt had loved her unconditionally. And she'd returned the feeling. She supposed that at first her own love had been flavored with the desperation of a little girl clinging to the only pillar of stability in a wildly tilting universe. That desperation had softened into a growing sense of genuine affection that remained edged with gratitude. Sometimes she wondered how she might have turned out without her aunt's firm discipline and unconditional support. Aunt Pauline's love and approval had made it possible for her to grow and develop into a mature, responsible adult, but it was precisely the sense of obligation that had kept her mute when it came to certain topics.

In the shadow of her aunt's final resting place, Tess felt the effects of that silence like a constricting band around her chest, making it hard to breathe and slowing her steps as she made her way toward the crypt. Somehow she managed.

"My daughter, are you ready to begin?" Father Boutte asked.

As she looked into the kind, clear eyes, Tess felt a measure of equilibrium return. "Yes, I'm ready," she said, drawing herself up straighter.

In a firm voice, the old priest began to speak the familiar words of blessing for the dead and consolation for the living.

Not many people were gathered at the cemetery to hear the farewell. Some of the staff from the station. Those few of Pauline's friends who were still alive. And one paunchy, middle-aged man Tess didn't know. His face expressionless, he watched the service from the shadow cast by a crypt several yards away. Wishing he'd either leave her in privacy or stop eavesdropping on her grief, Tess deliberately turned away from him. But she felt his piercing stare drilling into the back of her neck. For several moments, he distracted her from the priest's words.

Chris Spencer, who'd been standing several paces in back of Tess, must have seen her shiver. Stepping forward, he put a steadying arm around her shoulder.

"Thanks," she mouthed before giving her attention back to the service.

The familiar prayers from her childhood were a comfort.

Later, after the few guests who'd come back to the house had left, Tess wandered into her aunt's room. On the bed was the suitcase she'd brought home from the hospital. She hadn't remembered seeing the locket Aunt Pauline always wore or kept nearby, and suddenly she was struck with an attack of panic. Quickly she began to search through the gowns and simple dresses. The locket was at the bottom, and when her fingers closed around it, Tess felt a profound sense of relief. She pulled it out and clicked it open. Her own picture, taken at her confirmation, was inside. Now, as she studied the girlish photograph, she could see a line around the outside. Was something underneath? After lifting out the picture, she tried to pry up the silver backing. All she got for her pains was a broken fingernail. *Sorry, Aunt Pauline. I'd better stop fooling with it, or I'll break it.* After putting the picture back, she turned to the mirror and fastened the chain around her neck.

BRAD EVERETT WAS HOLDING off on his threatened feature about Lisa and Erica. Instead, he'd scheduled a couple of shows on cosmetic surgery—complete with women who were willing to show before and after views of their breasts and buttocks to the viewing public. The ratings were up—which meant Everett was feeling smug and LeRoy was keeping his own counsel. Thank the Lord for small favors, Tess thought.

By Friday afternoon, when Chris came into her office and asked, "How are you doing?" she was able to answer, "Better than I expected."

They talked about her aunt for a few minutes, although Tess was aware that this wasn't just a social call. So she set down the interview list Stan would need to put the finishing touches on her French Quarter renewal story.

The news director looked apologetic. "I know you're supposed to be off this evening, but I need someone to cover the final round of the Southern Conference Computer Marathon this evening."

"Sorry, but I've got an appointment I can't break."

"It better be good."

"I'm meeting with Lisa Gautreau's aunt. Ernestine Achord." It was the first time since the incident with the tape that she'd talked about the continued investigation with anyone at the station. She hadn't dropped it. But she'd decided it wasn't prudent to advertise her plans, either.

Chris rocked back on his heels. "I was wondering if you'd hit a dead end and were holding off giving me the bad news. So you won over the aunt. I'm impressed. How did you manage that?"

"I haven't won her over yet. I just tracked her down through the funeral home that handled the arrangements for Lisa. Mrs. Achord was one of the relatives who met with the director.''

''The hotheaded brother was the other?'' Chris asked astutely.

''Yes. I was all ready for another slap in the face, but the aunt's willing to give me some background—if I come this evening. I'm driving out there later.''

''To Savannah Bayou? I can't really spare a video crew.''

''I wasn't planning to take one. At this stage, it's still off the record. In fact, it's not just an interview. Mrs. Achord invited me to dinner—which makes for a nice informal talk. If she has the right kind of information and agrees to being taped, we can do that later.''

''Well, good going.''

Tess nodded, pleased. The news director didn't often offer praise. When he did, she knew he was genuinely impressed.

The encounter might have terminated then. But Chris still stood in the doorway, an uncertain look on his face. ''It's rough country out there. I don't exactly love the idea of your driving out that way at night.''

''How come you weren't so solicitous the last time you arranged to have me hang around Savannah Bayou at night—and spring a miscreant from jail?''

He looked sheepish. ''Tess, you know how I get in the heat of battle. In retrospect, that stunt was probably a mistake.''

While they had been talking, people had been passing in the hall. Now, although Chris was blocking her view of the corridor, Tess had the sudden uneasy feeling that someone had stopped walking and was quietly listening to their conversation.

The crawly sensation wasn't something new. It had started the night of the tape. No, before that. The first time she'd thought someone had been going through the papers on her desk.

Chris misinterpreted her doubtful look.

"Besides, you had Ken with you. And a KEFT van. Tonight, you're on your own."

She lifted her gaze to his. "Chris, I'm all right. You don't have to worry about me." The reassurance was meant as much for herself as for him.

"I guess I'm feeling guilty about you and Roger squaring off over these two murders—or whatever they are."

Was it Roger out there in the hall eavesdropping? Tess wondered. Was that what this was all about? Had he stooped to spying on her to get an advantage in their imaginary race for the weekend anchor job? She raised her voice slightly. "He may be squaring off. But I'm not. And what happened at the meeting wasn't your fault."

Chris grinned. "That's what I like about you, Tess. You're one of the few people around this place who says what they mean. So what time are you leaving for your Cajun dinner?"

"In a couple of hours."

THE TALK WITH CHRIS had lightened Tess's mood. For days she'd felt as if she weren't getting much accomplished. Now she cleared a slew of folders off her desk and finished the scripts for several special reports. In fact, she was getting so much done that she kept delaying her departure. By the time she finally put away the last of the work, she knew she was going to have to push the speed limit to make it to Savannah Bayou on time.

Was that a subconscious acknowledgement that she really wasn't looking forward to this trip? Tess wondered as she slid behind the wheel of her little Oldsmobile. Her feelings about the bayou country hadn't changed. If she'd been able to get Ernestine Achord to meet her in town, she would have. But a couple of gentle hints hadn't elicited an offer.

Then there was Vance Gautreau to consider. Savannah Bayou was his stomping ground, and he'd told her to keep her nose out of his family's business. As she headed down the length of the parking lot, his darkly brooding face—the way it had looked the evening at the station—hung in front of her vision until she firmly banished it. She supposed she had good reason to be afraid of the man. Yet he'd saved her life—and he'd put the tape back when he'd thought it would get her into trouble. Or at least, that's what he'd told her.

At odd moments she kept recalling the encounters between them. Somehow, what she kept coming back to was how it had been when he'd wrapped her in the protection of his muscular arms. Usually she ended up focusing on how warm and strong they'd felt. Or the way his breath had gently stirred the top of her hair.

With a little self-mocking laugh, she acknowledged that he stirred more than her hair. He stirred something deep inside her that she hadn't known existed.

Did he feel the same way? she wondered as her thoughts turned to their last meeting. He'd barely touched her that night. But she'd known he was holding himself under strict control. Because he was attracted to her and didn't want to encourage the feelings? Or because he was hiding something important from her?

In reaction, her scalp prickled again and she gave her head a little shake. Any way she looked at it, Vance Gautreau was dangerous. If she was lucky, she wouldn't run into him on this trip to the bayous.

Banishing him from her mind, she concentrated on the rush-hour traffic heading northwest out of the city. If there'd been any way to make the appointment during the day, she would have found it. But her schedule and Mrs. Achord's simply didn't permit any different arrangement.

On the crowded road, drivers on their way home were jockeying for position, changing lanes and leaning on their horns. And some nut in back of her who was obviously in a tearing hurry kept riding her bumper. Glancing in the rearview mirror, Tess tried to get a look at his face, but a baseball hat was pulled down over his eyes. She had no trouble seeing his vehicle, however. His monster-size blue pickup was in danger of pushing her right off the road. Several times he honked impatiently at her. And more than once she had to jam on her brakes to avoid slamming into someone's bumper.

To add to her problems, her own car's steering seemed sluggish. If the appointment hadn't been important, she would have turned around and gone home. But there was a good chance that if she didn't show up, Ernestine Achord might well change her mind about their talk.

Tess let out a long sigh when she reached the exit from the highway. She was out of the worst of the traffic. But the feeling of relief was short-lived.

Coming back so soon to this flat, brooding country spider-webbed by waterways was like taking another expedition into her own psyche. Only she hadn't realized how difficult it would be to face this part of the world alone after dark.

Cursing herself for being so late, she switched on her brights. They illuminated the narrow road, but the landscape was already fading into contours of gray and black. The trees crowding on either side were looming shapes more menacing in their featureless bulk than in their details. There were no lights in the distance. No houses. And once or twice she caught a glimpse of the bayou—a ribbon of polished onyx in the dim light. Was there swamp beyond it?

Tess kept her eyes glued to the center of the headlight beam. Yet the foliage on either side of the road remained a dark blur in her peripheral vision that seemed to press closer and closer on either side of her.

A small animal scurried across the pavement, only a few yards in front of the car. Slamming on her brakes, she skidded to a stop and then started up again with a jerky motion. The car definitely wasn't responding as she expected. But she wasn't sure what was wrong.

In the next minute, there was another sign of life—headlights high and painfully bright in her rearview mirror—coming fast. Tess lifted her left hand to block the glare. In the next moment, she felt the other vehicle crowding her toward the side of the road. It was big and seemed to tower over her own car. Like the pickup that had ridden her bumper along the highway.

Yanking on the wheel, she tried to swerve out of the way. It took a tremendous effort to make the Oldsmobile respond. Then, suddenly, the vehicle was hurtling toward the underbrush.

For several frenzied seconds, Tess fought with the wheel, sure that she was going to plunge off the pavement and into the darkness beyond. Pulling with all her strength, she finally managed to bring the car back onto an even course again.

Panting, Tess lifted her foot from the accelerator and slowed to a crawl. For want of a better focal point, her eyes followed the red taillights of the other car as they disappeared into the distance.

She wasn't aware that her whole body was trembling violently until she felt her hands vibrating against the hard plastic surface of the wheel. It was slick with her own cold sweat. Wiping her palms against the skirt of her dress, she fought to keep from coming undone.

The first thing she'd better do was turn on the hazard lights. As she stabbed at the button, her mind continued to churn. Someone had come within a hair's breadth of rear-ending her. And even though her car had been in for a twenty-thousand mile check in the past month, there was obviously something wrong with the steering.

Another car passed, sounding its horn loudly, and Tess jumped. Whatever her options, she couldn't simply sit here half on and half off the road. She was sure to get hit.

And what exactly were her options? she asked herself bleakly. It looked as if she would have to choose between very unappealing alternatives. Driving a disabled car. Waiting on a lonely road for help. Or walking.

At the thought of stepping out into the darkness, a host of old fears clawed at her like unseen goblins mewling and raking at her flesh. Alone at night. In the bayou country. Unprotected. Vulnerable.

A shudder started at the base of her spine and traveled upward, making her whole body throb.

She wanted to climb into the back seat and curl into a ball like a frightened child. Yet she knew that in reality, huddling in the Oldsmobile was just as dangerous as getting out. She'd covered enough traffic accidents to know that anyone barreling down the road could smash into her car.

Well, she was only about five miles from Savannah Bayou. Probably the best thing to do was to drive very slowly into town and call Mrs. Achord.

Turning on the radio, she fiddled with the dial until she found a station playing a cheerful mix of golden oldies and light rock.

Hazard lights still blinking, she began to make her slow way into town—dismayed to find that in the five minutes since the near miss, the steering had deteriorated even more. If there had been any other option, she would have pulled over again. But she couldn't take the chance.

At least the country was more open now, and she didn't feel quite so hemmed in. When she came to a straight stretch, she was unable to resist the temptation to increase her speed a bit. As long as there were no turns, she should be all right. And the sooner she got to Savannah Bayou, the safer she'd be.

In the distance, she could see another set of headlights coming toward her. Fast and blinding. Like a few minutes ago. Except last time they'd been in back of her. Now they were full in her face.

Tess's pulse began to pound wildly at the base of her throat. All at once she was sure that the pickup truck had circled around and was coming back to her again. The notion was crazy. Yet the absolute conviction filled her mind.

Pulling on the rigid wheel, she tried to edge over to the side, out of the way of the oncoming car. The maneuver was a mistake. Her right tire sank into mud. And the headlights were still coming at her like a train in a railroad tunnel.

She could see nothing but the blazing headlights. Hear nothing but the squeal of rubber against pavement. Then a quick, sideswiping blow sent her car lurching off the shoulder.

As her temple banged against the mirror, Tess screamed. The pain and ringing in her ears were followed by the sickening sensation of free-fall. All at once there was nothing under the front wheels of the car but empty space—and beyond, the slick black surface of the bayou.

Another scream tore from her throat as the front of the car nosed down into endless darkness toward the solid-looking barrier of the dark water.

It wasn't solid at all, of course. The car broke through with a muffled splash. Then it rocked and sank lower. The mud below it made an eager sucking noise, like a great mouth trying to slurp in a tasty morsel.

Her head still ringing and her vision blurred, Tess clung to the steering wheel as if it were a life preserver. There was another dull thump as the car came to rest against some submerged obstacle.

It took several dazed, disoriented moments for Tess to realize that the awful plunging movement had stopped. But she wasn't safe, yet. Cold wetness began to gather around her feet.

The car was filling with water.

It was creeping up her legs, up her thighs, into her lap. Instinct sent her scrambling up from behind the wheel. As she moved, the car lurched again. Whatever was holding it up wasn't very solid.

With a little sob, she scrambled over the seat and yanked at the back door handle. It didn't move.

Chapter Six

The water was in the back seat now, lapping at her feet. Sucking in little gasps of air, Tess continued to yank fruitlessly at the door. Then reason penetrated her sodden brain. Like a schoolgirl struggling with a difficult algebra problem, she worked through the logic. Water was blocking the bottom of the door so it wouldn't open.

With fingers that felt as clumsy as wooden sticks, Tess grasped the window crank and began to turn. As the glass started to roll down, she gave a little sob of relief. First she stuck her head and shoulders out, then she wiggled the rest of her body through—and plunged into water over her head. There was an endless moment of mind-numbing panic as the bayou seemed to draw her down, down toward oblivion. But when her feet hit the muddy bottom, she automatically thrust upward. Clearing the surface again, she sputtered and sucked in a deep gust of air. Then, making certain of her bearings, she began to thrash her way toward the shoreline that bordered the road.

When her feet touched bottom again, she sank into thick mud. Half wading, half swimming, she struggled doggedly toward the bank, her skirt clinging in a sodden swath to her legs. She felt the bayou clutching at her clothing, trying to drag her down again into its wet embrace.

Somewhere in the darkness, Tess heard an ominous splash. Teeth gritted, she redoubled her efforts. Finally she reached the bank. Grabbing handfuls of cattails in her numb fingers, she pulled herself out of the water and lay panting in the coarse weeds.

Pushing the drenched hair out of her eyes, she looked back at the car. In the light of the waning moon, she could just make out its shape half submerged in the inky water. It must have hit a hidden cluster of cypress knees or some other obstruction.

Unconsciously, her fingers went to her aunt's locket around her neck, as if it were a talisman that had somehow kept her safe. Whether or not it was the source of her good luck, she was grateful.

The thought of being trapped in the car made her lungs freeze. Struggling for breath, she pushed herself to a sitting position. The next step was to drag herself up on rubbery legs. Standing, she realized that she'd lost her shoes on the muddy bottom of the bayou. Her purse was probably still on the front seat.

Somehow that made her feel all the more defenseless. Around her in the dark, she heard the sounds of the night. Insects. Little animals in the grass. If she wasn't careful, she'd start seeing glowing eyes in the deep shadows.

SHE WAS STILL HOLDING ON to a tree for support when another pair of headlights cut through the darkness in front of her again. Oh, God. In her present state, all Tess could think was that the pickup truck had come back. And she was out here on the side of the road—wet, shoeless and terribly exposed.

Turning, she began to stagger in the opposite direction. But she was trapped by the bayou on her right. And she couldn't cross the pavement. That would be an open invi-

tation for the man in the truck to smash into her and finish the job.

The vehicle skidded to a stop. Then heavy footsteps were
pounding toward her in the midnight darkness.

"*Dah! Que de diable?* What the devil?"

She was terrified of the inky water. Yet the unknown
dangers of the bayou were better than the known horror.
Desperately, she struggled toward the bank again. Just as
her foot slid in the mud and she began to tumble forward,
firm hands caught her and pulled her back.

"Tess."

Muscular arms shifted her around, and she began to flail
wildly, instinctively.

"Easy. It's all right."

"No."

"It's Vance Gautreau. I'm not going to hurt you." He
spoke in English now.

The familiar timbre of the voice penetrated her terror.

"Vance?"

"*Oui.*"

"What—what are you doing here?" Even as she asked
the question, relief flooded through her. Terror had given
her strength. Now she slumped against him. He caught her
easily and held her against his hard length, his fingers
touching her shoulders, her back. One hand went from her
sodden dress to her bedraggled hair, plucking a filament of
water grass from the blond strands.

"I was looking for you, *cher.* You were late, and Tante
Ernestine was worried." He tossed the grass away. "What
are you doing here like this? You're soaking."

"Someone in a truck ran me off the road—my car—"
She gestured back toward the half-submerged vehicle.

"Sacré bleu!" He followed the motion and saw the car. Then his gaze swung quickly back to her pale, upturned face. "You could have been killed. How did you get out?"

"I—I—climbed over the seat. And opened the back window—before the water..."

"I knew you were brave. Yes. And cool." His fingers traced over her cheeks, her lips.

"No, I panicked."

"You don't know yourself very well, do you? A woman should understand her own strengths."

"I know myself better than you do."

"Hush." His free hand traced along her shoulder and then her neck until both hands rested delicately on her cheeks. He lifted her face toward his and held her, not just with his light touch but with the burning intensity of his dark gaze.

There was a subtle shift in him, then. From seeming calm to tension. "A man must understand himself, too. I don't know what's happening between us. I tried to tell myself it was nothing. But it seems I can't get you out of my mind."

The hands that held her face compressed, rough and warm and urgent against her skin. She felt his breath fan her cheek—heralding the heady taste of him. Then he lowered his head, and his lips were on hers.

"Vance." His name was sighed out on a quick little breath. Her eyes shut. Her body clung to his.

Something powerful flowed between them. Heat. Hunger. Needs. She didn't know this man. And he was right; she didn't know herself. Perhaps in his arms she would find the truth.

She heard a moan as his lips moved over hers. Which one of them had made the small sound? Did it really matter?

No. Not when her senses were filled with the potent taste
of him. The masculine scent of his body. His hard length
pressed to her. Thigh to thigh. Chest to chest. Heartbeat
to heartbeat.

She forgot the car in the bayou. The sounds of the night
around them. Everything faded from existence except the
way it felt to have Vance making love to her.

Caution had evaporated like dew in the sun. They
swayed together, clinging, kissing, touching each other. He
pulled her closer, his hands sliding down her back to her
hips, anchoring her to him. She melted against his length,
a small sound of assent escaping from her lips.

A car cruised past, slowed. "Go for it, man! Get her!"

Vance's body jerked. Lifting his head, he followed the
trail of the disappearing headlights. Then he looked back
down at Tess. The confusion in his eyes mirrored her own.

"*Zut*, where is my mind? I need to get you somewhere
safe—and out of those wet clothes."

He swung her up into his arms. Closing her eyes, she let
her head rest against his shoulder. The sparks flying between them had taken her by surprise. No. That wasn't
true. She'd understood all along what would happen if he
took her in his arms again. To be honest, she'd been waiting for it. Her body. Her soul.

She looked up at him through a screen of lashes. He
stood motionless, holding her against his chest, and she
sensed that he was as befuddled as she.

He pulled himself together first. Striding to his red
Mustang, he settled her in the passenger seat, closed the
door and went around to the driver's side.

"I'm getting your car wet."

"The devil take the car."

As he started the engine, she began to shiver. His kisses
had heated her body. Now she clasped her arms around her

legs, settled her chin on her knees and pressed her lips together to keep her teeth from chattering.

After swinging the Mustang around to the direction from which he'd come, Vance turned on the heat. "It's not far. We'll get you warm."

"I'm not cold. I'm—"

"Reacting to what happened."

To her brush with death? Or the out-of-control passion that had flared between them? She didn't ask for clarification.

A few minutes later he turned off onto a rutted road that crossed the bayou on a narrow wooden bridge. Several hundred yards farther on, he pulled up in front of a sagging, one-story house. Tess saw unpainted siding. But the shutters were new. And a pile of lumber and construction blocks was neatly stacked off to one side.

"I'm not sure I would have found this place in the dark."

"I know. That's why I was searching for you. I'd already been down the road the other way."

"What were you doing here?"

"Tante Ernestine called me as soon as she finished talking to you the other day. I told her if she was going to meet with you, I was going to be there."

Tess glanced over at Vance as he cut the engine. He'd carried her to the car. She might be wet. She might have lost her shoes and her purse. But she was darned if she was going to have his aunt see him carrying her in. Before he could come around to her side of the vehicle, she had opened the door and stepped out. Gravel dug into the bottoms of her stocking feet as she made her way to the low porch. Vance moved ahead of her, knocked twice and opened the door.

As she stepped onto the porch, an elusive memory flickered at the end of her mind. She tried to hold on to it. But its substance was as flimsy as mist rising across the swamp.

Vance put a hand on her shoulder, urging her forward. Before she could reel in the recollection, she had stepped into the warmth and light of the little house. Impressions came to her in stages. First she was enveloped by mouth-watering aromas. Black-eyed peas. Gumbo. Shrimp or crayfish simmering in a rich, spicy sauce.

The sumptuous cooking essence contrasted sharply with the setting. The room was neatly but sparsely furnished. Simple wood furniture brightened by calico pillows and rag rugs. Everything precisely placed.

The tiny, white-haired woman sitting in a rocking chair near the window almost faded into the surroundings. Her clothing was drab and monotone, relieved only by the lacy pink shawl draped over her shoulders. Her face was deeply lined. Wide-set, doelike eyes faltered and then honed in on Tess as she took several steps forward.

"Where are your shoes, *ma cher?*"

Vance answered for her. "There's been an accident. That's why she's late. Her car went into the bayou, *Tante.* She's wet and cold, and she needs a bath and a change of clothes."

"*Ça c'est une affaire, oui!* How did this happen?"

"An accident," Tess repeated. "My steering wasn't right. Then a truck swerved across the road." She made the explanation brief.

Vance looked at her questioningly.

She shrugged. "Nothing like that's ever happened before."

"Don't you get the power-steering fluid checked in your fancy car?"

"Of course! I just had it in a few weeks ago and everything was fine!"

"For truth, the last thing she needs right now is a lecture." Ernestine stood and shuffled over to her guest. She reached out, her gnarled hand colliding with Tess's chest. "Wet, yes."

Tess stared down at the old woman, realizing for the first time that the liquid brown eyes were sightless.

Vance was beside his aunt, touching her shoulder. "You rest yourself. I'll get Tess what she needs."

"I can rest myself all day if I want, me. The girl must have a bath, dry clothes, a good meal, *hein?*"

Vance grinned. "You've already spent hours on the meal, you. Let someone else take care of the rest." Without waiting for an answer, he wrapped his large hand around Tess's arm.

Still not altogether herself, she let him lead her toward the back of the house.

"How does she manage?" she whispered.

"She knows the inside of this house as well as the lines in her own face." Vance ushered her into a small bathroom and turned on the taps in an old-fashioned clawfooted tub. "I'll be right back."

Tess bent to adjust the water taps. When she straightened, the damp dress pulled uncomfortably across her shoulders. Slightly befuddled, she reached for the zipper at the back. She'd lowered it about six inches before she stopped and dropped her arms. Where was her mind? She could hardly get undressed before Vance came back.

She was standing awkwardly in the middle of the room when he reappeared. A large fluffy towel and several items of women's clothing were piled in his arms. After setting them down on a wooden stool in the corner, he looked at the filling tub, then back at Tess, and she knew he hadn't missed the exposed skin of her back.

Tess quickly picked up a softly flowered cotton dress from the top of the pile and unfolded it. "This doesn't look much like your aunt's."

"It's Lisa's. She didn't take her old things when she moved to the city. You don't mind wearing it, do you?"

"No. Thanks for offering it."

He gestured toward a pair of thong sandals. "They may be a little big...."

"They'll be fine."

The water in the tub had almost reached overflow level. Vance brushed past her and shut off the taps. A natural gesture, yet an intimate one under the circumstances.

Tess's eyes went to his chest. She could see the imprint of her body clearly against the fabric of his blue work shirt. At least Ernestine hadn't seen it.

He followed her gaze. "There's a clean shirt in my old bedroom."

"You lived here?"

"Both of us did. Me and Lisa," he clarified. "After our mother died."

"Oh."

Before she could pursue the subject, he changed it. "I talked to *Tante*. You're staying here for the night."

"What do you mean? I can't stay here. I have to get back home."

"No, you don't. It's Friday night. Besides, you can't go anywhere unless I drive you."

Her chin came up. "I came out here for an interview with your aunt. I didn't expect to find you here. Are you holding me captive here or something?"

"If that's how you want to think about it. I'm going to do some investigating before you leave. At the moment, this house is the safest place for you."

"Why?"

"Because whoever forced your car into the bayou thinks you're dead. I presume you noticed they didn't stop to help you out."

The remark sent a shudder up Tess's spine. When it reached her teeth, she clamped them together.

He cupped his hands around her shoulders. "We have to talk about what happened. When you're feeling more like yourself."

Earlier in the evening she'd clung to him. Now she kept her hands stiffly at her sides. "What do you mean *you* have to do some investigating? We have to call the police."

He snorted. "This isn't the city with a bright and shiny traffic division and a homicide division and a burglary division. The police out here are Frank Haney or his deputy. If you want to report this to them, you'd better forget about the bath. You can say a passing motorist picked you up, and I'll drop you off in front of the jail, because if Haney sees you with me, he's likely to charge you with reckless driving—or decide I'm the one who ran you off the road."

"You can't be serious." Even as she spoke, her eyes went to the almost-faded marks on his face. The marks Haney had put there. She knew he had followed her gaze.

"*Oui.* You already know how he deals with scum like me." His voice was low and gritty.

"Vance, you're not—"

"Okay. Forget his opinion of me. The important point is that all he's going to do is tell you there's nothing to investigate. Unless you happened to get the license of the pickup." He raised questioning eyebrows.

"No. Of course I didn't get the license. When the truck came at me, the headlights were in my eyes."

"I thought he was behind you."

"He—he must have turned around and come back," she muttered, not happy with the implications. "But that's not the real issue. Somebody hit my car pretty hard. There may be a pickup with a crumpled fender. Doesn't Haney care about the law?"

"Only when it suits his purposes. He cares more about the money he's getting from Glen Devoe."

"How do you know?"

"All right. Maybe he's not on the payroll. But he has to look the other way if he wants to keep his job." Vance slipped his hands into the back pockets of his jeans. "I'll drive you down there if that's what you want."

Tess thought the whole thing over for a few moments. Finally she shook her head. "No."

"Then I'll be out in the front room if you need anything," he said quietly and left her alone.

Tess clutched a handful of her wet dress and stood staring at the closed bathroom door. Once, long ago, she was pretty sure she'd been outside the bounds of civilized society. Being there again made her feel confused and angry and strangely soiled.

Well, at least she could wash away the bayou mud. Maybe if she did that and changed into some clean, dry clothing she'd be able to think more clearly. When she'd sunk into the tub, the hot water began to do its work. Ten minutes later she was feeling not only clean but refreshed. After her bath, she towel-dried her hair and combed it out as best she could with her fingers. Then she slipped into the cotton panties and dress that Vance had brought. There was no bra. But Vance had selected a loose-fitting shift.

Before opening the door, Tess ran some more water, washed her sopping dress and underwear, and wrung them out. She hung them on a wooden rack by the window.

When she returned to the front of the house, only Ernestine was present. Vance's aunt was sitting in the rocker again, facing the door, her back rigid, as if she were waiting for bad news. However, when she heard Tess's light footsteps, she turned and smiled at her guest. "Are you feeling better?"

"Yes, thanks."

The old woman seemed to be looking at Tess's tangled hair. Then she gestured toward a folded towel with a new-looking comb and brush. "You'll want these."

"I'm all right."

"Go ahead, *cher*. I don't need them, me."

Further protest would be ungracious, Tess realized. Taking the offered articles, she returned to the bathroom and worked the snarls out of her hair.

Tess came back to find Vance closing the front door after himself. He'd changed into a white shirt that set off his dark good looks. Her eyes followed him as he moved to the kitchen and spoke in a low voice to his aunt. She nodded.

After washing his hands, he picked up a steaming platter and set it on the table. Ernestine was in the kitchen, too, spooning rice into another dish. Taking it in her hands, she turned toward the table.

"Is the path clear?"

"Yes," Tess answered.

With unhurried assurance, the old woman carried the dish through the door.

"Where have you been?" Tess asked Vance.

"Arranging to have your car towed. A friend of mine will take care of it in the morning."

"Thank you."

He hesitated for a moment. "I checked in town for the pickup you described."

"I guess you didn't find it."

He nodded.

Ernestine had seated herself. Vance took the chair at the other end of the table from his aunt and gestured for Tess to sit between them.

"You didn't have to fix all this for me," Tess protested as she served herself some gumbo and sprinkled rice on top.

"Vance made that gumbo. The boy, he thinks I'm going to starve if he doesn't bring me dinner at least once a week. But I can cook for myself."

Tess shot Vance a quick glance and then dipped her head, sure that no one but his aunt would dare to call dangerous, hard-bitten Vance Gautreau a boy. But it was an obvious mark of affection between the old woman and her nephew.

Forking up some chicken smothered in black-eyed peas, Tess chewed and swallowed. It was quite different from the Creole dishes her aunt loved to cook. But it was equally delicious. "You're quite a good cook."

The old woman sat up straighter. "When I started losin' my sight ten years ago, I was afraid I was going to have to give it up, me. But Alphonse, my husband, God rest his soul, he says he isn't goin' to lose out on the best food along the bayou. So he fixes the kitchen up—with everything in its place. Then he ties a blindfold over my eyes and stands me up at the choppin' board. The first time I try to cut up a chicken, I almost cut my finger off. But I learned."

"I don't know if I'd ever be able to do it," Tess murmured.

"You do what you have to, *cher*. You can tell most things by the feel—or the smell. And if you put them back where they belong when you're finished with them, that's half the battle. Cans are the big problem. But Vance puts big plastic letters on them for me. T for tomatoes. C for corn."

Tess glanced once more at the man sitting comfortably at the head of the table. Whatever picture she'd formed of him before, it hadn't included this kind of loyalty to a blind old woman.

"Alphonse and Ernestine took care of me and Lisa when nobody else gave a damn," he said, as if he had followed her thoughts. "Alphonse taught me my trade. There's no way I'll ever pay back what I owe him and Tante Ernestine."

"Knowin' you've made something of yourself is all the payback I want, boy," the old woman said. She inclined her head toward Tess. "I keep telling him to stop wasting his time fixing up this old house. I can't see the improvements, anyway."

"But they'll keep you from blowing away in a hurricane."

The old woman clicked her tongue.

They ate in silence for several minutes.

"This is almost like the dinners we used to have with you and Lisa," Ernestine finally said.

Tess could see at once that Vance didn't like the comparison.

"Tess isn't Lisa. She doesn't look anything like Lisa," he answered tightly.

"What does Tess look like, her?"

His eyes swept over their guest. "Blue eyes. Dark blond hair. I think she's missing her hot rollers right now."

"Is that the best you can do, boy?"

Tess saw Vance swallow. His gaze came back to her and held. "She's very pretty, even when her hair isn't curled. Her eyes are big. She's got thick lashes, but they're paler than they look on TV. Her face is delicate. Her nose is small. Her lips are soft."

"Soft?"

Tess saw a flush creep up his neck.

"That's how they look."

"Umm. Is she a small woman?"

"I'm five-five. I weigh 120 pounds. And I wear mascara on TV," Tess cut in sharply.

"Pardon, *cher*. You miss so much when you can't see the changes on a face. Or the hands move. So I think I shoot two birds with one bullet by asking the boy to describe you."

"Shoot which two birds?" Vance asked.

Ernestine laughed. "Well, perhaps it's really four birds. I know she's pretty. I know she makes your blood run hot—even though you're suspicious of her city ways. I know she doesn't sit back and let a man take over—or let a blind old lady get away with murder."

Tess flushed scarlet. But to her surprise, Vance joined in the laughter. "And both of us walked right into your line of fire, *Tante*."

"We all know one another better, eh?" the old woman asked.

"Yes," Tess agreed.

Ernestine cleared her throat. "I like you, Tess Beaumont. I'm sorry, me. When I ask you out here, I don't know it will put you in danger."

Chapter Seven

Tess's blue eyes locked on Vance's dark ones—trying to send him a silent message. Out of the corner of her eye, she saw Ernestine turn her head slowly from one of them to the other and fought the unsettling feeling that the old woman could see the communication.

Tess leaned toward her. "I don't think it has anything to do with you. On the highway as I was driving out here, a man in a blue truck kept honking and trying to push me faster. I think he was the type who'll go out of his way to teach an annoying woman driver a lesson—if he can get her alone on an isolated road."

Vance gave Tess an incredulous stare. She shook her head. Why let his aunt think that this was all her fault?

Still addressing Ernestine, she continued. "You've known men like that, haven't you?"

"*Oui, ma cher.* Especially poor men who curse their fate and take out their anger on their women. It could be true. But you may need to look further. You come out here to talk to me about Lisa. Don't you know her husband guards his business closely? Others who get in his way end up in the bayou."

"But he doesn't know I'm poking into his business," Tess argued. "When I went to his house, he wasn't home, and nobody knows I was there." She glanced at Vance, trying to discover if he'd also told his aunt about their meeting in the bushes. His expression was unreadable.

"Did you let anyone else know I was coming here?" Tess asked Ernestine.

"Only the boy, him. And Vance never blabs his business around."

"I know," Tess murmured.

"You say nobody knows about your investigation," Vance cut in. "Are you doing it on your own?"

"No. It's an assignment." She lifted her chin. "I could have ducked it if I'd wanted."

"So your boss knows about it."

"And everybody else at the senior staff planning meeting, but none of them wants to hurt—" She stopped abruptly.

"Which one wants you out of the picture?" Vance asked quietly. From the way his dark eyes bore into hers, she suspected he was thinking about their conversation the night she'd found the cassette on top of the shelves in the library.

"I wouldn't put it exactly like that."

"How would you put it?"

"There's another field reporter I've had some friction with. He's angry about a woman getting the good assignments."

"His name?" Vance prompted.

"Roger Dallas. In his mind, he's set up a competition between the two of us. He wants the weekend anchor job. As far as I'm concerned, he can have it."

"How dangerous is he?"

Tess turned her spoon over and over as she considered the answer—thinking about the times recently when she'd thought someone was poking through her office—or listening in the hall. "I assumed he wanted to intimidate me—or get the edge on me if he could. I didn't think he'd try anything—physical. And there's no proof it was him. It was dark. I couldn't see anything but lights coming toward me."

"Maybe we can get some proof. Starting in the morning when Lonnie hauls your car out of the bayou."

Tess nodded, unsure what to say. More than likely there would be no way to connect Roger to the hit and run. But every time she saw him now, she was going to wonder.

"Drop the investigation." Vance's hard voice broke into her thoughts. It was the third time he'd warned her off. What had he said about bad luck coming in threes?

"Is that why you wanted to be here? To persuade me to forget about it?"

"I'm here to find out what Ernestine thinks she knows—and how much trouble it's going to get her into."

The old woman tipped her head to one side. "I learned how to stay out of trouble years ago. Not like some." She stopped abruptly, and her blind eyes seemed to search her visitor's face.

A chill moved over Tess's skin, as if a cool wind had suddenly swept across the room. "What is it?" she asked.

"*Rien*. Nothing. Something from long ago just touched me. Before Lisa. It's of no importance now."

Before Tess could pursue the subject, Ernestine pushed back her chair. "Let me get the dessert. I have a bread pudding that shouldn't go to waste."

"This is a woman who knows how to change the subject when she wants to," Vance observed. "Did you make this bread pudding for me or her?"

"For our guest, of course."

"But I hope you remembered the way I like it," Vance teased.

"With lots of sugar and cream and raisins and nice crusty bread, *hein?*"

Ernestine knew a lot more than how to change the subject, Tess thought. She knew how to step in and bring the tension down a notch or two, as well.

While the old woman got the pudding and made strong, chicory-laced coffee, Tess cleared the table and Vance put the food away.

"You don't have to stir yourselves. Come back and sit down," their hostess called as she waited for them to finish.

"We'll be with you in a minute," Vance told her.

"She didn't need to go to all this trouble for me," Tess whispered.

"She loves it. Ask for her recipes and you'll top off her day."

For a few moments they all enjoyed the rich dessert and the strong coffee. And Tess did ask for some pointers on the dishes she'd enjoyed most.

Finally Ernestine wiped her lips with her napkin. "I know you came here to talk about Lisa. Thank you for indulging me."

"You have to wait for the right time for some things," Tess murmured.

Ernestine smiled at her. "Ah. The good God gave you wisdom." Then she settled back in her chair. "The thing you must understand is that Lisa hated being poor. And she hated people around her calling her names. They both hated that."

Tess looked from the old woman to the man at the end of the table, remembering their recent conversation about the sheriff and their first meeting—at the jail. She'd been afraid of Vance then. Despite the relaxed atmosphere Ernestine had tried to create, the fear was still there. No, it was a different kind of fear. Yet she felt as if some of the old woman's courage had rubbed off on her. "They called you names?" she asked Vance softly.

"*Un salaud*. Bastard, mostly," he tossed out. "Why not? It was true, and kids like to taunt one another with the truth. Jacqueline got pregnant with me when she went to work in the city. When she told her lover, he wouldn't take any responsibility, so she came home to have the baby. Then he changed his mind and felt guilty about her or something and brought her back to town. He didn't want me, so I stayed here with Ernestine and Alphonse. She made the mistake of getting pregnant again a couple of years later. I guess it was too much for him. I gather he made things unpleasant enough so that she came slinking back here for good. The three of us lived together for a while—a couple of miles down the bayou. But she was never very well." His face contorted. "No, let's not pretty it up. She was drunk almost every evening. Most of her income she earned lying on her back. So you see where people like Sheriff Haney get their opinion of me."

"You didn't do anything."

"Actually, I did. As long as you're going to be called names, you might as well live up to them."

"He wasn't a bad boy," Ernestine broke in. "He just ran a little wild."

Tess stared at Vance. He'd called his mother by her first name, as if they weren't even related, and he'd tossed off the account of his early life in flat, unemotional tones. However, he'd watched her carefully as he spoke.

The story made her chest tighten, but she knew he didn't want her pity. "How old were you when your mother died?"

"Eleven. It was better, really, with her gone. Ernestine and Alphonse took us in. For a few years, I hated Alphonse. He was pretty strict with me. No more staying out all night—or stealing beer from the back room at the Paradise Café or raiding fishermen's traps. But discipline was what I needed, and later I realized he was doing it out of love. Both of them were more loving parents than either one of mine ever was.''

The old woman reached out and fumbled for his hand. Vance took it and squeezed. ''They were poor, but they shared what they had with us,'' he said. ''Alphonse taught me to work with wood. That was a priceless gift. Maybe that's why I started to settle down. Because I saw I could accomplish something.''

No one spoke for several moments.

''It's late,'' Vance finally muttered. ''You should go to bed now, *Tante*.''

''Yes. But first I have to tell Tess one more thing. Lisa's story is—'' She stopped and fumbled for the right word. ''Complicated. She was fragile. More fragile than the boy. And she remade the world to suit herself.''

''How do you mean?'' Tess asked.

''She told herself stories. About how she wished her life was. And after a time I think she believed them. When she met Glen Devoe, she was living in the city—pretending that Vance and Alphonse and her mother and me were no more real than swamp mist. She wiped us out of existence and spun him a bunch of fairy stories about where she came from, and he believed her. She was so pretty. And a good talker.''

Tess looked from Vance to his aunt and saw the anguish etched on both faces. Whatever she'd expected to hear, it hadn't been this. ''Lisa hurt both of you terribly. But you both still loved her.''

''Yes. Even after she tells us to stay away from her so she won't be dragged down to our level,'' Ernestine said.

"My God."

"Then somebody ripped the fairy story to shreds. At least for her," Vance grated. "Somebody dragged her through the mud. Humiliated her. Raped her. Or she could have made it up for some reason of her own. Maybe it was because her marriage had gone bad. Maybe she thought if he felt sorry for her, Devoe would love her again. Or it could be she was trying to deal with something else that somebody doesn't want us to know about." He ran his fingers through his hair. "The devil of it is, I don't know what to think anymore."

"When I watched the videotape of the show, I knew she wasn't telling the whole truth," Tess admitted. "But I don't have any more facts than you do. I was hoping you could fill in the blanks. One thing I don't understand. If she wanted a place for herself, if she wanted to pretend she was a different person, why didn't she use her husband's name?"

"She did," Vance answered. "Then, on the TV show, she was suddenly Lisa Gautreau again."

Ernestine shook her head. "There's so much we don't understand. You comfort yourself as best you can. She had our love, her. All she had to do to get our help was ask. But she was too proud to let us share the burden."

"Or too frightened," Vance grated. "Or maybe she thought we wouldn't stand by her anymore. Maybe she thought we hated her."

None of them had any real answers. Silence reigned in the little room. Finally the old woman scraped back her chair. "I *am* tired. If you want to know more, we can talk again in the morning."

It was obvious that discussing Lisa had taken a lot out of Ernestine. Strangely, it had taken a lot out of Tess, too. "Yes," she agreed. "Let's continue in the morning."

PUFFING CONTENTEDLY on his cigar, Desmond LeRoy strolled to the sliding glass window of his twelfth-story condo and looked over the black velvet expanse of the Mississippi. Upriver, jewels glistened against the velvet— the lights of a barge as it made its slow way up toward St. Louis. He could imagine the crew in the lounge, honest, hard-working men. They were relaxing now, drinking cans of soda, eyes fixed on the television set. KEFT, of course.

He glanced at the gold Rolex on his wrist. Eight-thirty. So they'd be watching *Shoot to Kill*.

He pivoted, sweeping his arm in a semicircle like a king surveying his domain, following the broad movement with his gaze.

He'd been through some tough times, and not so long ago, either. He'd even made a couple of mistakes along the way. But that was all behind him. Now he only had to look to the future.

He couldn't see the station's transmission tower. But he knew it was out there in the dark—beaming the KEFT signal in a wide circle like rays from the torch held aloft by the Statue of Liberty. Like they used to show on the old RKO news. Or did he have that mixed up?

How many of the ordinary people out there were watching? Thanks to Larry and Brad and Chris and the news team, more and more of them were tuning in.

The thought of all the common folk turned toward the flickering light of the TV, all watching his station, brought a warm glow to his chest. He let it build, let the pleasure grow and swell. At first it was very sweet. Gratifying. Like the rush from a line of good coke. Only better. Then the pressure started to balloon—until it was wedged against his lungs, making it hard to breathe.

Triumph expanded into fear.

People came at you with plans and propositions. But somewhere along the line, if you weren't careful, you lost control. Events could compel you forward. And you knew you were the one who was going to be sitting up the creek in the wire canoe if it all went bad.

He puffed rapidly in and out on his cigar. The nicotine helped. Like Larry said, you had to take chances for ratings—for the station. It was worth the whole game if you won. Market shares got you commercial bucks. Money got you power. Respect. Security. The things he'd wanted—needed—all his life.

IT WASN'T EASY FOR TESS to get to sleep. She had come here for information about Lisa. As she lay in the narrow bed in her borrowed white nightdress, she wished she could make sense of the story Ernestine had told her. But she'd never met Lisa, and her mind kept straying away from the troubled young woman to her brother and how it must have been for him growing up. A father who didn't care. A mother who'd abandoned him and then come back to her hometown to lick her wounds. It was a pretty good bet Jacqueline Gautreau had taken out her frustration on her children. Probably she'd even made them think they were the cause of her misery. What did that do to a child? Well, she knew what it had done to Vance. It had made him bitter and reckless. Maybe he'd even been headed for prison until Alphonse and Ernestine took him in hand. That had been a stroke of luck. But had it come soon enough?

Tess squeezed her eyes closed. When she tried to imagine what Vance—and Lisa—had to overcome, she shuddered.

Then she drew up her knees under the covers. Really, they'd talked more about Vance tonight than about Lisa. And Ernestine had made sure the conversation had gone in that direction—as if she'd wanted the eager reporter to have a better understanding of "the boy."

Well, it had worked. She did have a much better idea of what drove Vance Gautreau. Unfortunately, thinking about his childhood had an unsettling effect on her. Not simply because she ached for what he'd endured, but also because somehow the talk around the dinner table had brought back an echo of her own dim past. It was like distant music vaguely heard. The notes failed to generate any concrete images. Only shadows flickering in her mind.

She suspected the echo also had to do with the place where she was spending the night. The low wooden house. The narrow, lumpy bed. The night-blooming aura of the swamp all around her. Rich and loamy. So far away from the familiarity of the city where she'd lived all these years. And far away from the problems of KEFT.

The air was hot and sticky. Still Tess scrunched down in the bed and pulled the worn quilt up to her chin—as if she were a child trying to hide from monsters.

She knew the reaction was irrational. She should be safe here. In Ernestine Achord's little house. With a woman like her, you could believe in the fundamental goodness of humanity. Yet outside in the dark, some sort of doom seemed to hover. This was a land of violence. Not just nature's violence. Man's violence. Bad things happened out in the swamp beyond the reaches of civilization. Things she didn't want to think about.

Perhaps it was hours later when Tess awoke. Or perhaps she wasn't really awake—but in some strange state between sleep and consciousness. Still, she knew what had made her sit up in bed with the skin on her arms prickling and her pulse pounding at her temples. She heard his voice. The leader. He had brought the monsters.

Her body began to tremble uncontrollably. They were here again—in this house at the edge of the swamp.

Huddling under the covers with only her eyes showing, Tess peered into the darkness, her heart thumping painfully against her ribs. Tonight she couldn't see their shapes, but she could hear their booted feet and their raspy whispers, as if they were talking urgently and trying not to wake her up. Straining her ears, she heard one speak her name.

The whispers grew lower. Or were they receding? Did she hear a car starting? She was too frightened and confused to tell. The only thing she was sure of was that this time she wouldn't wait for the front door to splinter. This time she wouldn't wait for the evil coming to hurt Momma—and her.

"MOMMA. I'M FRIGHTENED, Momma."

Perhaps she hadn't even spoken aloud. But there was no answer. Once again she was defenseless, alone. Once again, she surrendered to a small child's blind terror. Get away. Before they got to her, too.

In the dreamlike mist, the window seemed to float in front of her. Momma had told her if the monsters ever came, she might have to get out that way. Now it was impossibly far away.

Boards creaked as she tiptoed furtively across the floor. Had they heard? Quickly, she thrust the groaning sash up. This time it wasn't such a long fall to the ground. But the hem of her nightgown caught on the rough wood, and she heard it rip.

Heart pounding, she stood gasping in lungfuls of the damp night air. Then, blinking in confusion, she stared up at the moon. It was pale and waning. Wrong. All wrong. But it gave enough light so that she could make out the shapes of trees in the inky blackness.

Did that mean the monsters could see her?

With a little cry of dismay, she started to run through the thick, wet underbrush.

"*Cher.* No. It's dangerous out there. Come back."

A woman's voice. Momma? Was momma calling her? No. Momma had told her to run. It must be a trick. A trick so they could grab her.

Insects buzzed around her face. Night creatures slithered through the rank weeds and snatched at her feet. Holding the sobs in the back of her throat, she moved in a frenzied zigzag path, trying to avoid them. She had to get away. Or they were going to grab her and do it to her, too. The terrible thing that started with Momma's scream.

Confused, she shook her head. Had she heard Momma scream? Or was that long ago?

"Tess. *Arrêt, pour l'amour de Dieu.* In the name of God, wait. Tess."

She stopped—hesitated, confused and uncertain.

"Don't take another step. There's quicksand out there."

Vance. Vance's voice reached out to her, cutting through her terror and confusion.

Shaking her head, she tried to clear away the broken cobwebs of the dream. Tried to sort the present from the past. What was Vance doing here? In the swamp with her and Momma. No, not with her and Momma. With his Tante Ernestine.

He was still talking, his words slow and reassuring. Turning, she stood still as a statue.

"That's right. Don't move." She heard the relief in his voice.

He was moving swiftly toward her, shirtless—wearing only a pair of jeans. She could hear the mud sucking at his feet, the breath slicing in and out of his lungs. He had almost reached her. Only fifty feet of smooth, flat ground separated them.

And then something happened. Cursing, crying out in surprise, he went down through the brown surface.

"Vance!" Tess screamed his name as she saw his legs disappear, screamed again as she saw the thick mud sucking at him like a huge, hungry mouth opening in the ground.

She was still disoriented—still unable to completely throw off the dream. But there was one certainty in the wildly tipping universe. She had to get to him before the mud swallowed him whole.

"Vance. Oh, God, Vance."

His arm came up, waving her frantically away. As he thrashed, he sank lower into the goop. "Quicksand. Stay back."

The harsh command in his voice and the sudden terrible knowledge that she was making things worse stopped Tess in her tracks. Still, she had to reach him.

Heart in her throat, she got down low on the ground and very carefully edged toward him, stretching out her hand.

"Tess. *Pour l'amour de Dieu, non.*"

"But you—"

"Please. Don't come any closer."

She stopped moving and heard him let out the breath he'd been holding.

His voice was pitched low, meant to reassure. "When you're in the swamp a lot, you learn how to survive. I know how to float in this stuff. You just have to relax and pretend it's water. You can even swim out sometimes."

Was he lying? Trying to keep her from panicking? Crouching down, she looked again and saw that his bare arms were spread wide on the surface of the sticky mud.

"You—you're floating."

"*Oui*. I told you."

"How long can you do that?"

"A long time, if I'm careful. But the edge of the pit is unstable. That's why I went in. And if I try to pull myself up, it's going to crumble."

"I have to get you out." Wildly, she looked around for a rescue line and saw nothing.

"We can do it if we work together." She saw his vision draw inward as he concentrated. "I left a pile of lumber beside the house."

"I saw it!"

"Get one of the boards."

Before he finished, she had already turned and started running back the way she had come.

She heard Ernestine calling anxiously from the window. "Vance? Tess? Tell me what's happening out there."

"Nothing. We're all right," Vance answered in French.

"Please. What is it?"

"We're all right," Tess repeated as she pulled a two-by-four from the edge of the pile. "Don't come out. We'll be back in a few minutes." And pray God it's true, she added silently.

The lumber was heavy, but she dragged it back across the rough ground toward the swamp. When she returned to the pit, Vance was still floating near the top, and he'd moved closer to the edge. But now his expression was doubtful as he eyed the board. "With all this mud dragging me down, I'm too heavy."

Tess's mind streaked back to the pile of building materials. "The foundation blocks. We can use the foundation blocks." She dropped the board and was off again in the darkness.

The concrete was far heavier than she'd thought, and she could hardly manage. But she gritted her teeth, hoisted one of the large blocks into her arms and concentrated on putting one foot in front of the other. Finally she dropped it on the ground and stood swaying and panting beside the pit.

"Are you all right?" Vance called out urgently.

"Yes."

She didn't spare the breath to ask him the same question. Nor did she let panic swallow her up. He had sunk lower. But his arms were still spread across the top of the mud.

"You look like a ghost in the night. A ghost wielding a big stick," he said.

"I hope I'm more help than that."

"You are."

He waited while she slid the board toward him, but he didn't grab hold. "Will it go through the hole in the block?" he called.

Tess inspected the rectangle and the hole running through the middle. Maneuvering the block to the end of the board, she jammed the wood into the opening. It was a tight fit—which made the whole thing an excellent anchor.

"Sit on it," Vance called. "Hold it down."

As he moved to grasp the wood, the mud gave a slurping noise, and he settled even lower in the thick goop. She heard him curse.

Pressing herself down with all the strength in her slender body, Tess held her breath as Vance fought to lever himself out of the deadly trap.

The thick goop was reluctant to yield up its newfound prize.

Tess wanted to scream in frustration. She forced the sound back down into her chest. The last thing she wanted to do was let Vance see how frightened she was. Instead, she clenched her fingers around the block and prayed silently.

Vance was panting now, and she realized with a terrible catch in her throat that the mud must be compressing his lungs. Hardly able to breathe herself, she watched him struggle and finally gain several inches of freedom.

He was dragging air into his lungs in painful gasps now. In the moonlight, his face was flushed and glistening with perspiration. With strong hands, he grasped the wood. His mouth set in a grim line, he strained upward, hauling himself up the board by brute force.

Tess offered silent thanks as she saw his chest come free.

He was getting out. He was going to make it. Then in the next second, the soil at the edge of the pit gave way and the makeshift lifeline dropped. With a curse, Vance lost the ground he'd gained and sank back into the muck.

Chapter Eight

After a terrible moment of uncertainty, the board stabilized. Tess could hardly bear to watch. Yet she couldn't bear not to. Her eyes remained glued to Vance's straining hands and his set features. Inch by inch he hauled himself upward, regaining the ground he'd lost. Then, with a mighty heave and a growl, he flopped onto solid earth.

At the same time, the pressure broke and Tess tumbled backward with a little shriek of surprise. Vance was beside her, pulling her up.

"Are you all right? Are you hurt?"

They both asked the questions simultaneously. Her arms went around him, and all the anguish and fear she'd been struggling to hold back whooshed out of her. She was half sobbing, half laughing hysterically.

"*Cher*. It's all right, *cher*." He pulled her to a sitting position, holding her, rocking her.

For several frantic heartbeats she clung to him, and he held her as if he might never let her go again. She wanted to stay there in his arms, but there was someone else they had to consider. "Ernestine. She knows we're out here. She knows there's something wrong, and she's worried."

"*Oui*, she came into the bedroom to tell me you were gone. She must have been frantic," Vance agreed as he helped Tess up. They were both covered with mud. "What a mess," he muttered, sliding his hand down his body and flipping a clump of muck onto the ground.

Somehow that broke the tension, and Tess started to giggle. "I think it's just mud," she managed. "At least it just smells like mud."

He threw back his head and joined in, letting the laughter carry away some of his own tension.

"Come on, we'd better go," he said.

She looked down at his bare feet. "Your boots! You lost them."

"*Non.* I didn't wear them. They're still beside my bed."

As they approached the house, Tess spotted Ernestine standing on the porch. One hand grasped the front opening of a faded robe. The other gripped the wooden rail in front of her. Her blind eyes were turned anxiously toward the swamp. Seeing her made Tess quicken her step.

She heard them coming.

"Vance. Tess. *Pour l'amour de Dieu.* Are you all right? What happened?" The apprehensive questions reached into the darkness.

Vance covered his aunt's hand with his own. "We're fine. Just muddy," he answered in French.

Ernestine's free hand slid over his bare chest, and she gasped in a sharp breath. "You were in the quicksand. For truth."

"I'm fine."

Tess gulped. "It's my fault. I—I thought someone was in the house. Men."

"There were men. Friends of Vance who heard about the two of you out on the road. They found the car and wanted to know what happened."

"I think I made them part of a nightmare."

The old woman tipped her head to one side. "I heard you get up and jump out the window, *cher.*"

"It—it was a stupid thing to do. I'm sorry I caused so much trouble. I can't explain it...." Her voice trailed off as she saw Vance watching her closely.

God, what a mess she'd made of things. Including almost getting Vance killed. He was waiting patiently to hear why she'd been such an idiot, and there was nothing she could say that anyone would understand. How could she explain how the house and the swamp and the trauma of the evening had transformed her into a frightened little girl? How could she explain something she didn't really understand herself?

"Go get cleaned up. You'll feel better," he said.

"Yes. Thanks." With a quick nod, she mounted the porch steps. Stopping in her room, she snatched up the light cotton dress she'd worn earlier. Then she closed the bathroom door and stripped off the ruined nightgown. For the second time that evening, she stepped into the tub and turned the hot water on full blast. Vance was in much worse shape than she, and she knew she should have let him go first. But now that she was alone, all she wanted to do was get clean and disappear. If she'd had her car, she would have driven back to the city. That, however, was impossible. She was trapped here, and she was going to have to make the best of it.

Tess was back in the bedroom with the door firmly closed in less than ten minutes. There was no lock on the door. She wished there were.

After slipping on the cotton shift she'd worn earlier, she stood in front of the window toweling her hair dry, putting a lot of effort into the vigorous rubbing because that was better than letting herself think. The terror had been with her so long, and she had never confronted it, not even

with Aunt Pauline when she'd wakened screaming in the
night. She couldn't start now.

After finishing her hair, she began to listen for signs of
other activity in the house. She heard the bathroom door
open again. A few moments later, the water began to run.

Tess lay tensely in bed as the shower cut off again. Then,
her ears tuned, she followed Vance's progress as he moved
around the darkened little house. For frozen minutes she
waited for him to return to his own room. He didn't.

As she sensed rather than heard the knob on the bedroom door turn, Tess burrowed down into the protection
of the covers once more. Eyes closed, she detected only the
sound of her own ragged breathing. But she felt Vance
watching her. Maybe he just wanted to make sure she was
all right. Maybe he'd go away.

She let some of the tension ease from her body when the
door closed again. But the relief came too soon. In the next
second she heard him striding across the worn cypress
boards toward the bed where she lay huddled.

One large hand pulled the covers away from her face.
Then he brought his mouth down close to her ear. "I know
you're only playing possum."

She stared up at him through a screen of lashes. His hair
was still wet from the shower. And his fresh shirt was half
unbuttoned. The combination was incredibly sexy, although she suspected he'd simply been in too much of a
hurry to bother with such niceties.

When Tess didn't respond to his comment, he threw the
covers all the way off and hauled her to a sitting position,
pressing her backward against the pillows.

"Vance, please."

His expression was half regretful, half stern. "I can see
you'd rather avoid me, *cher*. But I assure you, we're going
to talk. *Maintenant*. Now. And someplace where we won't

disturb *Tante*. She's had enough excitement for one evening."

So had everybody else, Tess thought. But Vance's hand was a steel cuff around her wrist as he helped her off the bed. Knowing that if she made any noise, Ernestine would come to investigate, Tess let him lead her quietly to the front of the house, out the door, and down an overgrown path that took them to a small three-sided shed.

The missing wall was open to the bayou and to the moonlight. Tess shrank away from the light, away from the dark glow of Vance's eyes.

"Alphonse used to store some of his equipment here. And this is where he used to bring me when I'd done something wrong." He jerked his head toward the wide length of leather that still hung on a nail in the wall. "He'd hold on to me with one huge hand and take down the strap with the other."

"He beat you with that thing?" Tess quavered.

"For my own good."

"But you were just a boy."

"A very angry, undisciplined one. Alphonse used to say, 'I'm taking the boy out to the shed,' and Ernestine's face would go white. But she didn't stop him. Later, she'd make sure we had one of my favorite dishes at dinner." He shook his head. "I don't know why I'm telling you any of this. We're not here to talk about my childhood. We're here to talk about yours."

Tess pressed her lips together. She didn't want to explain—she didn't know how to describe—what had happened to her. And she didn't want him to see the moisture gathering in her eyes, threatening to spill over the rims. Her head was bowed and her face was turned slightly away from him—which was only one of the reasons that the gentle touch of his strong, masculine hands on her shoulders took her by surprise. Gently, he turned her toward him.

As he gazed down at her, she realized he had the ability to confuse her as no other man had. She'd thought he was angry when he brought her out here, but his face displayed a more tender emotion. When he spoke, his voice was raw. "I didn't ask for this, *cher*," he muttered.

"Ask for what?" Tess whispered.

"To care about someone like you. To care about someone I don't understand."

She hadn't asked for it, either. She hadn't even wanted to come outside with him. Still, she felt something warm and vibrant unfurling inside her chest. Rising on tiptoe, she brushed her lips lightly against his. "Someone like me?"

He drew in a quick breath and his hands clenched at his sides. "A woman from the city—where they use people like me and throw us away."

"Like your father did with your mother?"

"*Oui.*"

"And Lisa's husband?"

"Yes."

"I'm not like them."

"I know." He stared down at her as if he weren't quite sure she was real. "I saw how scared you looked when I was thrashing in that muck. You ran back as fast as you could and dragged that board over. And the concrete block. It was too heavy for you. But you did that for me." His face became grim. "I shouldn't have asked. I could have sucked you down into the quicksand with me."

Tess shook her head quickly. "I wasn't thinking about that. I was remembering everything I'd heard about people who never came out of the swamp. I was worried about getting you out of that pit."

"Oui."

She felt her heart thumping against her ribs again, and a fine tremor skittered through her body. This time she knew it wasn't terror that she felt.

"Tess—" His mouth brushed hers with the same light touch she'd used.

She moved a fraction of an inch closer, but still only their mouths touched. They nibbled at each other's lips, drank in each other's breath, deepening the kiss by slow, sensuous degrees. The moist warmth of the night surrounded them. The warmth of excited discovery flowed between them. It was fueled by the danger, the fear, the awareness of each other that had been building between them since the moment they'd met.

They were a man and a woman asking questions, seeing answers, in the only way they could. More tremors swept over her. He drank them eagerly from her lips. Then he murmured something low and sensual as his arms lifted to gather her close. Abruptly they changed their mission and his hands came down gently on her shoulders.

"Non. I'm not going to take advantage of you like this." His voice was raw, as if it had been filtered through ground glass.

Tess blinked.

"You're not . . . I want . . ."

"Cher, I know you'd rather do anything else than talk about what happened before you jumped out the window."

She nodded almost imperceptibly.

His thumb stroked over her lips and he gazed down into her upturned face. "You did something very brave for me. Don't be a coward when it comes to yourself."

Tess swallowed painfully.

"I understand why you didn't want to say anything when we came back from the swamp. But let me help you. Whatever it is, don't lock it inside of yourself. I did that once. It almost destroyed me." His hand tightened on her shoulder. "You need to talk—while the memory is fresh."

Wordlessly, she searched his face. It would have been a lot easier for him to let the whole thing go. Yet here he was, pressing her to unburden herself.

"I don't know how to start," she whispered.

"Just do it. Starting is always the hardest part."

She sucked in a steadying draft of the humid air. "I—I—told you. A nightmare. From being out here. Surrounded by the swamp. And the men in the house." She waited tensely for some sign of derision. He only smiled down at her reassuringly.

"Does this happen to you often?" he asked.

"No. Not for years. Well, sometimes," she amended. "Usually when the moon is full. Like the night I got you out of jail."

"You had a nightmare like this one then?"

"Yes. When I went to bed."

"What happens in these dreams?"

She could feel the cold sweat blooming on her skin, but she forced herself to go on. "When I was a little girl, my mother and I lived out here," she began in a quivering voice.

"*Ici?* Here?" She heard the incredulity in his voice.

"Not Savannah Bayou. At least, I don't think so. But somewhere out in the bayou country where the roads are narrow and the trees press in on either side and Spanish moss reaches down for you like—like—witches' fingers."

"An interesting description."

She shrugged. "I don't know the exact place. I don't remember much. We had a little house—something like

Ernestine's. With a porch. I remember that. I haven't thought about it in years. I haven't talked about it. But when I stepped onto Ernestine's front porch, some of the memories came back.''

He drew his arm around her shoulder and led her to a bench along the wall. They both sat down. ''It was very bad? You hated it out here?''

''Oh, no. Not at first. When I think about life before the city, it's like a dream. Or maybe a story in a book. Anyway, it's like something that happened to another little girl. And I can't be sure about what's real.'' She gave him an anxious glance. ''Do you understand what I mean?''

''Not exactly.''

''Maybe it's the opposite of how it was with Lisa. The story is there in my mind, but I'm not completely sure how it goes.''

He nodded.

Vance was right. Once she started, Tess found that the need to keep talking was like a painful pressure inside her chest. ''I—I—don't remember much about my mother. But we were happy. And she was good to me.'' Her eyes were unfocused, as if she were looking into the past. ''We used to go out in the swamp gathering plants. Momma had a flat wicker basket with a handle. She used to bring the leaves back and dry them. Sometimes they hung from the ceiling in bunches. I liked the way some of them smelled. Others were nasty.''

Vance was listening with great attention. ''There are plants in the swamp you can eat. And herbs some people use for home remedies.''

''I think we did eat some of the things that we picked. And I remember Momma brewing up medicines when I was sick. And spring tonic.'' Tess's voice took on a wistful quality. ''Now that I'm telling you, little things are popping into my head. We'd go trapping crayfish. And then she'd have a big pot of them steaming on the front of the stove. She used to hang out laundry in the sunshine." Another strong image came to her. "And she'd spend a lot of time sitting at the kitchen table typing on an old battered portable typewriter. At night, she'd cuddle beside me in bed and read me a story before I went to sleep." Suddenly Tess shuddered.

"Was there something frightening about the stories?"

"No. Nothing like that. I loved the stories. I used to try to make her keep reading." She took her bottom lip between her teeth. "Part of the reason I wanted to keep her there was because I was scared after she'd tucked me in bed and gone away. I was afraid of the night. People used to come to the house after dark. I'd hear them in the front room with Momma."

Vance's eyes turned hard, and the set of his jaw was rigid. Standing up, he crossed to the open wall of the shed and stood staring out at the surface of the water. All at once Tess knew she'd made him think about his own childhood.

She got up off the bench, crossed the space between them, and gently touched his shoulder. "What I just said. I—I—guess it made you remember about your mother."

He didn't answer.

"I'm sorry," she whispered.

His answer was sharp and instantaneous. "I don't want you to feel sorry for me!"

"Vance, I don't. Not in the way you mean. Not for the man you are now. You've proved how strong you are—how much you can accomplish. You don't have to prove anything more to me." She met his gaze squarely. "It's too bad your mother never knew that her son was solid and competent and very well equipped to take care of himself in the world."

"She wouldn't have cared."

"You can't know that. Perhaps she would. Maybe it would have made her feel better about her own life."

Vance shrugged.

"She must have been like every other girl once. With hopes and dreams for the future. She made some terribly wrong choices, and her life turned into a mess. I expect she felt frightened—and angry—and couldn't cope. The worst tragedy is that she couldn't give her children what they needed."

Vance remained silent for several moments. "I never thought about it like that," he finally said, pressing his fingers over the hand that still rested against his shoulder.

"You've risen above a very bad start in life."

"I had help. From Alphonse and Ernestine. He wasn't actually my uncle. A cousin, really. He didn't have to take us in, but he and his wife did."

"Don't minimize what you've done for yourself."

He looked bemused. "We came out here because I knew you needed to talk about yourself."

Tess laughed. "I guess I find you more interesting."

"With me it's the other way around." He folded his fingers around hers and brought her knuckles to his lips. "You're probably exhausted."

Before her courage failed, she went on. "Yes, but we kind of got off on a sidetrack, and I'd like to tell you about the dream—if you still want to hear it."

"I shouldn't have tried to force you. I'm the last man with the right to make you talk about painful memories."

"I want to—now. While I can reach out and connect with it." She gulped. "While you're here, and it's not so scary."

He came around to stand in back of Tess, folded his arms around her and pulled her tightly against him. She found it was easier to talk that way. Leaning her head against his shoulder, she closed her eyes.

"I guess I knew that something was happening—something was different. My mother looked pale. She didn't tell me, but I knew she was afraid. We didn't go out so much. At night, she'd lock the door and pull the curtains closed. And she showed me how to get out the back window—if anything happened." A peppering of goose bumps rose on her skin. Vance's hands stroked her arms until the shivering stopped. Then his fingers locked with hers again.

"Your mother was expecting trouble."

"Yes. That must be true. And then the monsters came. In the dark. When the moon was full."

"Monsters?"

"Not really. That's how I've always thought of them. Now that I'm grown up, I know they were men. And one of them was the leader. He brought them to hurt Momma. And me."

"But you got away."

"Out the window, the way she'd told me. And then I was running through the swamp."

He shuddered. "There are snakes out there. Alligators. Quicksand. You could have been killed."

Tess couldn't stop her body from trembling again. "I know. Things snatched at my legs. Vines, I suppose. And every rustle in the grass was an alligator coming to eat me. Then I went into the water. It was like tonight. With the car. Only I couldn't have saved myself back then."

Vance pulled her more tightly against himself, his arms enfolding her protectively. "What happened? How did you get out of the water?"

"Somebody fished me out. A man. He saved my life."

"Who?"

"I don't know who it was. I just know he was kind. He was singing to me. In French. A lullaby. Maybe he was a trapper. He dried me off and took me home, I think. And tucked me in bed. I don't remember much of what happened after that. Except that my Aunt Pauline came to get me. She took me home with her to the city."

"And she didn't say anything to you about what happened?"

"She never talked about it. Somehow I knew, without her having to tell me, that the monsters in the house and my night in the swamp was something we were never going to discuss. Or my mother. We never talked about her—about anything that happened before I came to live with Aunt Pauline."

"You'd met her before? Your aunt."

"Oh yes. She'd come to visit us. She brought me presents. And..."

"What?"

"Something I'd forgotten. She and Momma used to argue. About me, I think." Tess's brow wrinkled as she tried to remember more about it. But the details were a blur.

"So you went to live with her in the city?" Vance prompted.

"Yes. She was a very prim and proper lady. From the old school, I guess you'd say. But she unbent with me. In her own way she was like *your* aunt. We loved each other very much, and I was young enough so that she could give me a sense of security—a good foundation. But there was this deep dark secret we each understood the other knew about. And we never shared it."

"That's very strange," Vance mused.

"I know. But I knew I wasn't supposed to ask." Tess swallowed painfully. "I was afraid that if I did, somehow, she'd go away. Like my mother."

"How did she know something had happened? Or where to find you the morning after the men came?"

Tess shrugged. "I never thought much about that. I was just glad she came and got me."

"You must have been awfully frightened. Didn't you ask for your mother?"

"I must have. But I don't remember. I've blocked that part out. I'd blocked the rest of it out, too. Except for the nightmare. As I've been telling you, I've been remembering more than I ever had before. Thank you for helping me do that."

Vance squeezed her hands, his expression thoughtful. "Out here where men like Frank Haney look the other way when it suits them, sometimes the community takes the law into its own hands. It doesn't happen so much anymore. It could have happened twenty years ago."

"What do you mean?"

"It sounds as if there was some kind of organized vigilante action against your mother."

Tess didn't want to believe it, couldn't believe it. For years she'd hardly remembered anything about her momma. Tonight she'd brought back warm memories of a sweet, loving person. And she couldn't bear to have that image wiped away. "No." The instant denial sprang to her lips.

When she tried to pull away from Vance, he held her fast. "It couldn't have been anything like that!" she repeated. "What terrible thing could she have done to make everybody turn on her?"

He shook his head. "I don't know what she did, *cher*. Maybe nothing. Maybe I'm wrong. And there may not be any way to find out. If there was some incident, your aunt was following the unwritten code when she wouldn't talk about it.''

"From what I told you—a bunch of rough men in the house at night—you can't be sure it was the community. You're just guessing. Maybe there was a gang of thieves and rapists operating around here.''

"If there had been, I think I would have heard about them. People repeat stories like that. It's the other kind of thing nobody talks about. Because after the community has punished someone, when everyone realizes what their group hysteria has inspired, nobody wants to remember it. It's a conspiracy of silence. As if it didn't really happen. Or, if you want to look at it another way, if everyone's guilty and no one tells, then no one can be punished. Even years later, it's dangerous to go poking into something like that.''

Tess responded to only part of what he'd just said. "Aunt Pauline wasn't guilty of anything!''

"Perhaps not.''

All these years, Tess had been trying to deal with her own buried memories—her own private terror. Now there was a more important issue. "I've got to find out what happened!''

His hand stroked over her back and shoulder. "There's nothing you can do about it tonight. Come on. You need to sleep. So do I.''

The quiet words made her realize how hard it was becoming to hold herself together.

He was right. They'd both had a hell of an evening, and she wasn't coping very well anymore.

"All right,'' she whispered.

"It won't seem so bad in the morning. That's what I always told myself when I was a boy.''

She pressed her cheek to his shoulder for a moment. Then they started back to the little wooden house.

When they reached the front door, Vance hesitated with his hand on the knob. "Do you need anything? Something *Tante* might have forgotten?"

"No. Thanks. I think I'll be okay."

Vance opened the door quietly, and Tess tiptoed toward Lisa's room, aware that he was following her progress.

Without another word, she entered the bedroom and slipped under the covers. She'd expected that the turmoil of the past few hours would keep her awake. To her surprise, it wasn't all that difficult to get to sleep. Perhaps exhaustion had finally caught up with her. Or perhaps it was the knowledge that the bad dreams never came twice in one night.

Chapter Nine

Long after Tess had gone to bed, Vance sat in the wooden rocking chair on the porch, one booted foot resting lightly on the other knee. He'd made the chair a long time ago. In fact, it was one of the first projects he and Alphonse had completed together.

He didn't move. He might have been a night creature patiently hunting its prey in the sultry darkness of the swamp. But his seeming composure was hard-won. Behind the eyes that pierced the shadows, his mind refused to calm. Tonight he'd bullied Tess into confronting the terrible fears of her childhood. And he'd gotten more than he'd bargained for.

He'd thought he knew himself. He'd thought he had his life under control. Perhaps he had until he'd met Tess Beaumont.

Their relationship should have ended that first night where it began—outside the jail. But fate had thrown them together again. After that, he was the one who kept coming back and asking for more.

He squeezed his eyes closed to try and clear his thoughts. Instead, his mind began to replay the scene in the toolshed. He'd known how scared Tess was to start talking—to let the terror out. But she'd opened up with him in a way he was pretty sure she'd never opened up before. The knowledge made something inside his chest swell. Yet it was hard to hold on to the good feeling.

It had been difficult for Tess to dredge up memories from her childhood. His had been burned into his brain, into his soul. Even now he could still remember the day long ago when *Tante* had told him his mother was coming home to Savannah Bayou. He'd been full of secret joy. And hope. *Maman* wanted him, after all. It wasn't his fault that she'd gone away to live in the city. She wanted them to be a family.

Childish optimism had given way almost at once to the devastating reality. Jacqueline wasn't coming back to *him*. She was coming back because she was going to have another baby, and the man she lived with had kicked her out.

Vance's jaw muscles clenched. Life with the resentful, bitter woman who'd slunk back to Savannah Bayou was worse than anything he could have imagined. During their brief acquaintance, he'd learned how to keep her from hurting him. Not physically, of course. She was bigger than he was, after all. But he'd grown a tough skin so that she couldn't touch the inside—where it counted.

Before he was eight, he'd sworn that Jacqueline was the last woman who would have the chance to kill him slowly. He'd never broken that rule. Even as close as he was to *Tante,* they both knew there was a line that couldn't be crossed. But it had all worked out. He'd survived—no, he'd grown and thrived by being strong and self-sufficient.

He should be proud of that. Once he had been. Now he suspected that while he'd saved himself, he'd let Lisa down. He'd railed at her for not having the guts to do it his way. No wonder she hadn't come to him for help when she needed it the most.

A tremor went through his rigid body, and he clenched his hands around the arms of the wooden chair.

Maybe all his unfinished business with Lisa was the reason Tess had caught him off guard and come stealing past his defenses. Or maybe he was kidding himself. What if he'd been wrong all along? What if survival meant admitting he needed something he'd told himself only weak men wanted?

A stabbing pain of longing shot through him. He made himself conquer it the way he'd conquered all the other pain. Things were building too fast with Tess. He was being swept along by emotions he didn't know how to handle. And that was dangerous.

PROGRAM DIRECTOR Larry Melbourne smoothed his fingers over the shiny dome of his bald forehead, unaware that he was even performing the nervous gesture. Most evenings he came back to work after dinner and stayed into the small hours of the morning when no one else was at the station except the cleaning lady. It was a habit he'd gotten into at his last job, and it had become a way of feeling safe. Except that it was harder and harder lately to hold on to the illusion of safety.

Maybe it was time to move on again. No. Not yet. He was doing so well here. Another few months, if everything held together, and Desmond LeRoy would be raking in the ad revenues. Then he could . . .

He canceled the thought even before it formed. Where was he going to run to next time? Taiwan? Malaysia? Did they hire American TV producers in either of those places?

The phone on his desk rang, and he jumped. Then he glanced at the clock. After one. Who the hell would be calling him at work at this hour?

The phone continued to ring. Eight, nine, ten times. He stretched out his hand to pick it up, then snatched it back and scrambled out of his chair.

A wrong number. Just a wrong number, he told himself as he sprinted down the hall. Moments later, he was climbing into the little silver sports car he'd bought a couple of weeks ago when he'd been feeling confident. It was hard to remember that feeling now.

TESS AWOKE TO THE SIGHT of sun streaming in the window, the sound of birds warbling in the swamp, and the aroma of something delicious cooking in the kitchen. Chicory-laced coffee dominated. But she also caught the subtle scent of orange water and brandy and suspected that someone was frying *pain perdu*. Not the ordinary French toast of other regions, but the bayou's special "lost bread."

The tantalizing aroma drew Tess out from under the covers. From the strength of the sunlight, she guessed that the morning was fairly well advanced.

She'd slept very soundly. Last night someone had put the underwear she'd washed back in her room. And there were a couple of other cotton dresses on the chair. Quickly she put one on and went to brush her hair and wash her face.

Fifteen minutes later she joined the man and woman in the kitchen. Ernestine was sitting at the table, a mug of coffee clasped in her wrinkled hands. Vance stood at the stove frying the bread.

"Did you sleep well when you got back to bed, *cher?*" the old woman asked even before her guest's feet crossed the threshold.

Tess felt color stain her cheeks. So Ernestine knew they'd been together later. How much had she guessed about what had been going on out in the shed? "Fine. Thank you. And you?" she murmured.

"As well as can be expected at my age."

Tess glanced up to find Vance watching her as if there were only the two of them in the room. Pulling out a chair, she quickly joined her hostess at the table and then wondered if she should have offered to help. "I—is there anything I can do?" she asked.

"*Non*. Just relax," Vance answered. "I like to cook breakfast when I have time. I wanted to let you sleep, but I was going to come and get you in a moment. How are you feeling?" It wasn't simply a polite question. She knew from the timbre of his voice that he was concerned about her.

"Better. I'm sorry I caused you so much trouble last night," she murmured.

"Don't worry about that. You were upset. I'm glad you're better now." As Vance poured her a mug of the aromatic coffee and set it before her on the table, she was aware of the intimacy of eating breakfast together. Like lovers who were feeling awkward with each other. No. Not quite like that, she amended as she added milk and sugar and took a sip. They weren't lovers, and they had a chaperon. Probably that was a good thing.

Vance brought a platter of the *pain perdu* to the table and slipped into the seat opposite his aunt. For a few moments they were all busy passing the food. Vance and Tess poured maple syrup on their French toast. Ernestine used the honey.

"It's wonderful," Tess approved after her first forkful. It was tempting to simply appreciate the food and the relaxed atmosphere of breakfast with a charming old woman and her nephew.

"Ernestine's recipe," Vance told her. As he finished off two pieces and helped himself to another, he seemed content to enjoy the morning and the company, too.

Yet this wasn't exactly a normal domestic scene, Tess reminded herself. Whatever had happened in the past twelve hours, she had come here on business. Although she hadn't achieved much, perhaps there was something else she could accomplish—something personal. She chewed thoughtfully for another few bites. Then she inclined her head toward Ernestine. "I guess you've lived around here for a long time."

"Seventy-five years, me. And my family, 200 years." There was a note of pride in her voice.

"So you must know a lot about the area?"

"Oh my, yes. I have cousins and friends all along the bayou from upstream down to the gulf."

"Have things changed much?"

Ernestine's face took on a nostalgic look. "If you mean, can the families still make a living off the land, it's hard now. But the old ways die slow. A rich widower, he marries a young girl half his age. His neighbors show up for the wedding night banging pots and pans and scraping washboards. They don't leave until he invites them in for food and wine."

Tess smiled, delighted. "And what happens if he just ignores them?"

"They come back every night for the next month."

"Maybe I can do a story on the local customs," Tess suggested. "Umm, do people still go out in the swamp foraging for plants and—uh—herbs?"

"Some do."

"Did you ever hear about a local woman who—"

Before the sentence was out of her mouth, Vance had reached across the table and pressed his hand over hers.

"Non," he mouthed.

"A woman who what?" Ernestine asked.

"I think Tess needs to get her car," Vance broke in as he pushed back his chair. "Lonnie called this morning to say he'd gotten it out of the bayou. Perhaps we'd better go and see about it."

The statement was couched politely enough, undoubtedly for his aunt's benefit. But Tess knew it was an order. She pushed back her chair and stood up. "I'm truly grateful for your hospitality, Mrs. Achord."

"I enjoyed the visit. I'm sorry you have to leave so soon. Can't you have another cup of coffee?"

"Uh—no. Thank you, anyway. And thanks for putting me up for the night. I'm sorry about all the extra fuss I caused."

"It wasn't your fault. I hope there isn't too much trouble with the car."

"We'll get things straightened out," Vance told her. Then, his face set in an unreadable mask, he marched Tess out the door and toward the car. Not until he'd backed up and started down the narrow dirt road did he speak.

"Didn't you understand what I was telling you last night? I said poking into that mess with your mother could be dangerous. If you want to get yourself in trouble, that's one thing. But don't pretend to be interested in a story on the local customs so you can pump Ernestine for information."

"I'm not pumping anybody for information. I'm just asking questions. I'm a reporter. That's how I'm accustomed to getting facts. And I thought your aunt might be able to help me."

"Believe me, *cher,* whatever happened to your mother has nothing to do with *Tante.* Don't try to get her involved."

"Come on, Vance. It was twenty years ago. How could it hurt her now?"

"Twenty years ago, *oui*. And in all that time, *your* aunt never let you talk about it. Why do you think that was?"

"I don't know."

"That's right. You don't."

HE'D WANTED EVERYONE to think he was out here lounging on his houseboat. But driving into town every time he needed to take care of personal business was getting old, Glen Devoe thought as he climbed into his Mercedes. It was time to open up the house again. The mental image of his meticulously restored mansion brought a satisfied smile to his lips. He was going to enjoy getting back to the amenities. Like the surround-sound theater with the movie-size screen that he put in downstairs. Or the sous-chef he'd stolen away from Commander's Palace. Reaching for his car phone, he dialed the man.

With no more than a peremptory greeting, he began to speak. "Henri, I'm coming back to town. So you'll have to stop lounging around in your lover's bed. I want crayfish bisque and tournedos with béarnaise sauce for lunch. And bananas Foster for dessert."

"Yes, sir." The answer came back loud and clear over the speaker. But then Glen Devoe was used to having his wishes carried out.

Which was why he needed to lean on his contact at KEFT. Things weren't going so well there. But they would. After all, he had the advantage of dealing with management, he thought with a satisfied smirk as he punched in the number.

He could tell at once from the indrawn breath on the other end of the line that his call had been anticipated with dread. Good. Sometimes the way to catch flies was with honey. Sometimes it was better to blow them away with an Uzi.

"What about the woman who's working on the Lisa Gautreau story?" he asked. "Has she been taken care of?"

"She's disappeared."

"Permanently?"

There was a slight hesitation. "I'm not sure. I'm trying to find out. My contacts out in the bayou country aren't as good as yours."

"Don't concern yourself with my business. Just do what you're told."

"I'm not your messenger boy."

"You're in my debt."

"But I've paid you back."

"That may be true one day." Without bothering to continue the discussion, Devoe pressed the disconnect button and turned his eyes back to the road. But wheels continued to turn in his mind.

Was it harder to control men or women? he wondered.

There were lots of women you could stop dead in their tracks with a little intimidation. Lisa hadn't been one of them. Neither was this woman, Tess Beaumont. Of course, he hadn't expected her to be easy. He'd already had too much experience with her type.

With men, now, you almost always had to get tough. Get them where it hurt most. Sometimes it meant breaking a few bones. Sometimes it meant quite a bit more. But he was prepared for that, too. His motto had always been Whatever It Takes.

TESS AND VANCE RODE the rest of the way down the long drive in silence. There was a distance between them now that hadn't been there the night before—or this morning.

She didn't like it. But as she glanced covertly at his strong profile, she suspected that he did. Perhaps he was even relieved. Things had been moving pretty quickly between them. Given what she'd learned about him, it would be strange if that didn't make him uncomfortable. It was scary for her, too. The difference was, her instincts didn't urge her to run in the other direction.

She wanted to say something that would make them both feel more comfortable. She knew there was no point in trying to sway Vance. He made his own decisions and his own judgments.

Maybe if she slowed things down now. Maybe if they could spend a bit more time together, he'd relax again. And there was something else she should do, anyway. When they reached the main road, she cleared her throat. "Uh, on the way to look at the car, could we stop and see where it went into the water?" she asked.

"If you want."

He turned left and drove slowly for a mile or two, stopping at a spot where the bayou curved. In the daylight, it was just another lonely stretch along the road, but Tess's palms were clammy as she peered at the sluggish brown water and the narrow gravel shoulder.

"Do you want to get out?" Vance asked.

Tess didn't. In fact, now that they were here, she wished she hadn't made the request to stop. But she opened the door and stepped onto the gravel.

She looked back at Vance. He was watching her, his hands wrapped loosely around the wheel. Instead of approaching the bank, she stood with her own hand resting against the warm metal of the car.

From where she stood, she could detect tire marks at the edge of the water, a few flattened weeds, and a place where some stumps sticking out of the water listed toward the opposite bank. Maybe they had stopped the car from going all the way under. Otherwise, there was nothing to indicate that anything out of the ordinary had happened here.

Last night this had been a place of terror. In the dappled sunlight she couldn't recapture the feeling.

"There's nothing much to see," she said as she got back into the car.

"I know. I was here this morning," he answered.

She turned her head toward him. He didn't say anything more. Instead he made a U-turn. Ten minutes later, he pulled onto another narrow side road. This one was paved with gravel. They'd driven only a few dozen yards before Tess could see that the weed-choked fields on either side were strewn with the rusting hulks of battered cars and pickup trucks. It was like a cemetery, only the remains were baking in the sunlight.

"Is this a repair shop or a junkyard?" she asked.

"You'll have to judge Lonnie by his work," Vance replied.

The scenery became more metallic the farther they progressed. But at least the vehicles weren't quite so rusted, Tess noted. Apparently the hopeless cases were the ones most remote from Lonnie's base of operation—which couldn't be too far away. As they traveled up the road, the strains of a traditional Cajun tune, complete with accordions, fiddles, triangles and an enthusiastic male vocal group, became louder.

By the time they rounded a bend and came to a stop in front of a low corrugated steel building set in the center of a circle of autos, the cacophony had reached a painful decibel level. Tess clamped her hands over her ears and got out of the car. Perhaps Lonnie was somewhere in the field of cars and had turned up his radio so he could hear. No, she took the speculation back as she spotted a pair of short, stumpy legs protruding from under a late-model Ford. One of them was flopping up and down in time with the ear-destroying music.

Vance, who seemed to know his way around the place, strode toward the boom box resting on a fifty-gallon drum. After turning down the volume to a tolerable level, he went over to the Ford and addressed the legs. "Where'd you put the car that went into the bayou?"

The mechanic didn't seem to resent having his entertainment interrupted. "Be wid you in a minute, *ami*," he called out.

Vance leaned against the Ford and waited. A few minutes later, a man whose short body matched the legs slid out from under the car. Standing up, he pulled an oil-smeared rag from the back pocket of his overalls and wiped huge, muscular hands.

He looked from Vance to Tess. "Guess we'd better not shake, he-he. You Miss Beaumont?"

As he spoke, Tess saw that there seemed to be more teeth missing than present in the front of his mouth.

"Yes."

"Got your purse out from under the front seat. 'Course, most of the stuff is ruined. And the money's wet. But it'll dry out, good as new. He-he."

"I appreciate that."

"You won't be drivin' that car of yours for a stretch. Not wid the engine all wet like that and the line to the steering fluid screwed up."

Vance, who had been leaning against the side of his car, straightened. "What?"

"Spotted him after I started workin' on the car. Come on back and I'll show you."

Heads together and talking too rapidly in French for Tess to understand more than a word here and there, the men strode into the building. Forgotten by the pair, Tess trailed behind. It took a moment for her eyes to adjust to the dim light. Before they did, she was afraid to move, lest she trip over some piece of equipment, but to her surprise the interior of the shop was as tidy as the exterior had been chaotic. As far as she could tell, not a tool was out of place.

Lonnie and Vance were standing on either side of the opened hood of her Oldsmobile, conferring like shamans deciding what treatment to use on a desperately ill patient. Both their faces were grave.

"Are you going to let me in on the bad news?" she asked as she approached the pair.

"Right here, see?" Lonnie reached down into the guts of the vehicle and twisted his fingers on a metal coupling. "This doohickey, he's supposed to be attached to this here hose. Only he's been worked loose."

Not so much the words, but the way he said them and the way his fingers twirled the metal, made Tess's chest suddenly constrict. "All kinds of things go wrong with cars. Couldn't something like that happen by itself?" she asked sharply.

"Not likely. You don't try to do the repair work on this car, do you?"

"No."

Vance came around to Tess's side of the vehicle and put an arm over her shoulder. For a moment he held her against his chest the way he had the night before when she'd told him about her nightmares. Then he leaned into the hood, bringing her with him so that her eyes were only a foot from the coupling. "Either the guy who usually works on this thing is a damn fool, or someone did a nice job of sabotage."

"I know as much about cars as you do about applying eye shadow," she muttered. "So you can point to any tube and bolt you want to, and I won't know how it's supposed to look."

"I guess you'll have to take my word for it. And Lonnie's."

Tess had heard the note of desperation in her own voice. There had been nothing to see when she'd asked Vance to take her to the bayou. No evidence, so to speak. She'd secretly hoped this visit to the mechanic would be as placid as the still water. It wasn't.

She was silent for several moments, then she nodded brusquely. "I didn't want to hear it."

"Who would?"

Unaware that she was shifting her weight, she pressed more firmly against Vance's chest, glad of the stability of his body behind hers. From those first panicked moments last night when she'd felt the dark water rising up to swallow her, she'd known deep inside that someone had run her off the road and left her to drown. But it was worse than that. They'd tampered with the line of her steering fluid first. Suddenly she felt as if she were standing at the edge of a dark bottomless pit, and the ground beneath her feet was sliding away.

The unsteadiness wasn't a complete illusion. It was lucky that Vance's arm tightened around her, because she needed someone to support her weight.

He began speaking rapidly again in French to Lonnie, who came back with what seemed to be counter-suggestions. Vance's voice became more emphatic. After several bursts of dialogue, they switched back to English.

"Lonnie will get back to you with an estimate," Vance told Tess. "And the work will be done well."

"Yes. Thank you. How long will it take?"

"A day or two," Vance answered. "He's got some other jobs that are promised first."

"I'm sure he'll do a good job," she responded automatically. It was an odd way to conduct business, as if she were only a bystander. Ordinarily she would have been annoyed. Now she knew she wasn't capable of dealing with the mechanic, or anyone else for that matter. All she wanted to do was get out of there. Away from her car, away from the hateful evidence.

Vance kept a tight grip on her as they made their way back to his car. After closing the passenger door, he started the engine, headed back down the drive and turned right. For a while Tess slumped in her seat and watched live oaks, cypress and tung trees speed past. When they turned in at another narrow side road, she sat up straighter.

"Is this the way back to town?" she asked vaguely, her mind still not quite functioning normally.

"No. We're not going back to the city."

"What do you mean? I have work to do."

Vance pulled into a half-circle drive in front of an elegant little Greek revival house. A moment later he was out of the car and had come around to Tess's side. Opening the door, he helped her from her seat with the same firm hand he'd used the night before when she'd been playing possum under the covers. "*Cher,* someone tried to kill you. Probably the story's all over Savannah Bayou by now, so whoever was responsible knows the attempt wasn't a success. You're not going home where they can try again."

"But—"

He began to propel her up the wide wooden steps toward the covered gallery. When they reached the top of the flight, he turned to face her.

"Don't lie to me and tell me you're not frightened. What, exactly, were you planning to do?"

Her thinking processes hadn't taken her that far yet. So she asked a question of her own. "Where are we?"

"My house."

"You're taking a lot for granted."

"I'm taking nothing for granted, *cher.*"

Tess didn't move a muscle except to raise her eyes. She knew what she was going to see. Still, it was difficult to cope with his ebony gaze. She saw defiance. Arrogance. And a challenge that did nothing to calm the pounding of her heart.

"This morning, I was pretty sure you wanted to get rid of me."

"That's right."

"Because of what I asked your aunt?"

He pressed his lips together for a moment. "*Non.* I was looking for an excuse."

"Why?"

Vance turned his palms upward in a gesture of exasperation. "Because I don't know what the hell to do with you. Because you're not my responsibility, and I should just drive you home. Because I know how I'd feel if something happened to you."

"How would you feel?" Tess breathed.

She thought from his expression he might not answer, and when he did, the look didn't change. Yet his words stole into her heart.

"The way I felt when I found out about Lisa."

"Oh, Vance." She reached out toward him, but he didn't move.

"*Cher,* I don't have the right to tell you that. *Pour l'amour de Dieu,* put me in my place, or something," he growled. He was standing the way he had the night before when he'd kissed her in the shed, with his hands stiffly at his sides. "I'm sure you know how to stop a man like me from bothering you."

She shook her head in denial. "I've never met a man like you before. I've never met anyone who was so absolutely competent, so absolutely sure of himself—except when it comes to us."

He acknowledged the observation with a tight nod.

"Vance, I think you set a lot of store by bravery. Well, don't try to make me into the one who's a coward."

She had his full attention, and her gaze held its own challenge now. "You can't turn off feelings. Neither can I. I don't pretend to understand what's happening between us, but I don't want to pull it up by the roots and toss it away before it has a chance to bloom."

She didn't catch what he said then. It didn't matter, anyway. When his mouth came down hard over hers, the little gasp trapped in her throat had nothing to do with protest.

Chapter Ten

She knew Vance was a man of strong passions. Yet always before there'd been an edge of restraint in their dealings. Suddenly, all the civilized barriers fell and more primitive forces reigned. His lips moved over hers with a savage desire that would have sent her running in the other direction if she hadn't felt the same wild need to taste this man, to know him, to consume him. And if the truth be told, she lacked the strength to run. She only had the strength to cleave to him.

Last night death had courted her in the darkness and almost won. Now she plunged into light too bright for human eyes.

This was life. This was Vance.

If you counted the hours they'd been together, she barely knew him. But she'd spent twenty-four years with Tess Beaumont, and she was discovering she barely knew herself. She *would* know him. And herself. Her lips opened for the invasion of his tongue. Her fingers dug into the corded muscles of his back. Her hips swayed against his.

"Tess. *Mon Dieu.* Tess. I lied when I said I didn't know what to do with you."

He fumbled behind her, and the door eased open. Then they were inside in the cool, darkened hall. She caught almost nothing of her surroundings. But she heard the door slam behind them, shutting out the world. At last, it was no longer the wrong place or the wrong time for either of them. And no need to restrain the cyclone of emotions that had been building between them since he'd first taken her in his arms. No, it had been building since that first time they'd laid eyes on each other in the sheriff's office.

Yet the edge of fear in her voice as she spoke his name made him raise his head.

"Cher?"

She cupped his face in her trembling hands, stroking her fingers against the stubbled skin of his cheeks. He turned his head, catching and caressing her fingertips with his lips and teeth.

"You're afraid." His tone was low and gritty.

"Yes."

"Then we'd better stop." His voice turned raw.

"No. I don't want to stop. It's not you I'm afraid of. It's the feeling of being out of control."

"Ah, Tess. Then we're on equal footing, after all." He took her hands in his, folding down her fingers so he could kiss her knuckles. Then his lips skimmed over her brows, her nose, the tender curves of her ears. When they finally came back to her mouth, they were gentle and persuasive rather than driving and aggressive. The tenderness brought a new, different wave of heat shimmering through her.

She knew he had felt it, too, as he crooked his thumb under her chin and tipped her face up to his.

"Will you come up to my bedroom, then?"

"Oh yes."

He took her arm and led her to the broad flight of stairs she'd barely noticed when they'd first come in. Only fifteen steps. But it was a long, erotic climb as he kept stopping to turn her to him for lingering kisses and touches interspersed with endearments murmured in French.

She discovered very quickly that he was a man who knew how to please a woman, how to tantalize her almost beyond endurance. His hands skimmed her breasts and then withdrew before she'd had her fill of his touch. His lips teased her throat. With each caress, each kiss, she felt the blood sing in her veins as her body melted against his.

"Vance, please." Grasping his hand, she tried to tug him upward to the landing.

His laugh was low and sexy. But he wouldn't be hurried. Near the top of the flight, he paused on the stair below her, trapping her between the banister and his supple body. Breath trickled from her lungs as he turned her in his arms. Now they were on the same level. Her face even with his. Her sensitized breasts against his chest. Her aching feminine softness cradling the hard shaft of his arousal.

The intimate contact was like the door of a blast furnace suddenly thrown open. With an exclamation of wanting deep in his throat, he drew her hard against his trembling body. Caught by the same force, she began to move against him, her urgency matching his. Suddenly the time for slow dancing was over.

"I need you."

"*Je te désire.*"

The words were punctuated by hot, unbearably hungry kisses.

Impatient now, Vance swung Tess into his arms, carried her the rest of the way up the stairs, and strode down the hall to his bedroom. Standing her on her swaying legs, he pulled the cotton shift up and over her head and tossed it out of the way. His own clothes rained unceremoniously to the floor.

Then they were both naked and vulnerable and wanting. Vance pulled her back into his arms. Flesh against flesh at last. Without stopping to pull back the spread, he dragged her down to the bed with him.

Dimly, through her own pleasure, she marveled at the tension she'd roused in his body—and the way he held back, waiting to be sure her craving matched his.

Her teeth grazed his shoulder. Her fingers dug into the muscles of his arms. "Vance. Now, please. Now."

"Oui, bien-aimée. Oui."

He moved above her then, filling her body, filling her senses, filling her heart. It was like a gift. A gift she could return in kind, in this private world that the two of them had made for themselves. They sighed and murmured little exclamations of gratification as they found a rhythm that pleased them both.

He took her up, over the horizon, into a world she'd only dimly imagined. And then she was clinging to him, calling his name, crying out at the unbelievable joy of her fulfillment.

She felt him follow her over the edge, heard his hoarse exclamation of satisfaction, and pressed her lips against his cheek.

They were both too stunned to move. Finally, he lifted his head and looked down into her half-closed eyes. Smiling up at him, she touched her finger to his lips and felt him smile back.

"You were right. You knew what to do with me," she murmured.

He chuckled.

When his body no longer covered hers, the air-conditioned temperature was suddenly cold against her heated skin, and she shivered.

"Are you chilly? Let me do something about the covers."

"I don't think I can move."

He reached around her and began to pull the spread down. "You only have to lift your hips—now."

She complied. Then they were under the covers snuggling close together, her cheek cushioned by the thick hair of his chest. After a few minutes, she felt him drag in a long breath and expel it slowly.

"What?"

Vance didn't answer immediately. Instead he stroked her naked back and shoulders, sending fine tremors down her spine.

"I know there's something you're keeping back," she murmured. "Don't make me worry about what it is."

He eased far enough away from her so that he could tip her face up toward his.

"I want to hold you and keep you safe, but holding you isn't enough. Last night after your car went into the bayou, I was pretty sure it was a deliberate attack. Now there's no other way to interpret the facts. We're not talking about an accident or a case of mistaken identity. Someone tried to make sure you wouldn't leave Savannah Bayou alive, *cher*. So I'm going to ask you a very important question, and I expect you to give me an honest answer. Are there any other stories you're working on that someone might want to make sure never get to the six o'clock news? Or is the Lisa Gautreau case the only one that's likely to get you in trouble?"

Tess thought for a moment. "I—no. There's nothing else."

"Then it looks as if you don't have much choice. Monday morning you go in to the news director or whoever you report to and tell him you're withdrawing from the story."

"No!"

The defiant syllable was met with a string of curses in French. "Who do you think you are, *cher,* the heroine of some action adventure movie where the bullets miraculously keep missing their mark and the good guys climb out of the car after it's gone off the bridge? This isn't make-believe. It's real life. Someone's afraid you're going to find out what happened to Lisa. And when you do, it will lead back to them. So unless you let them know you're off the story, you have about as much chance as she did."

"But she killed herself. I'm just trying to understand why."

His eyebrow arched. "Did she? We don't know that for sure. And suppose she really was there alone when she went into the bayou. We don't know what happened in the hours before she came down here. Maybe someone convinced her that her only way out was to disappear under the surface of the water."

Tess shuddered, but her voice carried the strength of her convictions. "Vance, everyone knows me too well. They know I won't give up the story."

"Not even to save your life?"

She pressed her lips together. "Maybe."

His face betrayed some deep inner struggle. "All right, then you'll tell them you found what you were looking for, and it's not worth pursuing. You talked to Lisa's brother, and he told you she'd been hospitalized for depression. That she'd tried to kill herself before. And this time she succeeded. End of story."

She found his hand under the covers and wrapped her fingers around his. "Oh, Vance. I'm so sorry." He turned his palm up and held on to her.

"Did Ernestine know?" she finally asked.

"That she was in the hospital? That she tried to take her life before?" His voice was gritty. "*Non.* She just assumed Lisa was ignoring us again."

Tess nodded.

"I let her think that." He paused, then continued. "That was a mistake. Maybe it would have been better to try and explain things to Ernestine."

"You did what you thought was best."

"Did I? I don't know anymore. I was angry that Lisa was ashamed of us. You know that pretty hairbrush and comb you were using? They were a present from *Tante* to Lisa. Only she didn't think the set was good enough, so she never took it out of the box, and she left it in her room when she moved out."

"That must have hurt."

"Yes. But I didn't help the situation. I was put off by Lisa. Not just by the little things she did. I mean the way she decided to get ahead in life. She was too much like Jacqueline for my taste." He went on in a very low voice. "The worst part is that I was angry that she wasn't strong enough to keep herself from getting sick."

Tess meshed her fingers more firmly with his.

After a while, he started to speak again. "But she was my sister, and I hurt for her. I tried to see her after the attack. I thought she might need to go into the hospital again, but she wouldn't talk to me during the week before she died. No wonder."

"Vance. Don't blame yourself."

He went on as if he hadn't heard. "I wrote her a letter. I never got to send it. After you sprung me from that stinking jail cell, I went home and burned it."

Tess brought his hand to her cheek. "I'm sorry. You tried to help when you thought she needed you."

"Maybe the wrong way. Maybe I was too hard on her. Maybe I'm trying to prove somebody killed her so I won't have to blame myself."

"Oh God, Vance, don't! You didn't make any choices for her."

Tess knew he was struggling to hold himself together. She lay beside him, holding his hand and not saying anything.

"Well, at least all this gives you an out," he finally said. "The bottom line is that you can tell your bosses at the station that Lisa Gautreau's brother is going to tear the place apart if that information is splashed all over the KEFT viewing area."

"I—I—guess Chris would respond to that."

"I hope you won't tell any of this to Ernestine."

"You know I wouldn't do that."

He nodded tightly and she reached out, clasped her arms around him and held him close. "Vance, the Lisa Gautreau story started out as an assignment that Chris sprang on me at the end of a very full day. But it stopped being just a professional interest a long time ago. This is very personal for me. I guess because of you."

For long moments his body remained as still as a heron waiting for a fish to surface. Then he bent to press his cheek against the top of her head.

"I wish it had worked out differently for her," she murmured.

"Then do me the favor of taking my advice. I don't want anything to happen to you because of Lisa."

"I—I don't want that, either."

"You're staying with me for the rest of the weekend so I'll know you're safe. On Monday we'll go into the studio, and you'll let everybody know you're off the story."

"But you're planning to keep on with your own private investigation," Tess concluded, "because you don't really think this is a simple case of a depressed woman taking her life."

"Yes. And not just because it stops me from feeling guilty."

"Then let me help you. No one has to know."

"You are the most stubborn woman I've ever met."

"Does that mean you'll let me share the burden?"

"I shouldn't."

"But you will."

"If it turns out there's something you can do."

She relaxed against him, letting the tension seep out of her body. Here in his bedroom it seemed as if no one and nothing could touch her unless he gave them permission. Yet illusion had to make way for reality.

"I don't know if I can stay all weekend. I'm supposed to be on call if they need me for something that comes up. I should phone and let Chris Spencer, the news director, know where I am. Technically, they could fire me for disappearing."

"Letting him know you're here defeats the purpose of hiding out. I'd prefer not to have to barricade the doors and windows and break out the rifles."

Yet she knew he would, if that's what it took.

"Telling Chris is okay. I can trust him."

"Can you? Can you be certain of anyone? How do you know he isn't the one who hid the Brad Everett tape?"

She was unable to answer.

He turned to her, his face hard and urgent. "Tell me about the staff. I already know something about Roger Dallas."

For the next forty-five minutes Tess gave Vance a run-down of the men at KEFT. She started with the members of the team she saw most often. Roger. Chris. Larry. Then she progressed to the talk-show host Brad Everett and owner Desmond LeRoy.

"On balance, not a very nice bunch of coworkers," he observed when she had finished.

"I'm afraid you have to be tough to survive in the TV business."

"You're not tough."

"Yes, I am."

"No. You're vulnerable. And compassionate. And you take too many chances. Maybe you're in the wrong line of work."

"I'm—"

His fingers covered her lips. "And you argue too much. Any one of those men could have gotten to your car yesterday and started that leak in the steering fluid. Any one of them could have followed you from the station and run you off the road."

"I won't argue anymore."

"You can call Chris from here."

"Should I tell him what happened?"

"No. And don't even hint about needing to talk to him Monday. You want to be able to watch his face when he hears you beg off the assignment."

Tess nodded, nibbling on her lower lip. "I guess I can tell him that I'm with a source who wants to keep some information confidential, and that I'll be in touch later to see if there are any messages."

"Fine. But I want to listen to the conversation. I want to hear his reaction when he finds out you're okay."

"He won't have any reaction, because he won't have expected anything to happen," Tess predicted.

To her great relief, she was right.

Luckily, no problems requiring her presence had developed. But Chris was glad she was back in touch.

"We'd better stop by your house and get you some clothes," Vance said when she'd hung up.

"Yes."

Forty minutes later, Tess was standing outside Vance's study, feeling awkward. Just before they were about to leave the house, he'd abruptly excused himself and disappeared.

He was gone for several minutes, and when he came back into the hall, there was a hard edge to his expression.

She waited for him to tell her what he was thinking. When he didn't, she found herself filling in the silence with the first words that came into her head. "Someone did a beautiful job restoring this place. I guess it was you."

"Umm."

"Do you—uh—do much work in the city?"

"Yes. I'm in demand with the yuppies who didn't lose their shirts in the recession."

"A good position to be in."

"If you're thinking about doing a nice upbeat little TV feature on me, forget it."

"I'm not stupid enough to think you'd like that."

"Tess. Are you feeling uncomfortable about us?"

"Are you?"

He shook his head as if he were in a trance.

She looked up to see that he was staring over her shoulder—at the stairs. In that moment, she knew he was remembering their slow trip up to his bedroom. He looked from the stairs to her, his eyes darkening.

He took two steps forward.

She backed up and found her heels against the lowest riser again....

His hands at her waist, he picked her up and set her on the step so that her face was level with his again.

He took several sipping kisses from her lips. "I'm never going to be able to climb those stairs without thinking about taking you up there, you know."

"Vance."

She wanted him to say more. When he didn't, she murmured, "Feeling this vulnerable is scary for me, too."

"*Cher,* I know the kinds of words a woman wants to hear from a man after they've made love. I've said some of them—even if I didn't mean them."

There was no way to stop the pain that bloomed on her face.

Gently, he cupped his palms around her cheeks. "I'm sorry. You're right. I'm feeling very exposed. I'm wondering how you got so close to me so fast. Not just making love. The things I told you."

"It was good for you to talk."

"I don't want either one of us to get hurt. I guess I think the best way to do that is to keep everything that happens between us honest. Right now, that's the only thing I can do."

That hadn't exactly been what she wanted to hear. Yet there was so much more that went unspoken between them. Her arms went around his neck as she brought her lips to his again. She tried to put her feelings of trust and acceptance into the kiss. As she felt his unguarded response, her heart leaped. Slowly the communication became far more than a kiss as hands began to stroke over shoulders and backs.

"We don't have to go to my house now," she murmured.

The suggestion didn't have the effect she'd anticipated.

Lifting his head, he looked down at her, his expression bemused. "*Cher,* the sooner we get in and out of there, the safer it will be."

"Vance—"

"Come on."

Holding out his arm, he ushered her toward the door.

"Where do you live?" he asked.

She gave him the address. "It's Aunt Pauline's house. My house now, I guess."

"You never moved out?"

"She would have been lonely."

"Your mother lived out here with the poor folks, and your aunt lived in a nice house in the city."

"It certainly wasn't a palace."

"So where were your people from, originally?"

"The city—I guess. At least, Aunt Pauline seemed to fit into that life-style as if she were born to it."

"Then how did your mother end up living at the edge of the swamp?"

Tess shrugged. In truth, she was glad he'd started the conversation. It helped keep her mind off more pressing problems. In his darkened bedroom, in his arms, she'd felt secure. As they drove toward New Orleans, she sensed a knot of apprehension forming in her stomach. He was right; she should be worried. "I guess I never questioned why we were out here. A child just accepts life the way it is." She heard her voice wobble slightly.

He found her hand and squeezed it. She didn't ask if he'd detected what she was feeling now. If he simply assumed she was reacting to thoughts about her past, it was all right with her.

"Don't you have any other relatives?" he asked.

"Not that I know of. Aunt Pauline never talked about anyone."

"Don't you find that strange?"

"I do now that you point it out. It's just something else I accepted. She and my mother could have been the last members of their family."

"Maybe she had some records or pictures or something."

"Not that I ever saw."

"Stored away."

"In the attic, I suppose. We used to keep some things up there. Christmas decorations and out-of-season clothes. But there were some boxes and a trunk way in the back that nobody ever touched. We could have a look at them."

His face became grim. "Not today. I'm sorry I mentioned it."

"Why can't we do it now?"

"Because it's not a good time to hang around your house."

Tess folded her arms and sat staring straight ahead. He was right. But she didn't want to hear it.

They drove in silence for several minutes.

It had been sunny when they started out from Savannah Bayou. Now dark clouds began to roll in like waves sweeping over the land at high tide. By the time they reached the city it was dark and the wind had begun to blow.

An inauspicious homecoming, Tess thought, feeling the knot in her stomach tighten perceptibly. What would she have done if she'd had to come back here alone? she wondered. Maybe called Chris. Which might have been exactly the wrong thing to have done.

Stop it, she told herself sternly. *Vance has got you suspecting everybody.* Yet now she had to face the fact that he was right to be cautious.

Tess didn't speak to him until she had to give him directions. He raised his eyebrows slightly as she steered him onto fashionable St. Charles Avenue. But he'd soon discover that Aunt Pauline's home was a modest Victorian cottage in one of the least lofty sections of the Uptown area.

He slowed down and seemed to be studying a wrought-iron fence that needed repair. "Tell me when I'm a couple of blocks away."

"Two more streets and you'll be there."

Vance approached her abode with the wariness he'd used the day they'd both shown up at Glen Devoe's.

When they finally drove by, Tess peered at the facade, watching the wind tear at the ficus trees in front. As far as she could tell, everything was exactly as she'd left it. Yet there was no way to be sure when she couldn't see past the closed shutters facing the street.

"How many rooms?"

"It's small. Just the living room, dining room, kitchen, three bedrooms—I use one for an office—and one bathroom."

"The entrance is on the side?" Vance asked.

"Yes."

"Too bad. That means anybody could be hiding back there in the shadows." He pulled up to the curb in front of one of the houses down the block. "You sit tight. I'm going to check things out."

"I'm coming with you."

He shot her an exasperated look.

She wasn't going to explain that her insistence didn't come from bravado. All the fear she'd repressed was suddenly turning her skin icy, and she desperately needed to counteract a strong desire to turn and run. When Vance got out of the car, she followed him up the sidewalk, arms wrapped around her shoulders. Let him think she was simply warding off the sudden drop in temperature.

The wind whipped at her hair, and she swatted stray strands from her face. A few fat drops of rain fell, and thunder rumbled threateningly in the distance.

"Wait," Tess called. But the wind carried her voice away as Vance disappeared into the shadows of the covered doorway. Should she rush forward or hang back? She had ample evidence that Vance knew how to take care of himself. But what if someone did take him by surprise? Maybe it was better if she were in a position to run for help.

To her relief, he reappeared a moment later. Then her eyes snapped to the pistol in his hand, a pistol that must have been hidden under his jacket.

"Give me your key," he demanded.

"Where did you get that gun?"

"From the locked drawer in my desk."

"Why didn't you tell me?"

"I didn't want to worry you."

She might have argued. Instead, she fumbled with her still-damp purse for the key. Taking it from her hand, he inserted it in the lock and eased the door open.

Tess stood outside with her heart thumping while he turned on lights and made a quick inspection of every room.

"I think you're okay. I guess whoever tried to get you wants to go the accident route."

His casual words were far from comforting, and her nerves were still jumping as she stepped into the living room. She was glad she didn't simply have to stand there looking alarmed, since the answering machine was beeping.

Vance reached out his hand to stop her as she crossed to it. "Do you think it's going to explode?" she asked.

"After the trick with your car, I don't know." He picked up the machine and gave it the once-over before pressing the button.

"Tess, this is Ken Holloway. I have to talk to you. I have some information you'll want to hear about that girl who drowned herself, Lisa Gautreau."

Chapter Eleven

Tess's eyes shot to Vance's.

"Who the hell is this guy? What does he know about my sister?"

"He's the guy whose camera you pitched in the bayou."

"Wonderful. He's going to be thrilled when you show up with me."

A smile touched her lips. "I can explain that you make a better second impression." She extracted her personal directory from the drawer under the phone and dialed her coworker's number.

"Hi. This is Ken," his cheerful voice began. "Sorry we didn't connect, but I'm out doing the town. If you'll leave your name and number, I'll get back to you as soon as I can."

Vance uttered a Cajun expletive.

Tess's answering machine was still beeping. "Let me see what else I have. Then I can start calling around and find out if anyone knows where Ken went." She pressed the play button again.

"Ms. Beaumont, if I were you, I'd drop the Lisa Gautreau story." The voice was low and whispery—obviously disguised. Yet it tugged at Tess's subconscious—like a hand reaching out of an open grave to drag her in. All at once she felt as if a bowl of ice cubes had been pressed against her spine.

"I—I—know that man," she gasped.

"Who is it? Somebody at the station?"

Tess tried to bring the insubstantial memory into focus. She didn't realize she had started to shake until Vance put his arm around her shoulder.

"I told you to leave it alone," he grated.

"Maybe you're right," she said in a low voice.

She saw him relax slightly. Then he looked from Tess to the machine. The light was still blinking. "I guess while we're here, we'd better find out who else called," he suggested.

She felt her throat tighten, but she hit the play button once more.

"Tess. Where in the name of all that's holy are you?" It was Ken again, and his voice had taken on an urgent, desperate quality. "It's Saturday, noon. I'm getting out of town for a few days. But I need to talk to you first. Alone. If you come home this afternoon, I'm at Legacy Cemetery Number Three. About two hundred yards straight back from the main gate, there's a double crypt with two vases of stone flowers in front. Meet me—" The message clicked off before he'd finished whatever else he was going to say.

Vance's face was hard. "I don't like any of this. First someone warns you off. Then your friend sets up a meeting in a cemetery, of all places. Does he usually go in for melodrama—or investigative reporting?"

"No. He usually just works the camera. But plenty of people know he was with me when I went out to Savannah Bayou the first time. One of them might have approached him."

"And told him to get out of town. You realize this might be a trap."

Tess shook her head. "Ken is my friend. He probably wants to meet some place where we won't run into anyone we know."

"With friends like yours who needs enemies?" He came back at her with the old cliché—only now it made the tight feeling return to her stomach.

"Ken isn't one of the bad guys," she repeated.

"You keep telling me that. Well, who is?"

"I—"

"Then *I'll* meet him."

"You can't, remember. He'd run the other way."

They stared at each other, both aware that somewhere along the line, priorities had changed.

"I told you I'd quit the story. This isn't about the TV news," Tess whispered.

"You're doing it for me?"

"You. And the truth."

"I don't like this. I don't want to put you in any more danger," Vance muttered.

"You won't. You'll be with me. You can drop me at the gate and double back. I won't go near the meeting place until I know you're watching."

"All right."

They had come to pick up extra clothes for Tess. Now they were in a hurry, so she only grabbed a sweater and pulled it on. As they stepped outside, she felt as if they were stepping into twilight. Purple clouds hovered over the street like a dark shroud, and the wind had risen to near gale proportions.

"Your friend could have picked a better time for a rendezvous," Vance observed as he zipped his jacket. "I hope he's found some shelter."

"I hope so."

"He better have something important to say." Vance hurried Tess to the car. When he opened the door, the wind tried to rip it from his grasp. Cursing, he urged Tess inside and slammed the door shut behind her.

Legacy Cemetery Number Three had once been on the edge of the city. Now it was in a run-down neighborhood off Esplanade. The rain was still holding off as they made a quick pass by the arched front entrance, but Tess expected the heavens to open up at any moment.

"I can't take you up to the gate, in case somebody's watching," Vance said.

"I know."

As he pulled to a stop around the corner, he leaned toward Tess. "Wait a couple of minutes before you go searching for that tomb. I'm not coming in the front way so you won't see me. Don't act like you're expecting reinforcements. I'll be where I can see you."

"All right."

Tess hunched her shoulders against the rising wind as she fought her way up the sidewalk. Large drops were splashing on the ground, and she wished fervently that she'd grabbed a raincoat instead of the sweater.

Above the trees, a jagged fork of lightning split the sky. It was followed by a drumroll of thunder close enough to shake the ground. By the time Tess reached the archway, more drops were thudding around her.

Ahead of her were rows of shadowy little buildings—a city of the dead. Peering into the murky atmosphere, she shuddered. A cemetery in broad daylight was bad enough. A cemetery under these conditions was like something out of a slasher movie.

Straining her eyes, she tried to locate the crypt Ken had specified. All she could see were crumbling buildings surrounded by weeds. The stone flower baskets were nowhere in sight.

Tess shivered as rain suddenly began to pelt her hair and shoulders. Ahead of her and to the right was a green canvas tent set up beside one of the crypts. Although it was probably meant to shade a funeral party from the sun, it should provide her with some refuge from the storm.

Her heart was pounding thickly in her throat. Sprinting ahead, she made it to the shelter as the heavens opened up. Then she tried to keep her teeth from chattering and almost succeeded.

Tess jumped as lightning lanced the sky and thunder rumbled over the necropolis, the vibrations dislodging bricks from some of the aging vaults.

"Tess . . . Tess . . ."

Was her overactive imagination playing tricks on her, or was someone calling her name?

"Ken? Vance?" No one answered, but as the rain let up a bit, she thought she saw a flash of white through the gloom.

A man in a white shirt beckoning to her? Uncertain, she hesitated under the canvas.

"Tess. Oh, God, Tess . . ."

She was sure she heard her name again, only this time it was like a desperate plea for help.

"Ken? Are you in trouble? What?" she called out. When he didn't answer, she began hurrying toward the spot where she'd thought she'd seen the shirt.

The weedy grass was soaked now, and her feet sank into the ground as she made her way between the low buildings. As she reached out to steady herself against one of the tombs, her fingers dislodged several bricks. Fetid air from within drifted toward her, and she gagged.

Snatching her hand back, Tess stumbled forward in the
dim light, trying not to touch any more of the walls as she
went.

Wisps of fog had begun to rise from the ground, making it harder for her to see. It was impossible not to feel
slithery shapes oozing from the dank ground and plucking at her legs. She knew it was her imagination. She hoped
it was her imagination. Still, she had to press her lips together to keep from screaming.

Ahead, to her profound relief, wavering in the misty atmosphere, the stone baskets appeared. Almost there.
Thank the Lord, Tess thought as she ran the last few steps.

"Ken?" she called out to him again, but he still didn't
answer. Maybe he was hiding. Maybe he was afraid to give
himself away. Or maybe she couldn't hear him above the
thunderous pounding of the pulse in her ears. Then she
saw the white shirt again. Actually, she saw no more than
a stiff, shirtsleeve-clad arm protruding from the side of the
sepulcher. It moved as if to urge her to hurry, and she
sprinted forward, rounding the corner of the little building just as a distant flash of lightning snaked across the
deep purple of the sky.

Ken was standing, awkward as a scarecrow, in the
shadow of the building. His clothes were dripping, his hair
was plastered to his scalp, and his face was drained of all
color—except for the little round red hole in the middle of
his forehead.

Tess's mind tried to reject what she was seeing. Yet her
brain refused to stop processing the visual images.

"Ken. Oh, no. Oh, please, no."

As if she were a mother trying to get the attention of a
wayward child, she stretched upward and plucked at his
stiffened arm. His sightless eyes didn't change direction,
but he swayed toward her like a marionette hanging on

slack strings. It was then that she saw the rope cinched up under his arms and around his chest—the rope that must be holding him erect.

Her eyes traveled above his head, up the length of hemp anchored to the stone cross at the top of the roof gable. The sight of the hateful rope freed the scream that had been frozen in the back of her throat. It ripped from her lungs—the long, loud wail of an anguished mourner.

Even as she screamed, even as she knew there was no help or comfort she could give him, she was clutching at his body, trying to tear him down. She succeeded only in pulling him forward so that his weight fell against her shoulders.

Thunder cracked again. Vaguely she realized that she hadn't seen any lightning first. It was the wrong way around now. She felt the heat flash past her face.

The crack came again, and this time there was a ringing in her ears and a searing pain across the top of her head.

"Get down, *cher*. For God's sake, get down." Confused, she realized that someone was shouting at her. Like an apparition, Vance was lunging toward her from out of the rain. In the next moment he was looming over her, shielding her body, dragging her away from the man she had come to meet, the man who was beyond help.

As Vance threw her to the ground, the air whooshed out of her lungs, and she fought for breath.

"Ahh..."

"Someone's shooting at you," he clipped out, as he dragged her across the wet grass and around the side of the sepulcher. When she was out of danger behind the brick wall, he rolled over and freed the gun from the back of his waistband.

There was another loud report. At the front of the building, a patch of brick and mortar crumbled. Seconds later, Vance returned the fire, shooting into the mist and darkness at an enemy he couldn't see.

But no more volleys came from the shadows. When Vance stopped shooting, all Tess could hear was the awful ringing in her ears. Dazed, she pushed herself erect and pressed her hand to the back of her head where it throbbed. Her palm came away wet and sticky, and she gasped as she stared down into the red mess.

Vance had rolled back toward her. When he saw her upturned hand, the color drained from his face. "*Mon Dieu.* You're hit."

"No, I . . . must have . . . have . . . bumped . . ."

He was beside her in an instant, bending her head forward against his chest so he could search her scalp, his fingers pushing aside her wet hair. She heard him let out an exclamation of profound thanks.

"It just creased your scalp, thank the good God. A bullet cut across the top of your head."

"Oh."

"Head wounds can bleed a lot."

"Oh." She repeated the same dumb syllable.

"Does anything else hurt?"

Tess struggled to make her mind work. "Just my knee, where you pushed me down."

"I'm sorry."

"It's all right. Better than a bullet through the middle of my head." She glanced back at Ken and couldn't hold back a little choking sob.

Vance folded her into his arms and soothed his hands down the freezing skin of her arms. "*Cher,* you're so cold. Why didn't you wait?"

"I heard someone calling me."

"Come on, we're getting out of here."

"What about Ken? We can't just leave him like that. And shouldn't we wait for the police?"

"There's nothing you can do for him now, *cher*. We'll call the police as soon as we get to a phone. It's better not to stay till they come, because they're just going to ask a bunch of questions you can't answer. You don't know what happened here before you arrived, and neither do I."

Vance was right, she supposed. He was reaching for her hand to help her up, when she snatched it back. "What about...I mean, maybe he...maybe...there's something. Some clue. Don't we have to look?"

He swore under his breath. "Unfortunately, you're right. Stay here. I'll be back for you."

Tess wasn't about to stay there by herself. Ken had called her and asked her to meet him here. He must have been shot while he was waiting for her. He'd been her friend. She should be helping. Still, it was several moments before she could get to her feet and make her legs function.

When she reached the front of the crypt, she found Vance methodically going through the dead man's pockets.

"My God, aren't you even going to get him down?" she quavered, aware that her voice was verging on hysteria.

"The less I disturb the scene, the better for the police."

"Sorry. I guess I didn't think of that."

"I told you to wait for me," he clipped out.

"I can't do that." The words were high and strangled.

Vance pressed his hand over her shoulder for a second. "I'll be quicker than you." Swiftly he went on with what he was doing. After finishing with the pockets, he patted down the body. Then he reached for the dead man's left hand.

She couldn't see what he was doing now, but he was taking longer. "Did you find something?"

He made what she took to be a negative sound before beginning to search the steps and the ground around the tomb. "If there were any footprints, they've probably been washed away or trampled on by us." He turned back to Tess. "Come on. We've pressed our luck long enough. Let's go."

Adrenaline had been keeping her upright. All at once Tess wondered if she had the strength to make it back to the car—wherever it was.

Vance must have seen the fatigue sweep over her face. "Come on, *cher.*" Swinging her up into his arms, he started for the gate. She was too wrung-out to protest. Instead, she leaned her head against his shoulder, closed her eyes and snuggled into his warmth.

For just a moment he stopped and pressed his lips to the side of her face. Then he kept moving toward the archway.

When they reached the car, Vance opened the trunk and got out a blanket. After wrapping it around Tess, he opened the door and lowered her to the seat.

Eyes closed, she leaned back and drew her knees up, hugging them tightly against her chest.

A few blocks from the cemetery, Vance pulled into a gas station with a pay phone at the edge of the parking lot. When Tess looked up in alarm, he pressed his hand over hers. "I'm going to call the police," he explained as he exited the car.

Tess nodded slightly. As the door closed, tears began to leak from behind her closed eyelids.

"Well, they're probably on their way over there now," Vance said a few minutes later as he climbed back behind the wheel.

Tess didn't respond. Her shoulders had started to shake as the trickle of tears became a flood.

"*Cher,* what is it? Are you hurt? Is it the gunshot? What?"

Unable to answer, she shook her head.

Vance drove the car around the back of the station where some trees shaded the tarmac. Cutting the engine, he pulled Tess up and into his lap.

As he rocked her in his arms, he murmured low, soothing words in a mixture of French and English. She pressed her face against his shoulder and sobbed, unable to stop, unable to get control of herself. It was a long time before the well ran dry. Finally she lay limp against his damp shoulder.

"*Cher?*"

She fumbled in her purse for a tissue and blew her nose. "Ken . . . he's dead . . . because of me." The last part was a trembling gulp.

"*Non.* You don't know that."

"He called me. He had some information about Lisa. Somebody didn't want him to give it to me."

"You don't know what happened. How did they find out where he was meeting you unless he told them? For all you know, he could have been involved. It could have been a trap for you."

"Then what happened? Why is he dead?"

"Maybe he and his friends had a disagreement."

"No. That's not how it happened," she insisted. "He sounded upset. Maybe they held the gun to him and forced him to make the call."

Vance didn't look convinced.

When she stared at him challengingly, he sighed. "All right, we're going to find out." She'd never heard his voice more soothing.

Maybe that was the last straw. His condescending tone. But suddenly, it was all too much, and Tess couldn't cope—with anything. The fear, the tension, the guilt, the frustration.

Or perhaps it had something to do with the bullet that had slashed across her scalp, leaving her with a throbbing headache. She had passed beyond rationality into some other state where she could only react like a wounded, bewildered animal caught in the jaws of a trap. Her friend was dead. Her friend and two women. And somebody was trying to kill *her*. For a moment that terrible realization threatened her sanity.

She thrust it away and focused on something else. "How are we going to find out what happened to Ken? How? Tell me how."

When Vance opened his mouth, she hurried on. "We don't know anything! We don't know about Lisa. Or Erica Barry. And if that isn't bad enough, you won't let me find out anything about my mother."

"*Cher,* that's not true. And it's the least of your worries at the moment." He sounded weary.

"Oh, is it? You don't even understand the way I feel, because you didn't have a good relationship with your mother."

She saw him flush. Then his expression closed.

"Maybe it's the one thing I can do something about," she rushed on. "But you won't let me ask your aunt any questions. And you won't let me get those boxes out of the attic."

"Tess, I know you're upset...."

The tears began to flow helplessly once more. This time he didn't reach for her. "You're damn right I'm upset."

As he started the engine again, her body jerked. "Take me home. I'm a mess. I want to take a shower and change into something that fits properly."

"All right." He started the car.

She hadn't expected cooperation. When she threw him an incredulous look, he shrugged. "You're not going to get any more arguments from me."

"Fine." Leaning back, she pulled the blanket up around her shoulders and closed her eyes. Anything beyond brooding was too much effort. However, after a while, she began to wonder why it was taking so long to get home from Legacy Cemetery Number Three. The drive over hadn't been this long, had it?

Her eyes drifted open and she saw that they were no longer in the city, but on the highway.

"What?"

"Are you feeling any better?" Vance asked in a conversational tone.

"Where are we going? I asked you to drive me home."

"I am. To my house."

He was doing it again—taking charge without a by-your-leave. Thwarting her. "I don't want to go to your house."

"You're not in any shape to know what you want."

She straightened in her seat, looking at him with shock and fury. "You were lying to me, you bastard."

His face contorted as if she'd slapped him, and she knew at once how he'd taken the insult.

"I'm sorry," she mumbled. "I shouldn't have said that."

"I've heard it before."

"I guess I should have picked a better word. You pig, maybe."

"It's best to stick with honest reactions. Then people know where they stand with each other."

"Vance, for God's sake, stop it. You're blowing this out of proportion. I'm angry because you're not letting me make decisions for myself. You'd be angry if someone did that to you."

"Decisions for yourself!" He snorted. "We're not talking about accidents anymore. Whoever shot at you could have gone straight back to your house. They could be waiting there."

She couldn't think of a ready answer to that. Instead, Tess folded her arms and pulled up her knees. After several moments of strained silence, she slid Vance a sidewise glance. His hands were rigid on the wheel, and his eyes were focused straight ahead on the road as if there were no one in the car but himself.

She'd uttered a couple of careless words, and he was acting as if she were invisible. No, it was more than a few words. It had been building as her hysteria had built. A little while ago, she'd thrown his relationship with his mother in his face. That must have hurt, too.

She didn't know how to approach him anymore. All at once she felt very alone and very afraid. The only thing she had to hang on to was her anger. With him. With the whole damn situation. With whoever was stalking her. In fact, anger was the only thing she could clutch as they rode home in silence.

She'd hunched down in her seat and withdrawn so far into herself that it was a surprise to find the car coming to a stop in front of his house.

"Probably you want to take a shower," Vance said as he opened the door and got out of the car. He might have been talking politely to one of his customers about porch molding.

"Yes. Thanks," Tess answered, striving to match his tone. Opening her own door, she climbed out and stood swaying in the driveway, her knees barely able to support her weight.

She knew Vance was aware of her reaction, yet he made no move to steady her.

"There's a bathroom downstairs. You can use that one. I'll go upstairs." Without waiting for an answer, he started toward the house.

Tess followed, still trying to clutch her anger like a protective blanket. She could feel it ebbing away as she climbed the stairs to the gallery.

She wanted to grab Vance's arm and make him stop and listen to her, except that she wasn't even sure what she wanted to say.

As she stepped into the front hall, the view of the stairs hit her in the face, and she felt her heart squeeze so tightly that for a moment she was afraid she was going to faint. Turning quickly away, she ducked into the bathroom and pulled the door shut.

After stripping off her muddy clothes, she adjusted the taps and stepped under the water. It wasn't until she'd begun to lather her hair and felt a stinging pain that she remembered the bullet that had cut across the top of her head. Gingerly, she probed the wound. It was only superficial, and the blood had dried—so she simply washed the shampoo out of her hair again without disturbing the forming scab.

She might have stayed under the pounding spray all afternoon. However, the hot water finally began to give out, and she shut the taps off. When she stepped out of the tub, she found a pile of clothes neatly folded on the washstand beside the door.

Vance had been here, she thought as she held up a pair of man's cutoffs and a blue polo shirt. Even when they were barely communicating, he was still thinking about her needs. Maybe that meant something.

Quickly she slipped into the pants. Although they weren't too bad a fit, the shirt hung well below her knees. At least she didn't have to wear the muddy dress. And she could clean up the sandals outside if he'd lend her a rag and a bucket of water.

She wondered where Vance was, until she caught the smell of something spicy wafting toward her from the back of the house. Following her nose, she found him in the kitchen, stirring the contents of a cast-iron pot on the stove. He didn't glance up when she came in.

"What are you doing?"

"You missed lunch. I thought you'd be hungry." Again his tone was polite and impersonal. On the surface, everything was dead calm. Yet Tess could feel echoes of tension vibrating around them in the still air.

"Do you want to eat?" she asked quietly.

"It's been a long time since breakfast. I could have something," he allowed.

"What are you cooking?"

"It's just leftover shrimp gumbo."

"It smells good."

He didn't reply, and the conversation came to a halt. For another minute or so he stirred the soup. Then he turned the heat down and cleared his throat. "I've been thinking. Maybe I was wrong to jump to conclusions."

All at once hope bloomed inside her chest. "About us?" she asked in a shaky voice, taking a rapid step toward him and reaching out with her arm.

For the first time since the drive home, he gave her a direct look. It was the same look he'd given her the night she'd come to get him out of jail, and it made the little bud of hope inside her freeze and die. "No. About your mother. Maybe there is something you can find out."

Chapter Twelve

"You don't have to put yourself out on my account," Tess whispered, knowing she couldn't manage anything louder.

"It will help fill the time."

"What did you have in mind?"

"Research. We can go as soon as we've finished."

"You don't have to fill any time. You can just take me home."

"I said I'd keep you safe until Monday morning. When I give my word on something, I don't go back on it," he said stiffly.

Turning away, he got two bowls from the cupboard and spooned gumbo into each. Then he set the table with spoons and napkins. They sat across from each other. He ate. She forced herself to swallow a few spoonfuls of the gumbo. Perhaps it was good, but she couldn't tell.

Dipping her head and stirring the soup, she glanced up at him. He looked perfectly relaxed. She wanted to scream.

Instead she willed her mind to function. He'd been this way before, when they'd driven to Lonnie's. When he'd been looking for excuses to detach himself from her. This time was worse, because they'd gotten closer. And then she'd lashed out at him. Now he was shielding himself the way he'd told her worked best—by withdrawing.

She knew for damn sure he wasn't going to do anything to change the situation. Was she strong enough to make him understand he was giving up too easily?

Vance finished eating and leaned back in his chair. She saw his gaze flick to her bowl, but he didn't comment on her lack of appetite. Probably that was too much personal interaction for him.

"All set?"

"Where are we going?"

"Charter University Library. I did some renovation work for them. So they let me use the facilities whenever I want."

While she gathered her courage for something more meaningful, she continued the impersonal conversation he'd begun. "Will they let me in dressed like this?"

"If you put your shoes on."

"Suppose I don't want to go."

"*Cher,* you told me how important this is to you."

As he moved away to open the refrigerator, Tess got quietly out of her seat. When he turned around again, she was standing right in front of him.

"Don't," she whispered.

"Don't what?" His voice didn't change at all, but his eyes had frosted over. "Don't help you see if there are any articles about your mother? An obituary, at the very least? Maybe we can pick up some clues about what happened. Or there may be something about her background."

She wasn't listening to the recitation. "Don't treat me like I'm some stranger from the city."

"I can't control my reactions." Although his lips moved, his body might have turned to stone. Yet she could see a fine sheen of perspiration on his skin.

"I think you can."

When he didn't answer, she took a step forward, slipped her arms around his muscular body, and pressed her cheek against his chest.

This time he was the one who growled "Don't." Yet he didn't pull away. And he was far stronger than she.

Tess held him tightly for a moment, knowing that the focus of what she said would have to be on her. On how she felt, on what she'd done and why. Not on him.

She began to speak quickly before her voice broke, her face half buried in his shirt. "Vance, for years I've kept so many anxieties—so many fears—deep inside because there was no other way to deal with them. It was like a boiling pot, but I thought I had it all under control—except maybe when the dreams came bubbling over the edges and spilling down the sides, and I'd wake up in a cold sweat. But now so much more has been dumped in. And this afternoon, I couldn't keep the lid on any longer. It was safer to be angry than frightened. I'm sorry."

She felt a tremor shake his body. The first uncontrolled reaction she'd sensed since the terrible moment when he'd closed her out. Other than that, he didn't move.

"Vance, I fell apart after finding my friend, Ken, hanging like a dead steer in a slaughterhouse and having a bullet slice across the top of my scalp. Does my reaction to that have more weight on your mental scales than how it was when we made love this morning?"

He muttered something low and guttural. Then he wrapped his arms around her shoulders, pulling her into his strength.

With a little sob, she clung to him.

"Don't cry, *pour l'amour de Dieu.* Don't cry."

"I...can't...help it."

She felt his lips brush her forehead. His hands stroked up and down her back.

"I shouldn't have taken out my feelings on you," she whispered.

"But you've been through a devil of a lot. Anyone would have cracked." He uttered a short, self-deprecating laugh. "I did, too. But with me, the damage doesn't show quite so much."

"Oh, Vance. Don't do that again. Don't pretend I'm invisible."

"*Cher,* I've been protecting myself like that for a long time."

"You don't have to be that way with me. I promise. If I hurt you, if I make you angry, tell me."

"If I can."

As lightly as raindrops sliding through tall grass, his fingers moved through her hair and found the injury. "Does it hurt?"

"It's all right."

Touching her cheek, he stared down at her. "I think you must be like the Acadian women who trekked down here from Canada when the British exiled them. You look so damn fragile. But you're not."

Tess smiled up at him. "And I think you're like the men. Everything they had was ripped away from them. But they found a way to survive. Together."

"Ah, Tess." His lips came down on hers. It was a kiss that began tenderly and ended in a rush of raw passion. He devoured her mouth. She returned the urgent assault, her hands moving over the strong muscles of his back and shoulders and into his thick, dark hair. When he finally lifted his head, they were both breathing raggedly.

"*Bien-aimée,* trusting anyone is hard for me. I'm always ready to find reasons why it won't work. And I usually do."

She saw him swallow slowly, his eyes watching hers, as if he were afraid the simple admission would be enough to drive the wedge back between them. It had just the opposite effect because she knew what it must have cost him.

"I know. Oh, Vance, I know. Feeling this way about someone is new for me, too. It scares me a little, too. But I don't want to run away from it." There was so much she wanted to say to him. So much she knew he wouldn't accept. Instead, she covered his face with sweet little kisses that he began to return. Leaning back against the refrigerator, he pulled her with him as they continued to kiss and touch, relearning the caresses that had brought them both pleasure, and finding new joys.

The first time their lovemaking had been fierce. This time it was slow and gentle, a communication of tenderness and caring as well as passion. It was several hours later before either one of them remembered about the library.

AS THEY DROVE AWAY from Vance's house, Tess gently touched his shoulder. He took his hand off the wheel for a moment to press her fingers.

"There's something I should ask you," she said in a low voice.

"Umm?"

"What did you tell the police when you stopped and made that call after we left the cemetery?" she asked.

His expression became watchful. "You're sure you want to talk about it?"

"I can handle it now."

"Just that they'd find a murder victim in Legacy Cemetery Number Three. Then I gave them the approximate location and hung up. There isn't much more either one of us can tell them—except that whoever killed Ken was waiting for you, too."

Tess nodded. "The—the—person who murdered him will know I kept the appointment. And they'll know I got away."

"But they'll also be pretty sure they've scared you off the story."

"Yes." Tess closed her eyes for a moment. "Vance, even when Lonnie showed me the damage to the car, there was some part of me that still wanted to think it was some kind of accident."

"I imagine it's hard to make yourself believe someone is trying to kill you."

"A bullet across the top of your skull is pretty convincing."

Vance draped his arm around her shoulder and dragged her against him. Tess moved into his warmth and rested her head on his broad shoulder.

After several miles, Vance cleared his throat. "How old were you when you came to live with your aunt?"

"It was before I started school. I think I must have been about four or five."

"So we know the approximate time period to start looking."

"Yes."

A half hour later, they arrived at the campus. Tess had never been in the venerable old college library. It was all dark wood and polished tables with green shaded reading lamps. But Vance was right, the students bent over the stacks of books on the tables were wearing everything from cutoffs to tie-dyed T-shirts and rubber sandals. She didn't look a bit out of place.

"What restoration work did you do here?" Tess whispered as they made their way to the reference desk.

"Some of the paneling and the ceiling molding were damaged when a drain upstairs overflowed."

Tess glanced at the walls and the molding, but she couldn't tell which Vance had fixed and which was the original. That was quite a tribute to his skill, she decided.

After a brief conversation with the woman behind the desk, he led her down an air-conditioned corridor to the periodical reference room. Like most libraries, this one had stored older periodicals on microfilm. Vance asked for some likely selections and they each sat down at one of the reader-printers.

"What do you usually look up?" Tess asked as she watched him expertly thread the film.

"The home section. When I'm working on a house, I can sometimes get the period details I need from old photographs and descriptions. I also check the rare books about architects and old construction methods."

"You're resourceful."

"I've had to be. Was your mother's name Beaumont?"

"No. Otelie Hugo. That's about the only thing I really know."

"That's an unusual name."

"Yes." Despite everything she'd said earlier, now that Tess was sitting in front of a machine that might provide her with some information, she felt a strange reluctance to start her search.

She looked over at Vance. He was spinning the wheel, moving the film forward. Tess fingered the knob for a moment longer. Then she began to run through the film. It was a relief when she came to the end of the first reel.

"Nothing?" Vance asked.

She shook her head and threaded another one onto the machine.

After a while Vance got up and returned his film to the attendant. Then he went over to one of the computers in the corner and sat down. In about twenty minutes he was back, with a sheet of paper in his hand.

"Look at this."

Tess felt her throat tighten. "What do you have?"

"I got to thinking—instead of looking through old newspapers, why not do a computer search of your mother's name." He handed her the paper. "So I tried the article index."

On the paper was a list of bibliographical references:

"Medicinal Plants of the Louisiana Delta," by Otelie Hugo, Ph.D.

"The Water Hyacinth as a Fuel Source," by Otelie Hugo, Ph.D.

"Folk Remedies of the Louisiana Delta Area," by Otelie Hugo, Ph.D.

As her gaze skimmed down the list, Tess felt her scalp prickle.

"Otelie Hugo, Ph.D," she murmured as she counted the entries. There were eight. "Could there be two women around here named Otelie Hugo?"

"It doesn't sound likely."

"What about her thesis? That would be in the data base, wouldn't it?"

"I imagine."

Tess had already gotten up and was crossing the room to the reference librarian. "Pardon me," she began. "I'm looking for some information about this woman. She wrote about the Delta area, and I think she lived here about twenty or twenty-five years ago."

"I don't know how much material we'd actually have in this building, but we can do a computer search, if you'll wait. It will take about half an hour," the librarian told her.

"Yes. Thanks."

Vance took her arm. "Come on, there's no use sitting around biting your nails while you wait."

That was exactly what Tess would have done. Instead, she let Vance lead her out onto the campus. He seemed to know his way around, because he steered her away from the knots of students talking and studying on the lawns to an iron gate. Pushing it open, he ushered her into a walled garden with flagstone paths that meandered under shade trees and between beds of flowers and herbs. It was a quiet, peaceful place, and also very beautiful.

"Thank you," she murmured.

"No charge." Hand in hand they began to stroll past beds of roses, variegated sage and yarrow. It was a bit like stepping into another world. At least that was the way Tess felt. Or perhaps it was simply the strange turn that events had suddenly taken.

Vance was the right companion for the occasion, because he didn't try to make her talk. And he didn't comment on her trembling hand.

Finally she drew to a stop in front of a bed of fragrant roses. "I feel so strange."

"Mmm."

"I've wanted to know about my mother for so long. But I never expected anything like that." A sudden image flashed into Tess's mind, and she turned quickly to Vance. "I told you she used to sit at the kitchen table and type," she whispered. "Maybe she was writing the articles."

"*Oui.*" He looked at his watch. "Come on, it's time to go back."

When they returned to the library, there was a black-bound manuscript sitting on the reference desk.

"Otelie Hugo's dissertation," the librarian informed them. "It seems she went to school right here at Charter. Her maiden name was Beaumont. Which was how she was listed in the undergraduate commencement program. Her major was botany.''

As she heard the name, Tess's scalp contracted again. Vance moved closer.

"Her thesis is titled 'Folk Remedies of the Delta Region.'"

"The same as one of the articles," Vance said.

"Is—is—there anything else?" Tess whispered.

"An item in the alumni bulletin saying she died while doing research in the bayou country." The librarian handed the magazine across the counter.

Her breath frozen in her lungs, Tess turned quickly to the marked page. It was a very brief announcement of her mother's death. No mention of a daughter. No mention of a husband. Or a sister, for that matter. The frozen breath sighed out of her lungs. "She was only twenty-nine," Tess murmured. "Just a few years older than I am now. Who gave them the information, I wonder." She looked back at the librarian. "Is there anything else?"

"I'm sorry. That's all we have. If you want to put in a request, I can get the articles for you. But it will take a couple of days."

"Thanks. Can—can—I have a look at the dissertation?"

"Of course. But there are only two copies, so you can't check it out."

"I understand."

Vance left her alone and went off to inspect the books on the shelves in another part of the room. Tess picked up the oversize black-bound book and took it to one of the tables in the corner. Her mother had written this. Her mother had held this very manuscript in her hand, Tess realized with a little gulp.

She began to read the first chapter. After a few pages, she started skimming through the rest. Finally she closed the book again. She'd thought reading her mother's words would give her a sense of connection. But it was impossible to merge the warm, loving woman she'd started remembering with the person who had written this dry, academic text. It was so flat. So impersonal. But then that was probably the way all dissertations sounded.

Vance must have been watching her out of the corner of his eye. Almost as soon as she put the book down, he was back at her side.

"Learn anything?" he asked.

"Not really. I didn't take botany, so it's too technical for me."

"Do you want to photocopy some of it?"

"No. We can go."

It had been Vance's idea to come to the university library, but he seemed relieved to get out of the building and drive away from the campus.

Despite her lack of reaction to the thesis, Tess was beginning to feel the stirrings of excitement—the same excitement she felt when she got a handle on a story. Besides, it was a lot more gratifying to find out more about her mother than to think about being a murderer's next target. For a while, as they drove back toward Vance's, she sat quietly beside him making plans. Finally she touched his arm.

"Thank you for making me go there."

"You didn't find out much. I thought you'd be disappointed."

"No. It's like my research for a story. I interview people, look at videotapes and read current materials. But one thing I've learned is that when you start to dig up information on a subject, you're going to find more. I can go back to the registrar's office next week and ask to see my mother's admission application. If they make it a privacy issue, I'll show them the obituary notice." She stopped speaking abruptly.

"What?"

"I just remembered what happened when I started sending out college applications. Charter was one of the places where I wanted to apply because they had a good communications program. My aunt got upset when I told her about it, but she wouldn't give me any good reason why. I ended up going to Tulane. It was one of the few times we argued about anything. Now I think my aunt didn't want me to go to the same school as my mother."

"Why?"

"Afraid of bad luck?" Tess murmured, her fingers unconsciously seeking the locket around her neck.

Vance followed the movement. "You always wear that."

"It was my aunt's." She swallowed. "Do you think she's the one who sent Charter the information about my mother's death?"

"What about your father? It sounds as if your mother took his name."

"Then where is he?"

"I don't know, *cher.*" Vance didn't say anything. In fact, he kept his lips pressed together and his eyes on the road. Tess had learned to read him.

"What are *you* thinking about?" she asked softly.

He was quiet for several moments. Then he glanced at her. "That after you told me about the dream, I thought you might be like me—from the back country. Now I know your mother was a very well-educated woman from New Orleans who moved out there to study the plants in the swamp."

"So?"

"You're nothing like me. Your roots really are in the city."

"My mother's roots. We don't know about my father. Is Hugo a common name in the back country?"

"Not all that common. But there are some families."

"Then maybe he lived over on the next bayou, and she met him on a research expedition to the swamp. Maybe he was her guide and they fell in love. Then his people didn't want him to marry her, and my aunt was opposed to the match. But they disobeyed everyone and got married. Something must have happened to him, but she stayed on in the little house where they'd lived—and she kept on with her research."

"That's a very romantic interpretation. Probably about as close to the truth as a fairy story."

"It's as likely as anything else. Perhaps they were very different, and they overcame those differences."

"Most dealings between men and women are based on fantasy. Or maybe it's wanting the other person to fulfill some need. At any rate, it doesn't last. You don't remember your father. What happened to him? Did he leave your mother? Or did she leave him?"

Tess felt her chest tighten. "It doesn't always happen that way."

"With people from different backgrounds, it does."

"You're thinking about us, aren't you?"

He didn't answer.

She wanted to tell him that he was wrong—that she wasn't planning to leave, that she was falling in love with him. She kept the insight to herself. He'd just as good as announced that he still couldn't trust his own feelings—or hers. But then why should he? All his experience told him that it would end badly. And the only thing she could do to prove him wrong was to stick around and let him see how she felt.

Silently, she leaned her head on his shoulder and closed her eyes.

"I'm sorry," he muttered. "I didn't mean to make you feel worse—about your mother."

"I'm just feeling sad because of what I missed," she said aloud. But she was still thinking as much about the future as the past. What would it take, she wondered, to make this man who'd been hurt so badly comfortable with love? He'd been protecting himself by labeling their relationship a fantasy. But she knew it was very real. Not just for her—but for him, too. He cared about her, even if he couldn't tell her. In her soul, she knew that. The trouble was, unless he permitted his feelings to grow and develop beyond the first, exciting stage of discovery, they would die. And the idea of letting that happen made something inside her shrivel up.

Tess sat with her eyes closed for several minutes. When she opened them again, Vance had turned off the highway and was heading for his house.

There wasn't much she could say to him that he'd believe deep down. But perhaps there were other ways to make him see how she felt.

IN THE EARLY HOURS of the morning when he was sure Tess was asleep, Vance eased away from her in the wide bed. She murmured his name and reached for him.

"Shh. I'll be back soon."

He stood naked beside the bed, waiting for her to settle down again, his eyes storing up details. In the light slanting in from the bathroom, he could see her silky hair was tousled on the pillow. Tousled from his fingers. And her lips were swollen from his kisses. *Sacré bleu,* making love with her was beyond anything he could have imagined.

He knew she'd meant what she'd said in the kitchen this afternoon. He knew her lovemaking had been honest and passionate and giving. Yet he also knew that a brightly flaming fire could easily burn itself out. Whatever else might be true, Tess had turned to him because she needed help. And no matter what she might tell him now, he suspected that it was only a matter of time before she realized that the two of them operated in two different worlds that happened to have touched for a time. The knowledge was too chokingly painful to dwell on for long. Instead, he turned his attention to finding justifications for his actions.

For years he'd made his own rules and lived by his own personal code. He wasn't used to explaining himself to anyone, and he wasn't used to discussing his plans. Now, as he began to climb into the jeans he'd tossed so hastily onto the floor, he knew Tess would be angry and disappointed if she knew what he was going to do. More than that, she'd try to call the police. And that was one thing he wasn't going to let her do.

Chapter Thirteen

Tess had dropped her purse on the floor in the front hall. He could get her keys on the way out and have them back before she even knew they were missing. But that was the least of his problems now. At the bottom of the stairs, he sat down to slip on a pair of running shoes.

Next, he reached into the pocket of his jeans and pulled out the shiny silver object he'd found in the graveyard and hidden before Tess had had a chance to see it.

For long moments, he stood looking at the metal disk in his hand. It might very well be a clue to the identity of the man who had killed Ken Holloway. The man who was after Tess.

Vance grimaced. If he were a fine upstanding—no, a trusting—citizen, he'd head straight for the nearest city precinct station and hand over his evidence. Except that he'd had too much experience with bureaucracy and with police officers who were on the take—or who had more pressing agendas than protecting the public interest. They might just shove his offering in a drawer somewhere. Or they could turn it back to the owner and tell him where they'd gotten it. Which would put both Tess and himself in a great deal of danger.

So his options were severely limited. And he was going to have to work quickly.

He turned and glanced back up the stairs, picturing Tess warm and giving in his arms, and now sleeping so trustingly in his bed. He was used to taking responsibility for his own decisions. Taking responsibility for another person's life was something different. A shudder swept over his body. If his logic was wrong, he was putting Tess in jeopardy.

His jaw tightened. He had a long night's work ahead of him, and he'd better get going.

TESS WAS ACCUSTOMED to rising at the crack of dawn and getting to the station in time for early assignments. She woke Monday morning just as the sun was hitting the windowpanes, and her mind immediately flooded with sweet memories of making love with Vance. When she reached out and didn't find him, her body went stiff.

"I'm right here, *cher.*"

She looked up and saw him standing at the foot of the bed, dressed in jeans and a navy knit shirt. A black shadow of beard darkened his cheeks, his hair was mussed and there was a hint of tension around his mouth. Studying his face, she decided that he looked more like a man who'd been out all night on some clandestine mission than like one who'd just gotten dressed.

"You're up early," she murmured.

He sat down on the edge of the bed and stroked her hair away from her face. "I was at your house."

"What?" She pushed herself up, dragging the covers with her and folding them around her breasts.

"Were you planning to go into work this morning in cutoffs and one of my shirts?"

"I—no—" She stopped and looked beyond him where a suitcase rested on the floor. "But I wasn't planning to have you go through my closets and drawers, either."

His hand moved from her hair to her cheek. "I realize I was taking liberties. But I didn't want you going back there yet. Not even for a little while. Not until I'm sure it's safe."

"When will that be?"

"After you go in and tell them you're off the Lisa Gautreau story. And after we see how they react."

Tess swallowed. Last night it had been easy to put thoughts of the morning's confrontation out of her mind.

"Chris is usually in by eight-thirty."

"Then we've got time for a shower and breakfast." He took her hand and began to help her from the bed.

"Did you pack my robe?"

"Sorry, *cher*. I didn't think about that." He pulled her naked from the bed and into his arms, pressing her tightly against his body. His lips found her neck and then the tender flesh of her ear. And she wasn't inclined to complain about what he'd packed.

TWO HOURS LATER, Vance's red Mustang pulled up at the curb a block from the KEFT building. Tess sat in the passenger seat, dressed in the cream-color suit and teal blouse he'd selected for her. It was an outfit that had always made her feel cool and confident. Had he seen her wear it on the air? Or had he simply known her taste?

On the ride into town, she'd done a fairly good job of staying relaxed. As the confrontation drew near, she could feel every muscle in her body tightening up.

"This is the second time I've dropped you off when I wanted to go with you. I don't like it," Vance muttered. "But letting them know you're mixed up with me is a bad idea."

Tess swallowed and reached for his hand. Once her fingers closed around his, she didn't want to let go.

"Remember, it's better if you play your big scene in front of an audience. So the word spreads fast."

"Yes."

He leaned over and gave her a quick kiss.

"I'll be okay." She reached for the door handle. "I'll call you as soon as it's over."

"I'm sorry. I won't be home."

She waited for him to tell her where he was going.

"Let me phone you in an hour or so," he said instead.

"I could be out on an assignment."

He nodded. "We'll figure out when we can get together. Go on now. We'll both feel better when you've gotten it over with."

"Yes." *And I'd feel better if you trusted me with your plans.* The observation went unspoken. This wasn't the time for a lesson on the ethics of relationships. So she squeezed his hand for a moment before opening the door and stepping out on the sidewalk.

Shirley Barnes, the newsroom secretary, glanced up when she saw Tess. "You were a friend of Ken Holloway, weren't you?" she asked gently.

"Yes. I found out about it Saturday. It's terrible," Tess murmured.

"It's going to mean overtime for the other cameramen until we can get a replacement," film editor Stan Reardon observed. He'd been passing through the room and stopped to join the conversation.

"I—yes." Tess blinked. She had been thinking about Ken in such personal terms that she hadn't even considered how his death would affect the station.

Shirley clicked her tongue as she watched the play of emotions on Tess's face. "It's a real shocker—coming on top of the others."

"I assume the police have been here again asking more questions. Do they have any leads?"

Stan shook his head and looked expectantly at the secretary.

Shirley obliged him by continuing the recitation. "That's not all."

Tess's fingers wound themselves in the strap of her purse. "My God. What else?"

"Brad Everett came marching in a little while ago and told our esteemed leader that he's not going on the air this morning, or any other morning."

Tess's mouth dropped open. "What?"

Stan stood with his arms crossed.

Shirley continued. "I got it straight from Desmond's secretary. Mr. Let-the-Chips-Fall-Where-They-May says KEFT is a death trap, and he's getting out while there's still time."

"You mean he's not planning a story on the latest development?" Tess couldn't hide her sarcasm.

"I guess he's not so tough when he thinks his own skin's in danger of getting punctured," Stan said.

"But he has a contract with the station. Desmond will be livid. He'll sue the pants off Everett," Tess responded.

"Maybe he doesn't care. Or maybe there's an escape clause for hazardous duty. Desmond is behind closed doors with his lawyer now," Shirley reported. It sounded as if she'd already told the story several times.

"Well, I'd better get on with it," Stan murmured as he headed toward one of the editing booths.

"What did Larry say?" Tess asked, unable to drag herself away.

"He got that funny look on his face and locked himself in his office. He used to be the linchpin around here. Now, if you ask me, he's cracking under the pressure."

Tess stood numbly, trying to take in the latest revelations. Perhaps she should step into her office before she talked to Chris. However, as she started into the hall, she saw the news director standing outside her door.

"Where the hell were you last night when I needed you?" he growled, advancing toward her. "I'm short a cameraman. I don't need to be short a reporter, too."

Tess stared at him—unsure about how to take his insensitivity. He was short a cameraman because Ken was dead.

"The world doesn't stop, you know. There was a fire in one of the warehouses on the river, and I needed somebody on the scene," he continued.

"It's hard to deal with, isn't it? Everything happening at once," Tess murmured. "Is Desmond coming down on you?"

"You didn't answer *my* question."

"You couldn't reach me because I was with a friend last night."

He stopped and gave her an inquiring look. "Oh?"

She pressed her hands against her sides, aware that Shirley and several other staffers were looking covertly in their direction—anticipating some sort of juicy confrontation. And someone else had stopped in the hall, in the shadows where she couldn't see who it was. But she sensed interested ears listening.

Well, Vance had told her it was better to have an audience. Better still, she wasn't even going to have to mention him. Taking a deep breath, she began, "Chris, I know you're having a morning from hell. And this isn't going to help. I was coming in to talk to you about the Lisa Gautreau story." As the sentence ended, Tess's voice rose.

She'd thought she was going to have to fake hysteria. With the first words out of her mouth, she knew she wouldn't have any trouble sounding like a woman fighting for survival.

Chris shook his head dismissively. "Not now. I don't have time to talk about her now."

"I—I'm dropping the assignment."

"Oh, no, you're not! Larry's hardly been functioning for the past couple of days. I'm doing my job and his, and I don't need any more damn problems."

"I'm afraid you've got another one, Chris. Ken left a message on my answering machine Saturday saying he had some information about Lisa."

She had his full attention—and everyone else's.

"Naturally, I went out to meet him. But when I got to the cemetery he was already dead, and whoever killed him took a shot at me, too."

Vance had told her to watch for reactions. She had the satisfaction of seeing the news director's mouth drop open—and hearing collective gasps from around the room.

Before Chris could recover, she rushed on. "So that's why you couldn't get hold of me. I was hiding. And trying to decide what to do. I've never ducked an assignment before. I've gone down into the city pumping stations for you. I've flown in a hot-air balloon up the Mississippi and done a lot of other dangerous stunts. What I keep coming up with this time is that somebody is desperate to stop us from figuring out what really happened to Lisa. And I'm not going to make myself the next target by staying on the story."

For a moment Chris seemed at a loss for words. "That does put things in a rather different perspective," he finally said.

"Digging into Lisa's background isn't worth getting killed for."

"I can't argue with you about that." He put his hand on her shoulder and squeezed. "Tess, I'm sorry I lit into you. It's just that I'm under a lot of stress."

"Yes."

"But that's no excuse. A man is dead and all I can think about is how to redistribute his workload."

Tess covered his hand with hers. "Tell me if there's anything I can do."

The offer allowed him to click back into business mode. "Stay available for assignments." He paused a moment. "And would you mind checking the stories you have in production? I may need to have a couple of news features that are ready to go."

Tess nodded. She wanted to ask how the Brad Everett problem would affect their scheduling. Would the station be filling in with news features? Local programming? Canned material? She didn't dare bring up anything so sensitive now. "I'll get right on it," she told him instead.

"I'm sorry," he apologized again. "I know I can always count on you."

As he headed down the hall toward the executive offices, Shirley stared at Tess, her expression proclaiming that she didn't quite believe what she'd heard. "Is all that true?"

"Of course. Do you think I'd lie about something like that?"

The secretary shook her head. "It's just... no. I guess not. You've always been one of the few people around this zoo who plays things straight."

"Thanks." Another vote of confidence, sort of, Tess thought as she turned to leave the newsroom. Her mind still on her conversation with Chris, she started toward her office.

As she passed the bank of file cabinets in the hall, there was a roar of sound like a 747 landing directly on the roof. Or perhaps the building began to shake with the impact first. Afterward, Tess was never sure in which order things had happened. But she knew at once that she'd been knocked off her feet and had landed with a grunt of pain on her backside. For several seconds she sat on the tile floor dazed and too disoriented even to push herself up. The building was old, and this part had never been re-modeled. Now chunks of plaster were falling from the ceiling like ice rock from an avalanche. Folding her arms over her head, she tried to ward them off. One hit her on the arm, tearing her jacket and gouging a jagged hole in her skin. She cried out, struggling to push herself up. In that instant, the wall next to her buckled and more debris pelted down.

A bomb, she thought. It must be a bomb. Unless New Orleans had been hit by the mother of all earthquakes.

Behind her in the newsroom, someone was screaming for help. Someone else was wailing in pain and terror.

Tess was pulling herself erect using the handles of the nearest file cabinet when Desmond LeRoy came stagger-ing down the hall from the executive wing, cursing and shouting at the top of his lungs.

"You bastard! You bastard!" he screamed.

Tess managed to stand on rubbery legs and stretched out her arm toward him. "Please. Wait. There are people who need—"

He gave her a savage look and rushed on past, heading for the exit to the parking lot.

Tess stared after him, hardly able to believe that he would simply leave while staffers were in danger. Then a moan captured her full attention. Making her way as quickly as possible around the rubble on the floor, she headed toward the sound.

"Easy, easy. Take it easy and I'll get you out of there." The soothing words came from Stan, who was on his knees beside Shirley's desk. Only the secretary's legs were visible.

Tess dropped down beside him amid the chunks of white plaster and white powder that covered the floor. She drew in a sharp breath as she saw Shirley lying behind the desk. One of the columns that supported the ceiling had fallen over and was pinning her to the floor. Stan wrapped his arm around it and pulled, obviously making an enormous effort. But although Tess could see the muscles of his back and arms bulging, the heavy piece of metal didn't move.

He cursed and cast his eyes briefly at the ceiling, where more debris was filtering down.

"You'd better get out of here while the getting's good," he muttered.

Shirley moaned.

"We've got to get her, too." Tess gestured toward the length of metal. "Can you move out from under this thing if we can lift it up?" she asked the secretary.

"I don't know. I—I—can't feel my legs. But I'll try."

Tess grasped her hands around the pillar. "Say when," she instructed.

"Now," Stan grated. They both heaved, and the heavy weight came up slightly.

"Move," Tess shouted at Shirley. For a moment, she thought it wasn't going to work. Or they might make things worse by dropping the column back on the secretary. But Shirley managed to roll to the side and pull herself free just before Tess's strength gave out and the heavy weight came crashing back to the floor. She sat down, panting and feeling cold sweat pouring off her body.

Stan tried to help Shirley to her feet. She shook her head and gestured toward her legs. "No. Hurts."

He was just about to pick her up when two men in white uniforms came running into the room, wheeling a stretcher between them. Ambulance attendants. Thank God, Tess thought. Somebody must have turned in the alarm. She hadn't heard the siren. She'd been too focused on moving the obstruction to be aware of anything else.

"I think this woman's legs are broken," she gasped.

Stan gestured toward the still-buckling ceiling. "Come on. The building isn't safe. We're getting out of here." He helped Tess up and slung his arm around her shoulder. Then, like two drunken comrades, they helped each other toward the door.

A minute later she found herself sitting at the side of the parking lot feeling sick and unable to keep her arms and legs from trembling.

Stan whistled between his teeth as he gave her a careful inspection. She followed the direction of his gaze and saw that her arm was bleeding. She hadn't known.

"You're bad off yourself," he said. "You should never have been liftin' that pillar."

"Had to." Tess couldn't manage any more words as she leaned back against the wheel of a car and watched ambulances and fire engines arrive. Stan stopped one of the attendants and gestured in her direction. When he came over and saw her chalky face and bloody sleeve, he hustled her into an emergency vehicle. Several more victims were brought in. Then they took off for Tulane University Medical Center.

Tess wasn't one of the worst cases. As she arrived at the emergency room, she saw several unconscious staffers.

And Larry Melbourne was just being wheeled into the back on a stretcher. His eyes were wide and staring, and his jowly face was like wrinkled pastry dough, except where blood had dried on a gash across his high forehead. My God, she thought, was he going to die?

With so many casualties, Tess expected to sit in the waiting room for several hours. She was surprised that after a brief conversation with the nurse in charge, the attendants helped her into one of the curtained cubicles and let her lie down while she was waiting to be treated. Her own doctor could probably take care of her arm. Except that she didn't have the strength to haul herself up and away.

Tess was lying with her eyes closed, trying not to focus on the throbbing pain in her arm, when the curtain was whisked aside. Looking up, she expected to see one of the doctors. Instead, Vance crossed swiftly to her side.

"*Cher.* I heard about it on the radio in the car. I went over to the station looking for you. The place is a mess."

Tess nodded.

"When I couldn't find you, I didn't know...I was afraid..." She saw his Adam's apple bob. "Someone told me you'd been brought here," he continued in a gritty voice. "Are you all right?"

"Mostly." She gestured toward her arm and winced. "Just scraped up, I think."

He leaned over her narrow bed, carefully spread the torn fabric of her jacket and inspected the wound. "Not exactly a scrape. They should be taking care of this instead of just leaving you lying here."

"Other people are worse off. Larry had a gash on his head. He looked terrible. Shirley's legs..." It took too much effort to continue the exclamation. Her lids fluttered closed.

Vance found her hand and wrapped it in his larger one. Just holding on to him made her feel a little better.

With his other hand he brushed her hair back from her face. The gesture scattered plaster dust, and she started to cough. Vance muttered something too low for her to hear. "I'll be right back."

When he reappeared, he had a wet cloth in his hand. He pulled over the metal chair in the corner, then sat down and began to wash her face and neck, murmuring in French. Tess closed her eyes again while he worked.

"That feels good."

"It's about the only thing I can do for you."

"You can give me some information. You said you heard it on the radio. Was it just at the station? What happened?" she asked.

"Just at the station. A pipe bomb, they think."

A bomb. That's what she'd assumed. "Has anyone claimed responsibility?"

"Not that I heard. But it was in Studio Seven. The building's been declared unsafe, the station is off the air for the time being at least, and the owner—"

"Desmond LeRoy."

"*Oui.* Desmond LeRoy can't be reached for comment."

"Good Lord." Tess tried to sit up, but Vance's hand on her shoulder prevented it. "Studio Seven. That's the one they renovated especially for the Brad Everett Show. I heard from the secretary that he came in this morning, threw a fit about safety and quit."

Vance stared down at her. "*Sacré bleu!* I'd like to know how all this fits together."

Before they could exchange any more information, the doctor appeared. "Ms. Beaumont, I'm sorry we couldn't get to you sooner. How are you doing?" he asked.

"Not too badly."

His stern gaze flicked to Vance and the cloth in his hand. "Would you mind stepping outside while I do an examination?"

Vance's expression made it clear that he did mind, however he didn't make a fuss. "I'll be in the waiting room," he told Tess.

Half an hour later, with ten stitches in her arm, she walked slowly out front and found him.

Seeing her pale face, he was on his feet at once and at her side. "Let's get out of here."

"In a second." Turning back to the desk, she caught the attention of the nurse. "Can you tell me if the other people who were brought in from the station are all right?"

"No fatalities," the woman informed her. "We do have a number of broken bones and some external injuries. And one of the sound technicians is in surgery. We won't know anything on that for several hours."

"Thank you," Tess said. She would have liked to get a list of the victims, but she didn't want to hold up anyone's treatment by taking up the nurse's time. Instead she followed Vance outside and over to his car.

When he'd closed his door, he turned to her and pulled her carefully into his arms. His lips slid across her cheek, found her mouth and pressed. She sighed and moved into his embrace—into his kiss.

It was several moments before either of them broke the contact.

"Did you quit the story?" Vance asked.

"Yes."

"When I heard the radio report I just about went crazy. I thought they were still after you," he finally said.

She found his hand and laced her fingers with his. "That bomb was in Brad Everett's studio—not my office."

"*Oui*. And now the station's closed. And you don't have to hang around there for a while."

"Hang around! I was working for a living. Now I'm out of a job. At least until Desmond gets his act back together," she pointed out as the larger implications of the explosion sank in.

"That's true. But you're not seriously hurt. And what you need to do is come back home and take it easy for a few days."

Back home? Did he mean to his house? And then what? She was still too shaken to grapple with *those* implications, so she simply nodded.

Vance pulled out of the parking lot and headed toward the highway. After several blocks Tess became aware that he had speeded up. Then he made a couple of sharp turns that took them away from the direct route to the highway.

"What's going on?"

"Somebody's following us. Hang on tight."

Chapter Fourteen

Tess's heart began to pound thickly in her throat. She'd thought the terror was finished. Who was after them now? The same man who had forced her into the bayou?

She snatched quickly for the armrest as Vance swung the wheel again, trying to shake their pursuer. The car tipped and swayed as he screeched around the corner. Glancing in the rearview mirror, he cursed under his breath.

When she'd regained her balance, Tess twisted around to look behind them. A sporty little silver car was right on their tail. And with its power and maneuverability, it had no problem keeping up.

"I've seen that car before," she told him.

"At the cemetery when you were supposed to meet Ken?"

"No. In the KEFT parking lot. It's new."

"Get down." Vance started to push her below the level of the dashboard as their pursuer drew abreast of the Mustang. When Tess gasped in pain, he loosened his grasp on her shoulder. "Sorry."

She did a double take as she saw the driver. Larry Melbourne! She'd spotted him in the emergency room being wheeled away. Now a bandage partially covered the high dome of his forehead, but his bulldog jowls were clearly

visible. He'd made a remarkable recovery. With only one
hand on the wheel, he was frantically waving at them. "It's
Larry Melbourne."

"The station manager who turned the programming
upside down when he came in six months ago?"

Tess nodded.

"It looks like someone lit a fire under his seat."

Tess watched him pull up so close that the two cars were
almost touching. Perhaps the head injury had affected his
mind.

"He wants us to stop."

"Tough luck!" Vance stepped on the accelerator.

Larry sped up, too. In fact, he passed them and pulled
in front of the Mustang. Like a sheepdog cutting an animal out of the herd, he began to edge them toward the side
of the road. The way the truck had crowded her off the
pavement the night she'd been coming out to Ernestine's,
Tess thought with a gulp.

Vance swore. Tess saw that in a moment he would have
the choice of sideswiping trees and cars on the right, running into the station manager, or stopping. For several
seconds, he delayed the decision. Finally, he slammed on
the brakes.

Tess was thrown forward and then jerked back into
place as her seat belt caught and held.

"Okay?" Vance asked.

"Yes."

He reached for the door handle. But Melbourne was at
the side of their car before anyone could get out.

"Are you crazy?" Vance growled.

The threat in his voice would have made any sane man
back off. Melbourne held his ground.

"I've got to talk to Tess," he insisted. "It's important."

"Important enough to almost get us killed?" Vance gave the door a shove, pushing the other man back against the hood of his own car. Leaning over, he grabbed him by the collar. "Are you the one who's been trying to kill her?" he demanded.

"Of course not! And they're not after her. They're after me."

As Tess climbed out of the car and approached the two men, Vance stepped quickly between her and their pursuer. "He's dangerous."

"I don't think he's trying to hurt us."

"He damn near got us all killed."

"I have to explain," Melbourne insisted.

Tess recognized the hysteria in his voice, and his eyes swung pleadingly to her.

"It's all right, Larry," she soothed.

"No. I was out in the hall when you were talking to Chris. I can't let you go on thinking it was directed at you."

"What wasn't directed at me?"

"All the bad stuff that's been coming down around the station." He swallowed convulsively. "It's me they're after. I've ruined everything! Now I'll be lucky to get away in one piece."

Tess was still mystified, and she could see from the perplexed look on Vance's face that he wasn't following the conversation any better than she was.

"Who's after you?" Vance demanded.

"I don't know. The mob, if you have to give them a name." In the past he'd always spoken precisely. Now his speech was slurred.

"For what?"

"Gambling debts. In Las Vegas last year. See, first I was on a roll. Then I started losing bad. But I kept thinking my luck was gonna change." He shrugged. "Instead, I got flushed down the toilet. And I couldn't pay up."

"The mob came after you to collect on gambling debts?" Tess clarified.

"Bingo. They were going to break my legs and wreck my career. But there was no way I could pay out that kinda bread. So I skipped town. I thought they wouldn't find me because I changed my name. But they tracked me down here. And they wrecked the station like they said they would."

"You changed your identity?" Tess asked. "Then how did you get a job if you didn't have any credentials? Why did LeRoy hire you?"

"Because the scuzzbag was desperate to make a name for himself. I heard about him and figured out how to ring his bells. Then I talked a good line." For a moment the old confidence came back in his voice. "He needed somebody like me—somebody creative who wasn't afraid to take chances with the schedule to pull the viewers. First I practically worked for free—on a trial basis, pending getting my credentials. Then when he could see how well things were working out—a résumé was a moot point."

Tess stared at him. Gambling debts. A new name. A station manager with no credentials. The whole thing sounded like some sort of paranoid delusion. Yet as she looked back, she remembered that Larry had never mentioned anything about his background.

"You think someone killed two of Brad Everett's guests and a cameraman because of you?" Vance demanded.

"Yeah. And I'm not stickin' around to get clobbered."

"Why didn't they just go after you?" he persisted.

"Warnings. They thought they could make me pay up if they scared me enough."

"Has anyone contacted you?" Vance continued the line of questioning.

"They keep calling. But I don't answer the phone anymore." He glanced over his shoulder as if he expected a hit man to come charging out of the bushes. Then he took a step toward his car.

Vance leaped forward and clapped a hand on his shoulder. *"Arrêt."*

"For what?"

"If all this is true, you've got to tell someone else."

"Yeah, that's right. LeRoy oughta know, too. You tell him. I'll back you up with a letter. From Alaska or somewhere." As he finished speaking, he straightened and wrenched himself away from Vance. In the next moment, he scrambled into his car and shoved it into gear. Then he swung the wheel in a circle and peeled away.

"You could have stopped him," Tess murmured as she watched Larry disappear.

"Oui."

"Why didn't you?"

"Because I haven't changed my opinion. He's dangerous. The farther he is from you, the better." He moved over and draped his arm around Tess's shoulder. "Come on, let's go."

"His story sounds crazy. Do you think he was telling the truth?"

"*He* thinks he is. I don't know how all of that fits into the picture. But there are ways to check."

Tess nodded as she allowed Vance to escort her back to the car. When she flopped into the passenger seat, she realized that her knees were trembling again.

Vance climbed behind the wheel and started the engine. Locking her hands together in her lap, Tess tried to bring herself under control. It was difficult. Too many things were happening too quickly. Soon she wouldn't be able to tell black from white or up from down.

After glancing briefly at Tess, Vance didn't try to engage her in conversation as they sped toward Savannah Bayou. She was grateful. With the rhythm of the car rocking her, she could feel her mind closing down the way it had the day before—barricading itself into some quiet, peaceful place where nothing bad could touch her.

"We're here."

Tess's lids fluttered open. Startled, she looked around. They weren't at Vance's. He had pulled up in front of Ernestine's little house.

"What are we doing here?"

"It's safer."

Safer than what? Wasn't the danger over? But she was too foggy to question Vance's logic.

As they stepped onto the porch, she glanced questioningly at him. "Where's Ernestine?"

"Maybe this is the morning that one of her friends takes her shopping. Come on inside." His voice was low and gentle. "You need to crawl into bed and sleep."

"Umm." He was right about that.

He led her to the bedroom where she'd spent Friday night and gently helped her unbutton her blouse and pull her injured arm from the sleeve.

"There's no point in saving it," she said, as he laid the ruined garment on the chair.

"Or your skirt, either, I guess."

When she was clad in her slip, he pulled back the covers and she crawled underneath.

Moving over to make room on the narrow mattress, she reached for him, and he hugged her against his chest.

"I'm so tired."

"I know." He pressed his lips against her cheek. "I'll be back by the time you wake up."

"What about Ernestine? You can't leave her a note."

"Actually, I can. There's a magnetic board we use. With the same big plastic letters I bought for cans."

Some of the fog had lifted from her brain. "Where are you going?"

As soon as the question was out of her mouth, Tess could see he wished she hadn't asked. "I need to take care of a little business," he answered.

"Business? The same business you had this morning when you told me I couldn't get in touch with you?"

"Oui."

"What?"

"Just some things I need to do."

"Vance, are you ever going to trust me?"

"I trust you, *cher.*"

"Then tell me where you're going."

He didn't answer.

"Does this have something to do with Lisa?"

"It could."

"You never did intend to let me help you, did you?"

"Please, Tess, you're in no shape for anything but rest. And it's better if you don't get involved in what I'm doing."

"Is it against the law?"

She saw his Adam's apple bob.

"Vance—"

"*Cher,* stop asking me questions. You have to let me handle things my way."

She hitched herself up in bed. "Is it always going to be like this between us?"

"We'll talk about it when you're feeling better."

"Vance, I know you're used to making your own decisions. So am I. But if you want our relationship to work, it has to be a partnership."

"*Cher,* I'm sorry. I'm trying to keep you out of trouble, and for the moment you have to trust me."

"Yes, Vance, I want to trust you. Let me help—with whatever it is. Please."

She could tell by the closed expression on his face that her words were having no effect. "Let me be a little more plain. This isn't like after Ken was killed. I'm not having some sort of hysterical reaction to the bombing or Larry Melbourne. I'm thinking very clearly. Before we went back to Aunt Pauline's house, you said you wanted everything that happened between us to be honest. Well, this isn't honest. And if you walk out that door now, I don't know if I'll be here when you come back."

"How are you going to leave? Walk?"

"I—"

Apparently he wasn't really interested in hearing her answer. Before she could figure out the rest of the sentence, he had stalked out of the little room.

Tess lay staring at the empty doorway. A few minutes later, she heard the car engine start again. Well, so much for ultimatums, she conceded. Vance was too set in his ways to consider something as simple as another person's wishes when he thought he knew best. He was going to do what he wanted, whatever her feelings. Which meant there was really no point in sticking around. Except that she was dead tired, emotionally battered, and without transportation.

Seeking some sort of comfort, she burrowed under the covers and squeezed her eyes shut. But Vance's face continued to fill her mind.

Vance. His father had never wanted him. His mother had been incapable of giving him the love or support every child needed. Ernestine and Alphonse had finally stepped in, but by then his personality had already been formed, and he obviously had no idea what it took to make a commitment to a partner.

Tess swallowed to ease the sudden pain in her throat. When she could no longer control her anguish, the tears began to flow down her cheeks. What if she were willing to settle for less of him? she asked herself. No, if he couldn't make a commitment to her, why keep hanging on? It would be better to try and find some way to deal with the loss.

Thoroughly exhausted, Tess finally slept. At first she dreamed about Vance. Yet even her subconscious was unable to conjure up a happy ending for the two of them. Instead she fled back to the time before. She was a little girl again. With Momma. In the house near the bayou.

Memories that had been buried rose to the surface. She was playing with fragrant dried leaves while Momma crumbled a basket of them and put them into packets made of waxed paper. A woman came to the door and told Momma her little boy was sick with the flux, and Momma got out a little box of white powder and gave it to her. The woman thanked her and gave her some money and went away.

Then all at once the woman was there again. Only this time she was crying and yelling at Momma. And Momma kept shaking her head and saying she didn't understand what had happened.

Suddenly everything changed, and Tess was standing in the middle of the swamp bewildered, terrified and crying.

Aunt Pauline came gliding toward her across the dark water, holding out her comforting arms. Clasped in one of her hands was the silver locket. She gestured with it toward Tess.

"Aunt Pauline, where's Momma? What's happening?" she wailed.

"Look in the locket, child. Look—"

Her aunt's voice was drowned out by the sound of voices. Confused, frightened, Tess tried to hold on to the dream and Aunt Pauline's words. She was trying to tell her something important.

No, it wasn't Aunt Pauline, she realized with a start. She could hear someone else talking. Tess opened her eyes and blinked. At first she didn't remember where she was. Then it came sweeping back over her like a cold, early morning fog rolling in off the gulf. The explosion. Vance. The terrible sadness of knowing that he couldn't share himself with her when it counted most.

A stooped figure filled the doorway.

"Ernestine?"

"You're awake, *hein?*" the old woman said. Her lined face looked pinched, and the furrows across her brow seemed deeper.

"Yes."

"Lonnie was just here."

"Lonnie?"

"He brought your car."

"It's fixed, then."

Ernestine nodded. "I heard there was a bomb at the TV station. Are you all right? Do you feel well enough to get up?"

Tess pushed herself up against the pillows. She felt stiff, and her arm throbbed where it had been gashed. But she'd expected as much. "I think so."

"*Cher,* I've been waiting for you to wake up. I want to ask you a question."

"About Vance?"

"*Non,* about Otelie Hugo."

"My mother!" She felt an eerie sensation begin to tingle at the edges of her nerves as the afternoon's dream snapped back into her consciousness. For a moment she was almost ill. Then she pulled herself together.

"So the name was right, for truth." Ernestine looked pleased. "I've put some clean clothes on the end of the bed. Come on out to the kitchen and let me get you something to eat."

"I—I'm not hungry."

"Then we'll just talk." The old woman turned and shuffled off.

A few minutes later, Tess found Vance's aunt stirring a pot of soup on the stove. "That does smell good," she murmured.

"Eat a little bit. It will make you feel better."

Pulling out a chair at the wooden table, Tess sat down. Although she picked up the spoon in front of her, she was too excited to touch the soup. "My mother. How do you know her name? What can you tell me? Did you know her?"

Ernestine shook her head. "*Non.* I didn't know her."

"Then..."

"First a woman's odd name popped into my mind while I was straightening the house Sunday. I remembered she was someone who lived near here long ago. It stayed with me. Then...I started thinking about the questions you asked the other morning before Vance took you to see your car...and I wondered. But I wasn't sure they were connected until you told me."

"Vance didn't like my asking anything. He thought poking into what happened to my mother could be dangerous for you."

The old woman made a dismissive noise. "Sometimes the boy is too quick to make decisions for other people."

"Yes."

"He only does it when he cares about them."

"He cares about you," Tess said in a low voice.

"And you."

"I—" She felt her heart squeeze.

"Nothing I can say is going to make any difference. You'll have to settle that with him. This business now— about your mother—this is between you and me, *ma cher*."

Tess dug her fingers into a fold of clothes. "What can you tell me?"

"Not too much. But I know where Otelie Hugo lived."

Tess felt heat prickle along her nerve endings. "Where?"

"The other side of Antonville. About fifteen miles up the bayou. I have family there. And I recollect the talk about her—and her husband. He was from the back country, him."

So her fantasy had been right, Tess thought. Or maybe it was one of her buried memories. Maybe her mother had told her all about it, and she'd forgotten.

"But he had a scholarship to the university. They both came out here to study the plants. He was killed in a boating accident."

Vance had been wrong. Her father hadn't left her mother. He'd died.

"She stayed on with the little girl, her."

Tess jumped up and began to pace back and forth across the room.

"People didn't like them at first. I think they tried too hard to be part of the community. But after he passed on, she changed. She knew about tonics and remedies for sore throats and skin rashes and such like. And people came to her for advice.''

''Yes!'' Like the dream. ''Do you know what happened to her?''

Ernestine shook her head. ''*Non*, I'm sorry.''

Tess knelt beside Ernestine. ''Tell me about the house.''

''It still belongs to the university, I think. Maybe nobody else would take it.''

Tess felt her excitement mount. ''I have to go there. I have to see it. Maybe there's even some clue about what happened. Can you give me directions?''

''Don't you think it would be better to wait for Vance, *cher*? Didn't he—didn't he say someone was after you?''

''Yes. But that's all over now. Really.''

Ernestine nodded a bit uncertainly.

''I don't have to ask Vance's permission.'' Tess took the old woman's wrinkled hands between her own. ''A few weeks ago I did a story on surrogate mothers. And all the time I was asking questions, I kept wondering how it would be if you didn't know who you were. I know now it was me I was really thinking about. I was still afraid to face the past. So it only came out in nightmares. Like when I ran out into the swamp that night at your house.''

''*Oui*.''

''Don't you understand what this means to me? You're dangling a key in front of me. A key to the part of my life that's been hidden all these years. But you won't let me have it.''

Ernestine squeezed her hand. ''*Bien*. I can see this makes your stomach churn. If you must go now, take the road along the bayou to Antonville. Go through town. On the other side, look at the mailboxes. Look for the university name.''

''Thank you.''

"Don't be disappointed if you don't find anything. It was so long ago."

"Thank you." Tess jumped up and started for the door. Then she turned back guiltily toward the old woman. "Will you be all right?"

"*Bien sûr.* I'll wait here for Vance. And I'll tell him where you've gone."

The car was almost as good as new—except for the damp smell coming from the upholstery. But she couldn't do anything about that until she got back to the city.

After emerging on the far side of Antonville, Tess slowed her speed and began looking at mailboxes. From Ernestine's directions, she expected to come upon the right road immediately. It was several frustrating miles before she spotted a mailbox with Charter University written in black letters across the top. Behind it was a post with a No Trespassing sign. Her hands gripped the wheel, and her breath came in shallow little puffs as she turned in. The one-lane road was rutted, and scraggly trees, dripping with Spanish moss, seemed to press in against the car. All at once Tess could feel witches' fingers plucking at the back of her neck.

Stomping down on the brake, Tess came to a jouncing halt and reached for the gear lever to put the car into reverse, then stopped in the middle of the frantic action. She hadn't been willing to wait another moment to come here. She wasn't going to turn tail like a frightened deer and bound away. It was broad daylight. The bad things were all in the past. And she was sure she could bring back some more of the good recollections if she sat on the front porch and maybe walked through the rooms.

Concentrating on the warm patches of sunlight filtering through the branches overhead, Tess continued up the drive. She came upon the bungalow suddenly as she rounded a curve. It was low and weathered and—as she'd suspected—a lot like Ernestine's. She sat for several minutes, simply staring at the front windows. But there was no sudden rush of memory. Disappointed, she got out and started walking slowly toward the porch. Just before she reached the worn boards, it happened. Not a dream. A clear image of a blond-haired rag doll lying on the ground beside the steps. Blond like her. It had a red plaid dress, and its name was Evangeline. Only she hadn't been able to pronounce the whole name, so she'd called it Lynn.

Overcome by the clarity of the memory, Tess felt her pulse begin to race. She'd been hoping, longing, for something like this. Now it was happening. She sat for several minutes on the steps until her blood stopped pounding. Then, with a smile flickering at the corners of her mouth, she got up and wandered around the back. Two poles still stood about ten feet apart in back. They were leaning precariously, and the line on which her mother had hung the laundry was missing. Tess could imagine white sheets and cotton underwear flapping in the breeze, but she wasn't sure whether it was a real memory or her imagination. Perhaps this wasn't going to be as easy as she'd thought. Walking over to one of the posts, she ran her fingers along the wood, and the scene around her seemed to blur. Once again she was a little girl watching Momma hang out the wash.

"Aunt Pauline says bleach won't get the dirt out of my white pinafore."

Momma pulled the pinafore out of the laundry basket and held it up. "Well, it did. It worked like a charm. See how white it is?"

"Why did Aunt Pauline yell at you? Were you bad?"

"No, honey."

"Doesn't Aunt Pauline love you?"

"She just doesn't understand why I want to live out here." She knelt down and took the little girl by the hands. "Honey, if something—something—happened to me, would you mind going to live with Aunt Pauline?"

"Nothing's gonna happen to you, Momma!"

"Shh, baby. It's all right."

The long-ago scene shattered like a mirror dropped on a tile floor.

"Careful, you don't want to get splinters from that old wood," a man's voice said.

Tess's whole body jerked in pain. As her head came up, she found herself looking into a round face with a double chin and bushy brows. Perhaps he was in his early fifties. Perhaps soft living had aged him. At any rate, he was the observer who had been standing off to the side at her aunt's graveside service. Today he wore a white cotton shirt untucked over baggy trousers.

"Who—who are you?" she asked in a voice that she wished was steadier.

"Glen Devoe."

Chapter Fifteen

"Lisa's husband," she breathed, still caught up by the sound of his voice. "Have I met you before?"

He smiled engagingly. "Haven't had the pleasure."

"What are you doing here?" she demanded. "And why were you standing in the background at the cemetery?"

"I wanted to explain to you about Lisa. Then I decided not to intrude on your grief."

"How did you know I was here?"

"Folks along the bayou tell me things."

Before she could ask for clarification, he went on. "Please. I want to explain about Lisa. It will make me feel better. I was at Savannah Bayou the afternoon my wife went into the water. I tried to stop her, but it was too late."

He looked distressed. He sounded convincing. Yet she found it very difficult to trust him. "Why did she do it?" Tess asked.

"She was never quite right in the head. That was one of the things I found out after I married her. Didn't her brother tell you?"

Tess nodded.

"After she was raped, I kept trying to help her, but she just kind of closed up."

Was that the truth? Usually Tess was good at analyzing the subtle cues people gave off. But this man's voice kept getting in the way of the words, sending little zings of alarm up her spine.

Devoe sighed. "Lisa was always a mystery to me. I'd appreciate anything you could tell me. Do you know if— uh—she told her aunt about anything else that was upsetting her? I mean, besides the rape."

"Maybe you should ask Ernestine about that."

"I don't want to bother the old woman."

"I'm afraid my conversation with Lisa's aunt was confidential.

He sighed once more. "You're not being very helpful. I thought we could do this the easy way. But I'm going to get the information out of you, one way or the other." Pulling a gun out of the waistband of his trousers, he leveled it at her chest.

A wispy breath trickled from Tess's lungs. When Devoe took a step forward, she automatically took two steps back.

"No use tryin' to split," he said. His speech became more colloquial, as if a layer of civilization had suddenly been stripped away. His tone became gritty, and the grit tore at Tess's nerves like an open wound dragged across gravel.

"I made sure your car ain't gonna start."

He ignored her gasp and kept talking.

"What do you care about Lisa? She was *my* wife. What happens between a man and his wife ain't nobody else's business."

Tess continued to stare at him, hardly able to take in his words, hardly able to get past the awful sound of his voice. She knew it now. It was the voice from that terrible night long ago when the monsters had come.

"You brought the men to my mother's house," she breathed.

"Yeah. They're simple people. Superstitious, too. It was easy to stir them up. I just made sure a few of the folks who got herbs and stuff from your ma died."

Tess was speechless.

"You can bring in a ton of drugs from the gulf—and stash 'em where nobody'll bother 'em. 'Less some nosy bitch starts poking around," he growled.

Tess fought the nausea rising in her throat.

He was watching her closely now, the way a cat watches a wounded mouse before it reaches out to strike again. "Your aunt and I had a deal, you know. I'd get rid of your mother, and she'd get you."

Tess's hand jerked to the locket around her neck. "You're lying. She wouldn't have done that."

He tipped his head to one side. "Guess you'll have to take my word for it." His tone became more conversational now. "What I say around here goes. I've got plenty of money. Enough to help out people who need it. So when I came up with a plan to punish your ma for what I convinced them she'd done, they went right along with me."

It was hard to breathe now. "What happened to my mother?" she managed.

"She's in the quicksand."

"Oh, God." Tess covered her mouth with her hands and bit down on her fingers. The pain brought back some sense of reality.

"Where you shoulda been," Devoe continued. "'Cause now here we are—again. You meddlin' in my business— just like your mother. And Lisa."

He didn't seem to want a response.

"Lisa. Now, that wasn't so simple. She fooled me. I didn't know she used to be the skinny little kid living with the Achords. All grown up, she was so pretty, so sexy. So willing to please. That girl could—" He stopped abruptly, as if he'd suddenly remembered who he was talking to. "But there's a limit to how far a man will go for a woman—even if she's a great lay. She thought she could hold me up for more dough than she was worth. But a man's wife shouldn't oughta try to blackmail him. So I hired someone to teach her a lesson."

Tess gagged as she realized what he was saying. "You had someone rape—"

He cut her off. "Then she turns up on TV, and I've got an even bigger problem. I can't kill her, because now the whole thing's too public. In the city and all. But I can take her medicine away and replace it with something else. So she's guaranteed to self-destruct."

"You monster."

Glen Devoe did the worst thing he could have done. He smiled.

VANCE TOOK THE BUTTON out of his pocket and held it up against the large-size navy sports jacket. The circle of brass with the crest in the center was a perfect match to the one still attached to the expensive fabric.

Cursing under his breath, he clamped his fist around the button and stepped out of the closet. Like a man still trying to make certain of his location, he glanced quickly around the well-appointed bedroom. Rosewood furniture. A brocade spread. Silver-handled brushes on the dressing table. Only the best for the man who lived here.

Vance's ebony eyes narrowed. A button torn off a sports jacket. That still wasn't going to be enough for the police. He could have torn it off himself and said he found it at the cemetery. But it proved something. It proved that Tess was still in danger, whether she thought so or not.

His teeth clenched. First he'd been trying to find out about Lisa. Then somewhere along the line, preventing anything from happening to Tess had become more important. Which was why he'd spent every moment he wasn't with her looking for Ken Holloway's killer. This was the last guy he would have suspected. He'd come here finally because none of the other leads had panned out.

But he hadn't said anything to Tess. What if his silence was putting her in danger now?

Mon Dieu. He'd better get back to Ernestine's on the double.

TESS STARED AT Glen Devoe's beefy face. She recognized the look in his eyes. She'd seen it before when she'd interviewed public officials convicted of corruption. Like him, they tended to be out of touch with reality. Now she was pretty sure that for a moment he wasn't really seeing her. Perhaps his vision was focused on some past victory or even some past defeat. It didn't really matter which—if it gave her a chance to get away.

She had a split second in which to go with her gut reaction or capitulate. A split second in which he might pull the trigger and shoot her. With a silent prayer that she was right, she ducked behind the tree.

The shot came—too late to stop her.

Hidden by the foliage, Tess turned and sprinted into the twilight shadows of the swamp. It had been her nightmare for years. Even in the afternoon, it was dark and forbidding—a place of menace. Now it was her only refuge.

Tess heard the crack of gunfire behind her. Once, twice. She saw the bark of a tree inches to her left shatter.

"Stop, damn you!" Devoe screamed, equal parts anger and frustration coloring his voice.

She ignored the frantic order and kept running—from her terror—from the man behind her.

Her hands balled into fists even as she fled. Determination kept the terror from swallowing her. She couldn't let Devoe get her. Not when he'd filled in the blank spaces in her past. Not when she could tell the world what he'd done.

Clamping her teeth tightly together, Tess dodged around trees and patches of slippery mud. Thorns tore at her dress, and she heard the fabric tear as she wrenched herself away and kept going. Once she slipped and went down on all fours, but she pushed herself up and stumbled ahead.

Through the frantic drumming of her own blood, she could sense him puffing and crashing through the underbrush behind her. At least she was in better shape than Mr. Devoe. He was farther behind her now. Maybe she really did have a chance to get away. Hope surged in her breast, but she didn't let elation slow her up, either.

Another shot rang out. This time it was wider. Farther from its mark. How many were left?

A canebrake blocked her path. Tess began to claw her way through, but the stiff stems slowed her down. When she broke out onto the other side, she found herself facing a broad ribbon of mud that curved around her in a semicircle.

Panting, desperate, she tried to think of what to do. She couldn't leap across. And there was no way to know how deep it went. If she started forward, she might get stuck in the middle. Then she'd be a stationary target in Devoe's private shooting gallery.

There was a sudden rustle in the cane behind her. In the next moment, her pursuer staggered out of the foliage. His shirt was torn and several scratches marred his face, but his lips were curled up in a parody of a smile. "End of the line, honey. It's either me or the quicksand now."

Quicksand. Tess shuddered as she looked at what she'd thought was mud. Was he telling the truth?

"You're going to tell me what that bastard brother of Lisa's found out about her death—and about my private business," Devoe growled.

Tess slowly shook her head. "I'm not going to tell you anything," she said, repeating her earlier statement although now her voice was raw.

He kept the gun trained on her. "Well, now, we could trade. Wouldn't you like to go to your grave knowing the truth about your aunt?"

"You were lying."

"You'll never know unless you tell me what you know about Lisa. Or I could just shoot you in the shoulder or something that might—"

Tess heard the crack of the revolver, and every muscle in her body tightened as she waited for the slug to tear into her flesh. To her astonishment, it was Devoe who grabbed his shoulder and screamed.

"Drop the gun," a voice behind him growled.

When she peered through the cane, she saw Desmond LeRoy coming toward them. A familiar-looking cigar was clamped in his teeth. A not so familiar-looking pistol was in his hand. Thank God. He was a very strange kind of savior materializing out of the mist.

"Drop the gun, you son of a bitch," he repeated.

Devoe's face drained of color. Tossing the weapon to the ground, he sank to his knees at the edge of the mud, still clutching his shoulder. Blood began to ooze from between his fingers. "Please—"

"Shut up." LeRoy spat the cigar into the mud. It hissed and gave off a column of blue smoke. With a savage kick, he sent Devoe's weapon spinning off in the same direction. It landed next to the cigar. But it was much heavier and sank slowly below the surface.

Tess edged toward her boss. "Mr. LeRoy," she gasped. "Thank the Lord. How did you know where to find me?"

LeRoy's gaze didn't leave the other man. "The aunt. Mrs. Achord."

Tess nodded. They could turn Lisa's husband over to the police. She could tell them about what had happened to her mother. And maybe the information she had for Vance would soften his anger when he found out that she'd gone against his instructions.

LeRoy took a step toward the man on the ground. "You bastard. First you tried to make me your messenger boy. Then you tried to ruin me, didn't you?"

"No. Please. It wasn't me."

Tess stared at them, trying to interpret a picture that had blurred and suddenly reformed in a different configuration. They knew each other.

"Mr. LeRoy—"

The little man ignored her. "Oh, come on, Glen. You expect me to believe it wasn't one of your men who tried to sabotage the station this morning? Too bad for you the bomb in the men's room fizzled. The only one that did any damage was in Studio Seven."

Tess's head swung from one man to the other, as she struggled to understand what was going on.

"Why would I bomb you, Des? We work together real good. And we go way back, remember."

"Sure we do. Way back to when you needed money to finance your dirty business, and I was stupid enough to get sucked in. I would have ended up in the slammer, except that my mother cut a deal with the district attorney."

"I would have gotten you out of it if she hadn't stepped in."

"Sure." He spat out the syllable as if it were a curse. "I thought it was finished. I didn't know you'd hold it over me every time you needed a favor."

"Let me explain—"

"Yeah. Explain why Brad Everett broke his contract. Explain why my station manager is missing." LeRoy's voice rose like steam hissing through a faulty valve. "Explain how I'm going to attract viewers now. You can't deliver the viewers, you don't get the advertisers. And if you don't get the advertisers, you go down the tubes." With the last word, he aimed a savage kick at the wounded man. It connected with Devoe's chest. On a piercing scream, he tumbled backward into the muck.

The scream changed from pain to terror as the drug lord began to sink into the goop. Quicksand. It really was quicksand.

Tess stared in horror as Devoe began to thrash wildly with his good arm. It wasn't like when Vance had floated near the surface of the muck. He was going down. Fast.

"We can't— We've got to help him." Kneeling, Tess stretched out her hand toward the struggling man. No matter what he'd done, she couldn't let anyone die like this.

LeRoy wasn't taking any chances. With the flat of his palm, he slammed Tess backward. He was stronger than he looked. She tumbled to the ground, gasping at the impact.

"Stay where you are," he growled as the gun swung toward her.

Eyes bulging, arms lashing at the surface of the mud, Devoe struggled to extricate himself. "Help me. Help! Help—" he gasped.

"Please—" Tess whispered. "You can't just let him drown. We can turn him over to the police. He'll be punished for what he's done. Not just to you. To my mother."

"Punished! Fat chance. Half the police force is on his payroll. In town. Out here where he picks up his drug shipments. So stay where you are."

It was all over quickly. One last scream, and Lisa's husband sank below the glistening surface.

"Good riddance to garbage," LeRoy muttered.

The look in his eyes made the breath trickle from Tess's lungs. She had seen his face turn evil as he watched a man die. He was looking at her with the same expression.

"Ernestine knows you came after me," she managed.

"But she doesn't know what happened when I got here. Actually, I was too late to save you. Devoe had already shot you. Then he attacked me, and it was self defense."

"But the connection between you—"

"Nobody who's still around town knows. You're my most pressing problem now," he said.

"No. I'll keep quiet about all this." Even as she made the specious offer, she could see that he wasn't going for it.

"Oh, come on. You're not the kind who keeps quiet. Look at the way you've stuck with this Lisa Gautreau thing. You just couldn't let it go, could you? You had to keep digging and digging. Watching the videotape. Asking her brother questions. Pestering the aunt. I knew Glen was going to be mad as a nest of hornets. He'd already gotten on me about Lisa being on the show." He snorted. "As if I could tell Brad Everett what to do—"

"You were the one who put the tape on the top shelf."

"No. I dropped the word to Roger Dallas that I'd rather have him for the weekend anchor than you—that I wouldn't interfere if he slowed you down."

So he'd been using Roger. But that was doing things the hard way. "We had a meeting. You could have just told me to drop the investigation."

"You're wrong. How could I? Everybody would have wondered why I was backing off."

"Was that you that night in the pickup truck?"

"I don't do that kind of scut work. I have it hired out."

As they'd been talking, Tess had been edging away. She'd given Devoe the slip. If she could fade into the cane, maybe she had another chance. She could go back the other way—get to the road. Get help. Or maybe Vance was on his way over. Maybe he'd called Ernestine, too. Maybe he was worried about her. Or maybe he didn't care.

"Hold it." The ice in LeRoy's voice stopped her almost as effectively as the gun in his hand.

Yet she saw a flicker of uncertainty in his eyes, as if this whole interlude were more than he'd bargained for.

"You can't say Devoe shot me. His gun's at the bottom of the bog. They'll be able to tell the bullet didn't come from it," she tried.

LeRoy's face had set itself into grim lines. "This gun isn't registered to me. It could be Devoe's. But it doesn't matter. The bad stuff is almost over now. I can put this behind me and start rebuilding." He looked from Tess to the swamp. "And they're not going to find either one of you."

As LeRoy took a step toward Tess, he didn't see the patch of mud lurking under a covering of leaves. When his foot connected with the ground, his leg shot out from under him.

Seizing the desperate advantage, Tess went for the gun. Her hand connected with the clammy metal, and the weapon sailed into the air, landing on the quicksand.

"You bitch."

In the next moment, LeRoy twisted around and hooked his fingers into the hem of Tess's dress. The fabric tore as she wrenched herself away. For a moment she was free. Then he reached higher, his fingers scrabbling at her knees. They dug into her flesh and held.

Tess tried to twist out of his grasp. When that didn't work, she began to pound at his hands. But he held her in his terrible grip.

She could feel them both sliding over the edge of the firm ground. "No—please—don't. Stop. We're going in—"

But he was beyond hearing. He'd ceased to care about anything but preventing her escape.

He snapped back to reality as he hit the muck. Crying out, he let go of Tess and made a wild grab for a root hanging over the bank. He missed.

Tess followed him into the slime, but she was able to twist her body so that she landed several feet away. Terror deluged her as a vivid picture of Devoe's last minutes flashed into her mind. He'd gone down into the quicksand struggling and flailing as he pleaded for help.

Oh, God. It was going to happen to her, too. She was going to disappear below the surface of the muck. Even as she tried to pull herself up, she could feel the viscous stuff dragging her down into its wet, sucking embrace.

A scream broke from her lips. It was answered by an echoing wail of panic from LeRoy.

She could see him beating at the brown surface with his arms. It was all she could do to keep from imitating his frantic movements. Instead, she forced herself to remember what had happened when Vance had stumbled into the quicksand. He hadn't gone down like Devoe. He'd floated to the surface like a cork in a bucket of water. Well, not quite as buoyantly as a cork. But he'd kept his head above the deadly stuff.

Tess focused on the way he'd looked. He hadn't been wildly struggling. He'd hardly moved. In response, her own thrashing stopped. All at once, she realized she wasn't sinking any farther.

"You can float," she called to LeRoy. "If you stop struggling like that, you'll stop sinking."

"Noooooo!"

He paid no heed. Unable to watch him go down, Tess closed her eyes and tried to imagine that she was floating far away in a beautiful pool of warm water. Perhaps if she held absolutely still, she could stay like this for hours.

It was only a few minutes before she realized that wasn't going to happen. LeRoy's ripples were affecting her body. His struggles were sucking her down too. The muck pressed painfully against her chest, making it hard to breathe.

"Stop," she gasped out as she felt her lungs being compressed. "Hold still. Please."

He didn't answer. But he did slow his thrashing movements. Perhaps he was simply too tired to struggle.

Tess felt the quicksand grasping at her shoulders and squeezing the breath from her body. The terrible sensation sent panic sweeping over her. All her anguish came bubbling out in a strangled cry for help.

To her astonishment, the plea was answered. "Tess. For the love of God, where are you, Tess?"

"Vance!" she called out with all the strength she could muster.

"*Cher.* Keep talking to me."

"Over here," she puffed. "I—we—"

In the next moment, a haggard-looking Vance came crashing through the canebrake.

LeRoy reached out toward him. "Help," he gasped.

Vance didn't answer. Instead he pulled a knife from his pocket. Then he turned away and quickly began to hack at several of the canes. When they came free, he slid them to Tess.

"Not her—me!" LeRoy screamed, the sound cut in half by the pressure on his lungs.

Ignoring him, Vance maneuvered the slender pole toward Tess. Grasping the ends, she tried to hoist herself up, but the muck held her fast, and her mud-slick hands slid off the smooth surface.

"I...I...can't—"

"Wait." Cursing softly under his breath, Vance withdrew the poles. With the knife, he hacked several angled cuts along the ends, roughening the exterior. Then he slid the makeshift lifelines back to Tess. Again, she grasped the ends. This time, there was something to grip. She winced as the rough edges dug into her hands.

In the background, LeRoy was still screaming at Vance. Tess tried to blot out the sound as she concentrated on getting free.

"I can't go in there after you. Can you hold on?" Vance's voice was edged with anguish.

"I think so."

"I'll pull you out. You don't have to do any of the work," he promised as he began to haul the shafts back.

Tess gritted her teeth and clamped her hands to the sharpened surface. For long, terrible moments, she felt the quicksand hold her fast. Then with a slurping noise, it yielded some of its power. She was coming up. Slowly at first and then faster so that all at once she found herself collapsing onto the bank beside Vance. As soon as she was on stable ground, he dropped the poles and pulled her into his arms.

"Tess, *mon Dieu*, Tess," he breathed, crushing her against his chest. She held on to him just as tightly.

"Let me see your hands." He shifted his grip so that he could examine her fingers and palms. They were red and gouged from the cane. "I'm sorry. I didn't have any other way."

"I know. I know. It's all right." She pressed her face against his chest. "Thank you for coming after me. Thank you for getting me out." She wanted to cling to Vance and forget about everything else, yet she realized that LeRoy was still screaming at them.

Vance continued to ignore him. "How did you end up in there?"

"He pulled me with him. He shot Devoe and tossed him in—and watched him drown. He was going to kill me, too." She swallowed painfully. "But we have to get him out."

The look on his face was harsh. "Perhaps." Standing up, he took one of the canes and slipped it to the station owner, whose shoulders were now covered with the thick mud.

It took some effort for him to raise his hands. When he finally freed them from the mud and wrapped them around the splintered end, he screamed. "How the hell do you expect me to hold on to this damn thing?" he bellowed.

"The same way Tess did," Vance clipped out. He watched while the man in the quicksand took hold of the shaft, but he didn't begin to pull.

"Get me out of here," LeRoy whimpered.

Vance kept a grip on his end of the cane. Instead of pulling he reached into his pocket and brought out a shiny round disk. "This button came off your navy sports coat."

"Yeah, so what? Where the hell did you get it?"

"I found it in the cemetery. In Ken Holloway's hand, to be exact."

Tess gasped. LeRoy's face hardened.

"Suppose you tell me what happened."

The station owner was silent.

Vance gave a vicious tug on the pole. LeRoy screamed as the cut edges tore out of his hands.

"Tell me what happened, or Tess and I will walk away from here."

Tess gripped his arm. Briefly, he pressed his fingers over hers. But his dangerous gaze never left the man in the quicksand.

"No. You can't— Please—" the little man blubbered. "Get me out of here. I—I—can't breathe."

"Put the pieces of the puzzle together for me. Did you kill my sister? Ken? Did you bomb your own TV station?"

"Bomb my station? Kill your sister? Hell, no. You think I'm crazy or something? Devoe bombed the station. That's why I took care of him. The only other one I had to get besides Ken was Erica Barry."

Tess gasped. "You? But why?"

"She could tie me to Devoe." Despite his grip on the pole the mud was creeping up his neck. "Please—get me out of here—"

Vance shook his head curtly. "Talk."

For a moment LeRoy's eyes rolled madly and Tess was afraid he would lose his slender grip on sanity. Then he clutched the cane more tightly and lifted his chin. A stream of words began to pour out of his mouth so rapidly that Tess had to strain to understand him. "Erica was one of Devoe's honeys back in the good old days. She recognized me when she came to the studio for that program. Don't you see? I had to take care of her."

Despite the muggy heat of the swamp, a chill swept across Tess's skin.

"You gotta understand," LeRoy pleaded. "You gotta know what it's like to be there on the edge of success. To make it on your own. The station was finally paying off for me. I was just starting to make it big. Then of all the damn, stinking, rotten luck, *she* turns up on the *Brad Everett Show*. Right after Lisa made her surprise visit. It still would have been okay, 'cause I wasn't in the studio or anything. But I had to go out to take a leak, and she had to be coming out of the little girls' room. I guess I must have looked startled. She's so much heavier now, and the camera puts ten pounds on you. I didn't recognize her on TV. She didn't say anything. But I could tell she remembered me as soon as she saw me. *I* haven't changed that much. So I went to her house that night. I thought if I made it look like a ritual murder, the police would think it was some nut."

Tess swallowed around the grit clogging her throat. She thought she'd figured out Desmond LeRoy. She'd never come close to understanding the man she worked for.

"My sister—" Vance growled. "Why did she end up in Savannah Bayou?"

LeRoy had began to blubber. "Not me. Not me."

"Devoe drove her to it," Tess answered quickly. "He told me before LeRoy killed him. He switched her medication. He said she was poking into his drug business. Just like my mother."

"What?"

"Later, Vance. Later." She gestured toward the man in the quicksand. His face was crimson now, and his eyes were bulging out of his head. As he sank lower, a strangled, high-pitched wail like the cry of a terrified cat came

from his mouth. Tess's fingers dug into Vance's arm.
"Please— Get him out of there. Before it's too late."

"Hang on," Vance growled as he began to haul back on
the pole.

Tess held her breath, wondering if it were already too
late. Finally, with agonizing slowness, the station owner's
pudgy body began to emerge from the quicksand like a
shriveled raisin being pulled from cake batter. He kept his
death grip on the pole while Vance pulled. Then he was
flopping onto the ground beside them, where he lay panting.

Vance stared down at him with distaste. "We'd better
call the sheriff."

"He's right here," a gruff voice behind them answered.

Chapter Sixteen

Vance and Tess whirled to find themselves facing Frank Haney, the man who'd locked up Vance for tossing the TV camera in the water. He looked much as he had that night at the jail. His uniform was still rumpled and decorated with half-moon patches of sweat at the armpits. Perhaps the only difference was that the strands of hair across his scalp stood out at wild angles.

Vance's whole body tensed when he saw the beefy man. Tess laid a cautioning hand on his arm.

"Ernestine Achord called me," the sheriff explained, answering their unspoken question. His gaze shifted among the three people at the edge of the quicksand and settled on Vance. "When you took off like the devil was after you, I guess the old lady figured you were gonna need some help. I got here a few minutes ago and decided to see what developed."

Tess moved closer to Vance, remembering the last time the two men had confronted each other.

"Glen Devoe is in there." He gestured toward the quicksand, his eyes never leaving the sheriff.

"Yeah. I heard." He crossed to LeRoy, hooked broad hands under the man's arms and pulled him to his feet. "Come on. You have the right to remain silent, of course.

Except that these folks have already heard your freely given confession. And Ms. Beaumont saw you kill Devoe. Which don't put you in a very good position.''

LeRoy's head was bowed and his lips were pressed together. Either he meant to take the sheriff's advice, or he was too overcome to speak.

"I'll need a statement from you," Haney said, addressing both Vance and Tess.

"Right now we're going home to get cleaned up," Vance replied. His voice was even but underlaid with a note of challenge.

The sheriff gestured toward LeRoy. "You want to put this dude away, don't you?"

"Oui."

"Seems we agree on that."

Vance didn't reply.

Haney swallowed. "You've caused me some grief in the past."

"The feeling's mutual," Vance said tightly.

Tess looked from one man to the other. They were standing facing each other, neither one of them moving.

Haney tipped his head to the side, and Tess's muscles tightened as she waited for him to say something. The words, when they came, were a surprise. "You saved Ms. Beaumont and collared LeRoy."

Vance nodded almost imperceptibly. When he saw Tess staring at him, he cleared his throat and addressed the sheriff. "I'm glad you showed up when you did."

"Yeah, well it's going to be a lot easier to enforce the law around here with Devoe gone."

Probably the first civil words the two of them had exchanged, Tess thought. It was a start toward normal relations.

Vance and Tess were silent as Haney hustled LeRoy toward the road. "There's been a lot of bad feeling between him and me," Vance said when they were alone again.

"Maybe things will be better now."

"It could be," Vance allowed.

"He thought of you as a troublemaker. This time you're on the same side."

Vance laughed. "If you'd told me that would ever happen, I wouldn't have believed it."

Silently, they started back through the swamp. She should be feeling better, Tess thought. But now that the danger was over and she and Vance were alone, she could feel a new tension mounting. Nervously, she fingered the locket that hung around her neck.

"Something's bothering you," Vance said as they reached his car.

Tess nodded. A lot was bothering her. A lot that she didn't know how to deal with.

Perhaps Vance felt the same way. He started to open the door. Then he turned abruptly back to her. Instead of meeting her eyes, his gaze honed in on the silver oval clasped between her fingers.

"Why do you wear that?"

"It was my aunt's. I put it on after she died. To feel close to her. Now...I don't know...Devoe made it sound like she knew he was going to kill my mother...that she was in on it." Tess gulped. Then a tingling sensation rippled across her nerve endings.

Vance saw the look of shock on her face.

"What is it? What's wrong?"

"The dream."

"Your nightmare? Like the one you had at *Tante*'s house the other night?"

"No. When I went to sleep in Lisa's bed this afternoon, I dreamed something different. About Momma. And Aunt Pauline. She came to rescue me, and she was holding out the locket."

"Can I see it?"

Tess nodded. Vance reached around the back of her neck and found the catch. She held her breath as he unhooked it, feeling suddenly as if some important discovery were going to be made.

He snapped the locket open. Inside was the confirmation picture of Tess. He touched it gently and then ran his thumbnail around the edges. "Do you mind if I take it out?"

"Go ahead."

Underneath was a flat silver plate.

"Right after her funeral, I tried to get it up. I couldn't," Tess told him. "Maybe I didn't really want to pry any further."

Vance pulled a penknife out of his pocket, opened the smallest blade and inserted it carefully under the edge. The plate popped up. Inside a small compartment was a folded, yellow piece of onionskin paper.

Handing the locket back to Tess, Vance waited while she removed the paper with trembling fingers and carefully spread it open.

As she stared at the lines of tiny script, her heart started to thump. "It's addressed to me. Aunt Pauline wrote it." Softly she began to read aloud.

My dearest Tess,
I believe Mr. Devoe killed your mother. The only way I could take you home was to swear that I would never speak of her again. Forgive me for the burden I will carry to my grave.

"Oh, my God," Tess breathed. "She..."

"She had a terrible decision to make," Vance said, finishing the sentence. "I guess she thought caving in to Devoe was the only thing she could do."

Tess wanted to believe it. But it was a lot to take in. "She kept a diary. Maybe she wrote about it in there."

"Or left a more complete record for you somewhere. But right now, all you have to know is that she must have found out Devoe ran things in town and she had to choose between trying to avenge a dead woman when the authorities would probably have turned a deaf ear—or saving her daughter."

"When you put it that way, I can understand it better," Tess whispered.

"It's a lot to take in all at once," Vance said.

Tess nodded.

He shifted his weight uneasily. "Ernestine is waiting to find out what happened to you."

"Yes, she must be terribly worried. We'd better tell her we're all right."

Tess felt a cord of tension pulling her shoulders back against the car seat as they rode back to Savannah Bayou. A few hours ago she'd made it pretty clear to Vance that things couldn't work out between the two of them. He wasn't doing anything to make her believe otherwise.

As they approached the house, Tess could see Ernestine on the front porch looking anxiously down the road. It was a relief to be able to focus her attention on the old woman.

Vance bolted out of the car and hurried to her side.

"Did you bring her back?" she asked.

"*Oui.*"

"*Cher,* are you all right?" she called out when she heard Tess's footsteps.

"Yes. Thanks to Vance."

"Come in and tell me what happened."

"She's a mess, *Tante.* She was in the swamp."

"Then I can wait until you both bathe and change. If you're quick."

It was good to wash the mud off, Tess thought as she swiftly bathed. "I'm using up your supply of spare dresses," she told Ernestine when she returned to the living room.

"You're welcome to them." The old woman looked uncomfortable. "I'm sorry. That man. Desmond LeRoy. He said he owned the station and that he had to get in touch with you. But as soon as I told him where you were, I started to wonder if I'd made a mistake, me."

"He fooled a lot of people," Vance said from the doorway. He was wearing fresh jeans and a clean white shirt. Tess's eyes were drawn to the drops of water still glistening in his wet hair, catching the sun coming in the window. "After I found the button at the cemetery, I started looking for the jacket it had come from. LeRoy's closet was the last damn place I searched."

"You broke into his house?" Tess asked.

"Apartment," Vance corrected. "First I thought it was that other reporter—Roger Dallas. Then the news director, your friend Chris. Or Brad Everett. Or Larry Melbourne."

"You searched all their houses?" Tess asked carefully.

"*Oui.* That was why I couldn't tell you what I was doing," he added tightly. "In case you were questioned."

"The police—"

"Would have needed a search warrant. They couldn't try everyone. I could. They never would have pegged LeRoy. There wasn't really any evidence pointing toward him. I'd simply eliminated everybody else at the station."

They gave Ernestine a brief account of what had happened after Tess had left for her mother's house. Then Vance stood up and paced to the door. "We should go."

"Yes," Tess whispered. She knew they had both been deliberately putting off whatever it was they were going to say to each other. Now that the unavoidable was drawing closer, her heart was starting to pound.

"Do you want me to take you home?" Vance asked as he started the engine.

Tess's fingers dug into the edge of the seat. "No."

"Then where?"

"Your house is closer. We need to talk," she whispered.

Tess saw the look of relief flash across Vance's features, but it was quickly gone.

Ten minutes later they were both standing uncertainly in front of the steps that led to the gallery.

Vance closed the car door very deliberately. Then he turned to her. "*Cher,* don't torture me any longer. If it's all over between us, tell me now. I've got to know."

Hope unfurled in her chest. "I don't want it to be over."

With a low curse, he crossed the few feet between them and pulled her into his embrace. Her arms went around him and they held each other, swaying like trees clinging to the earth in a hurricane.

"I thought I'd driven you away," he muttered.

"Oh, Vance, I'm so sorry I told you it couldn't work. I thought you couldn't trust me enough to let me help you investigate Lisa's death. I didn't know you were trying to find out who was after me."

"I should have told you. I'm just so used to—"

"To playing your cards close to your chest."

He tipped her face up to his. "I didn't know you were a gambler."

"I've been afraid to gamble before. Now I know sometimes it's the only way to get what you want."

"*Bien-aimée.*" He held her more tightly.

"Vance, we haven't known each other for very long or under normal circumstances, either."

"*Oui.* But I'm very selfish. I need to be sure I'm not going to lose you. That we have the time to work things out."

"I think you'd have to make a concerted effort to lose me."

They smiled at each other, and he threaded his fingers through hers as they climbed the steps to the gallery.

Once they were in the living room, his expression grew serious. "*Cher,* do you forgive your aunt for what she did to you?" he finally asked.

It was the last thing she'd expected him to ask. "I—I— yes."

She heard him swallow convulsively and raised her face, her eyes searching his.

"Then perhaps you can forgive me, too."

She looked at him questioningly.

"I did the same thing, you know. I made decisions about what was best for you without letting you have any say in the matter. It's one thing to keep the truth from a little girl for her own good. It's quite another not to give a grown woman any choices."

"You understand that?"

"*Oui.*"

"You understand that a man and woman have to trust each other and rely on each other if they're going to make anything important work between them?" she asked, her voice not quite steady.

"I'm starting to understand. But I'm so used to taking responsibility only for myself. I thought that if I got into trouble, I'd be the one who had to suffer the consequences. Instead, you were almost killed because I wasn't there when you needed me."

"You came back in time."

"Thank the good God."

She knew how hard it had been for him to admit those things. Now she knew she had to take a risk, too. "I haven't exactly been easy to live with. Every time you told me something I didn't want to hear, I got angry with you."

"You were having a pretty bad time, *cher.*"

"Still, it must be part of the reason you've kept telling yourself that a woman like me—whatever that is—couldn't love a man like you."

She felt him go very still.

"It's not true, you know," she continued. "If I hadn't been falling in love with you, I wouldn't have gone to your bed." She rubbed her knuckles lightly against the stubble on his cheek. "Vance Gautreau, I love you *because* of your background."

She saw the guarded expression on his face. And the hope he was trying so hard to hide.

"How could you?" he asked in a fierce voice.

"I love you because of what you've been able to make of yourself despite a rotten start in life. I love you because you're intelligent and creative. I love you because you have so much strength. And so much tenderness hidden below that tough exterior. And because you'd take any risk for the people you care about. I love you. And it's been so hard to keep myself from saying that."

The breath stopped moving in and out of her lungs as he cupped her face in his hands and gazed down at her. "Don't put me on some kind of pedestal—or you'll be disappointed."

"Don't worry. I'm a realist. I also know you have a hot temper. And you're impulsive. And bullheaded. And *tête dur*—hardheaded."

He nodded. "All of those, *oui*. But I won't claim to be stupid, and I'm beginning to think the luckiest day of my life was the day you walked into that jail."

He looked at her with such tenderness that her heart seemed to stop for a moment.

"Je t'aime," he whispered softly. Then louder, "I love you, Tess."

All at once she was seeing him through a film of tears. Then he was kissing the corners of her eyes, kissing her mouth, holding her as if he would never let her go.

"We'll work it out. I promise," she managed between kisses.

"Oui. We have to."

"Take me upstairs. Take me upstairs very slowly. The way you did the first time."

"The famous stairs." He laughed softly. Then he swung her into his arms and carried her toward the front hall.

OVER THE YEARS, TELEVISION HAS BROUGHT
THE LIVES AND LOVES OF MANY CHARACTERS INTO
YOUR HOMES. NOW HARLEQUIN INTRODUCES YOU
TO THE TOWN AND PEOPLE OF

One small town—twelve terrific love stories.

GREAT READING...GREAT SAVINGS...
AND A FABULOUS FREE GIFT!

Each book set in Tyler is a self-contained love story; together, the
twelve novels stitch the fabric of the community.

By collecting proofs-of-purchase found in each Tyler book, you can
receive a fabulous gift, ABSOLUTELY FREE! And use our special
Tyler coupons to save on your next TYLER book purchase.

Join us for the fifth TYLER book,
BLAZING STAR by Suzanne Ellison, available in July.

Is there really a murder cover-up?
Will Brick and Karen overcome differences and find true love?

Harlequin Intrigue®

COMING NEXT MONTH

#189 ILLUSIONS by Jenna Ryan
Summoned to the castle of magician Cesare LaFortune
to witness his greatest illusion, Karoline O'Connor
entered a realm of evil that changed her life forever.
Her only hope of survival in Sainte Marie des
Monts, France, a land where madness reigned, was
Nicolas Demos, Cesare's nephew. Did she dare trust
a man whose power to look deep into her soul was
both exciting and frightening?

#190 DOUBLE VISION by Sheryl Lynn
Tarkington Smith felt that Kerry Byfield's testimony
had convicted an innocent man, not to mention his
best buddy. After a grueling trial, the cowboy
Casanova flirted shamelessly with Kerry—all to
convince her there was more to murder than met the
eye. But was there more to Tarkington Smith?

◆ H A R L E Q U I N
American Romance®

American Romance's yearlong celebration continues. Join your favorite authors as they celebrate love set against the special times each month throughout 1992.

Next month, fireworks light up the sky when Anne Haynes and John Westfield meet in a special Fourth of July romance:

JULY

S	M	T	W	T	F	S
			2	3	4	
5	4th of JULY			11		
			7	18		
19	20		23	24	25	
26	27	28	29	30	31	

**#445
HOME FREE
by Cathy Gillen Thacker**

Read all the books in *A Calendar of Romance*, coming to you one per month all year, only in American Romance.

If you missed #421 HAPPY NEW YEAR, DARLING; #425 VALENTINE HEARTS AND FLOWERS; #429 FLANNERY'S RAINBOW; #433 A MAN FOR EASTER; #437 CINDERELLA MOM; or #441 DADDY'S GIRL and would like to order them, send your name, address, zip or postal code, along with a check or money order (please do not send cash) for $3.29 for #421 and #425 or $3.39 for #429, #433, #437 and #441, plus 75¢ postage and handling ($1 00 in Canada), *for each book ordered*, payable to Harlequin Reader Service to:

In the U.S.
3010 Walden Avenue
P.O. Box 1325
Buffalo, NY 14269-1325

In Canada
P.O. Box 609
Fort Erie, Ontario
L2A 5X3

Please specify book title(s) with your order.
Canadian residents add applicable federal and provincial taxes.   COR7